Being Australia

Joe Jeney

I0561710

Light River Books
The World's A Better Place Because We Read Books…

Copyright Page

Being Australia
First Edition 2018
Published by Light River Books,
Melbourne, Australia

books@joejeney.net

The World's A Better Place Because We Read Books…™

Bonus Material: The Romance Of The Swag
by Henry Lawson (1867-1922)
Originally published in Sydney by Angus and Robertson 1907
To the best of our knowledge, the text of The Romance Of The
Swag is in the Public Domain. Check the copyright laws for
your country before downloading or redistributing this file.

Front Cover photo unsplash.com/@mkwlsn
Irrevocable, nonexclusive, worldwide copyright license granted
under the terms and conditions at Unsplash.com at the time of
download and use.

Back Cover Adaption of "Shearing the Rams" by Tom Roberts.

Dedication

In memory of
Laszlo, Joan, and AJ.

See you next time around.

Epigraph

"The land I love above all others-not because it was kind to me, but because I was born on Australian soil, and because of the foreign father who died at his work in the ranks of Australian pioneers, and because of many things. Australia! My country!"

Henry Lawson, *The Romance Of The Swag*

Contents

Preface

Being Australia deals with "second-generation purgatory." Not all of it is about this, not at all. It also deals with a young man's relationship with his nation and the way in which stories – sometimes quixotically - influence him and his nation both. Ed's dad, Zolli, figures throughout, too, because dads affect how boys relate to their communities. The story is about the demise of agriculture and manufacturing as national symbols and the rise of the service sector as something else. It's about the transformative power of education. It's about Australia's wish for independence and its reality of dependence. It's about love at its most hopeful. But second-generation purgatory is one of the story's differentiating aspects.

Second-generation purgatory involves locally born children who exist between the worlds of their heritage and their birth. They await an indefinable admission to something they can't see and might never find. The experience can include foreign-born kids too young to recall their birth country, though *Being Australia* doesn't discuss them.

I never intended to write about second-generation purgatory. I never knew it existed, not consciously. I saw it surface in rewrites of *Being Australia* and only then realized what it was and what my book, in part, was about.

Second-generation purgatory is widespread in our globalized world. It is as necessary and proper as any other ineluctable manifestation of human nature. Read into that what you will.

When things turn sour, which they won't always, specialists refer to a "second-generation identity crisis." I dislike the phrase. It suggests that individuals can't get it together. The experience is more socially involved than that. It's literally impossible for it to fall to one person's shoulders.

When things do go wrong, second-generation purgatory is nearer bigotry than racism, but might not be that either, bigotry. The markers – race, ethnicity, religion, accent, the spelling of one's name, eating habits and dress, being called out on one's parentage etc. - are not the main game. They merely identify those who must endure purgatory. Equally.

Despite this, being told to "wait your turn" and to "go back where you came from" doesn't help. You can't go back to where you never came from. And when you have the cure for cancer, or other contribution to make to your society, "waiting your turn" harms everyone.

Governments harm everyone again when they revoke citizenship as a form of punishment – which must by definition target first and second-generation immigrants - rather than responsibly punish their citizens as citizens. It's one thing to selectively grant citizenship. It's another to willy-nilly demolish citizenhood. If citizenhood is optional, so too is the government. Chipping at cornerstones, any, brings the wall down, which makes for very unstable societies.

I mention this here because I can't help myself. Citizenship revocation doesn't actually figure in the story.

On another score, the purgatorial "sufferers" can be their own worst enemies. In proving they're one of the team, they become its zealous advocate. They overstress nationalisms. They self-destructively appropriate insults or fall prone to "Uncle Tom" syndrome, which is to say they become needlessly self-deprecating. They project the mistreatment they personally experience onto others. They ingratiate themselves rather than express gratitude. They publicly shun their heritage as if it were time wasted.

Or they go through life sensing a stacked deck. They believe they can never be one of the team. Some of them join "anti" teams to belong or to make a point. Ned Kelly, contemporary street gangs, and "homegrown terrorists" who fight for foreign causes bear this out.

Second-generation purgatory as a concept is useful because it offers a key to understanding issues that confront us as a community. The concept has explanatory power.

***

Being Australia came of actively refraining from writing novels and choosing a career path antithetical to storytelling.

I consulted that Knowledge-Fount, the Internet, and discovered a surprising amount of cogently argued blogs as to why it was futile for anyone to write stories. I was very miserable that day, I can't remember why, and indulged in the pathetic luxury of self-pity.

Yet I still needed a salve for my psyche. I wasn't about to give away writing entirely, so I commenced writing a journal.

The journal explored a moment in my life that occurred decades earlier when I cheated destiny or fulfilled it, I still don't know which. I know I cheated the destiny others expected of me, whether they or I wanted it.

Everyone should keep a journal. It would cure the world's ills.

At the same time, ever-wholehearted America granted me permanent residency (which unhappily I couldn't later pursue.) Nevertheless, I thought to sit the Californian Bar Exam, which would involve writing cursive in six-hour blocks, give or take. To get my hand in, I wrote for a couple of hours before work each day, like training for a marathon little by little. No surprises, my impressionistic journal provided the forum for these exercises.

The combination of these forces – giving up the writing of novels and studying for the Bar of California – meant that, like existence, *Being Australia* should never have been but was anyway, and now is.

Unevenness remains. The story isn't there totally. But what novel ever is? Yet it is a novel to its core.

It is not an autobiography, as you might expect, forged in the gentle fires of journaling as it was. It isn't even a *roman à clef* (a type of novel based on real life.)

It drew on my experience, recollection, and imagination, yes. But it drew on them in the same way that *Europa: A Thousand Years of Oil* drew on my experience, recollection, and imagination of ice and snow while I wrote a science-fictional tome set on another world, a moon of Jupiter. As soon as my recollection entered *Europa*, it became fictional.

Being Australia remains fictional in another regard. Textbooks relate facts on page twenty that remain facts on page two hundred, whereas "facts" in novels are fictional devices. At the beginning of the story, it's a "fact" that Australians won't die in the "country of their clay." (You'll see why.) But this "fact" changes in very real ways after Ed Kaspar hones his views. Story "facts" illustrate character perceptions and mood rather than textbook "truth" as such.

Certainly, *Being Australia* does not offer social comment. Nor is it a history. It can't be, given the mash-up of characters, timelines, and circumstances throughout.

Being Australia remains a story about imperfect Ed Kaspar, and his travels, not imperfect Joe Jeney and his far less interesting travels.

Joe Jeney
Belgrave, 2018

Acknowledgments

Thanks to John Turner for his kindly direction during the final stages of writing the novel. His suggestions were supportive and illuminating.

They were the words of a friend who knew that honesty and frankness never overstep the mark.

Being Australia

ED KASPAR'S AUTUMN job at the packing shed in the hills around the dry city of Adelaide suited him in the lead up to the shearing season. But that Thursday morning his boss, Bill O'Brien, the packing shed owner, bowed to social pressure and closed the shed with half of his fruit on the trees. A local current-affairs TV show outed him for underpaying backpackers. It was unfair, and the TV show never really got it.

"I pay for quantity," he told a camera at his front gate, "like all the picking industry." Protesters jeered.

Paying for quantity let him employ kids who couldn't get work to save themselves but needed a way to extend their travel visas, which working in rural Australia let them do.

Picking and packing jobs required skills and experience. Some workers worked at it for thirty years. They traveled the countryside along regular work routes with entire families in tow. They were good at their jobs, and they earned real money.

He never got to say that to the camera.

One kid wanted a hundred bucks an hour on his first day in Bill's packing shed, and when he didn't get it, he ran to the TV show.

The TV show, without any real idea of what was in play, and with even less inclination to find out, railroaded Bill O'Brien on screen, an easy-going soul, and turned him into TV public enemy number one. Now protesters stood at his gate. They stopped workers from walking the steep drive to the packing shed, a simple outbuilding with two faded forklifts parked to the side, dormant today. There went Bill's business.

"No one respects farmers anymore," he told Ed and Quinn, Ed's co-worker, aside.

He would sell to property developers who paid for views

15

of city lights and the ocean.

The Adelaide Hills would be down one more apple farm.

"I'll get your money, boys. You earned it."

Dog poop hung from his boot. He checked for the smell without finding its source as he walked to the main house. It gave him a hunted, harried look.

It was hot for late May. The winter was a couple of weeks away. The 1984 harvest was miserable. What fruit remained on the trees would waste.

Ed Kaspar stayed in the bunkhouse for the previous week. He lived an hour's drive away in a small town at the edge of the Valley to the north of Adelaide. He hadn't known old Bill O'Brien from Adam when he came looking for work, which was the week after he turned twenty. But Bill let him stay in the tiny, basic bunkhouse with another guy, Quinn, a year his senior.

Quinn was from Port Pirie, a lead smelting town close to the arid agricultural area that characterized most of the South Australian interior.

"I have shearing work to go to," he told Ed after they tidied the small room. They sat on their respective bunks while they awaited their wages like prisoners in a cell on their release day. "I can try to get you a job, you know, in the sheds, if you want."

Ed better head home to see his mother, Jean, who herself was trying to find work for him as a roustabout with a shearing contractor. Nothing was settled yet. He told Quinn this.

"I'll keep an eye out," Quinn promised.

Quinn didn't look like a regular shearer, not a shearer out of a nineteenth-century Henry Lawson bush ballad anyway. He had long, straight, chestnut-brown hair. He covered it with a black baseball cap, however hot or cold the temperature. He wore big lace-up boots. He sort of presaged a young Kurt Cobain look, still years away.

Ed Kaspar, on the other hand, was tall with strong

16

footballer's legs, though he hadn't played football for a year. His shoulders were rounded and powerful.

He loved hard work, and his powerful body came in useful for that. He loved exhausting himself in physical labor. In hard work, he found a reason for being.

And the way in which he decided to bring it together, the work, the freedom, the experience and the implosion and explosion of self, was in outback employment.

His mother, Jean, and father, Zolli, were immigrants, Jean from Britain, Wales more specifically, and Zolli was Budapest born. His parents had no claim to Australia's outback. Therefore, Ed Kaspar had no claim to it by inheritance. But Jean gave him books to read, plenty of books to read. The most recent book she gave him she purchased in hardback from the local newsagent across Main Street in his hometown. A collection of stories by Henry Lawson, it included his volume "The Romance of the Swag."

A "swag" was a bushman's bedding and possessions rolled into a bundle. The "romance" was the adventure of carrying it from job to job in the Australian outback.

Since reading Henry Lawson's tales of the bush, Ed wanted to "romance the swag."

When he was a kid, his father, then a wine merchant – which was before he returned to the building trades - held a hammer in one hand and a pen in his other hand. "Do you want to work with this or this when you grow up?"

A kid's future was always somewhere called "when-you-grow-up."

Zolli told his children that he set aside provision for their university educations. Back then, higher education wasn't free. Families couldn't even get a loan for it.

Maybe Zolli set aside the money. Ed didn't care.

Even as a kid, a regular job sounded too regimented to him, whether delineated with a hammer or a pen. And now, a young man, Ed wanted to annihilate himself in hard physical work while romancing the swag. He wanted to live the life that Henry Lawson wrote about a hundred years earlier.

Maybe his father recognized this in him decades later when he suffered a stroke and slipped toward death in a nursing home. Grabbing the arm of a much older yet still quite young Ed, he told him that he - Ed - always was a "romantic."

Zolli wouldn't have a "Don Juan" ladies-man romantic in mind. He would mean a "dreamer" romantic. An idealist.

It would take one to know one.

For now, Jean hunted for shearing work for her son, and Ed hoped she found something by the time he returned home from Bill O'Brien's capsized packing shed later today. Otherwise, he turned down Quinn's offer for nothing.

Bill O'Brien walked into the bunkroom. Flies followed him even this late in the year. The dog poop gave them a lead. Streaks of tears lined the dust-covered old face. He paid Ed and Quinn, shook their hands, and that was it.

"Oh," he said, "leave by the top gate. Protesters out front."

The young men nodded.

***

SOMETIMES LIFE GOT Ed down, usually on gray days, on days that were windless, when rain landed flat from the sky. As if from a flatness above.

Sometimes on hot days, and on bright days, life got him down too.

Mostly when Ed drank too much beer, or when he overate, a sort of chemical self-hatred made him want to beat his chest.

He always found reasons to feel guilty about something. Or to feel stupid for saying something dumb while he was drunk.

"Did I say that?" he would ask, sitting bolt upright at two in the morning.

Unlikely anyone remembered what he said, however stupid. Especially his friends. If he said something overwhelmingly stupid, maybe they might make fun of him

18

while the urge lasted. Otherwise, life moved them along quickly.

Girls might remember longer, because words, what he said, was felt harder by girls.

Ed sometimes felt he remembered things forever. He didn't know if he was cursed or blessed.

***

DOWNTOWN ADELAIDE SHONE in the late autumn midday rain. Ed parked his green Ford in a rooftop bay on a seven-story mixed business building. Below, North Terrace was thick with Thursday traffic in a dynamic way. Rain and its gray flatness failed to curtail the downtown thoroughfare as it would the quiet of the countryside or, for that matter, the loneliness of the suburbs. Rain along the city streets of Adelaide made people run and turn from one another and duck open umbrellas, and in this, rain brought excitement with it.

"Sorry," people called. "'Scuse me," others called.

They ran in the rain as if they waltzed without rules.

Ed roused from tiredness. That was the one thing about the physicality of work he didn't want. Tiredness. Now and then, tiredness crashed him. But today the midday rain made the city streets shine.

He never visited a city apart from Adelaide. It was "the city" in his mind. He hadn't visited Melbourne, several hours' drive away, Adelaide's closest neighbor.

"Man, I can't believe you've never been there," Mark Georgiou chided.

Back in school, Mark passed through the great metropolis in the back of his parents' station sedan squeezed between his two sisters on their way to relatives in regional Inverloch.

Conversely, Ed's folks avoided the city when the family drove to the Victorian Alps one year.

If Ed visited Melbourne, he would visit every major city in the world from New York to London to Paris to everywhere.

From what he knew, Melbourne was not downtown New York or London. Not by any stretch of the imagination. In no way was Melbourne another Paris, despite having a "Paris end of Collins Street." But if a city were big enough, which Melbourne was, he would see, hear, and smell what he saw, heard, and smelled around him, and it would be all he knew. Then he would learn that Adelaide was not big. It was not small either. But it was not big. Adelaide would never be all he saw, heard, and smelled around him. In Adelaide, the world was out there, somewhere. Always.

The sun broke through the clouds. Immediately, the day felt warm again, probably too warm for late autumn.

Ed stepped from his car, the beautiful, green five-year-old Ford sedan that rode like a Mercedes, so his father, Zolli, said. From the rooftop park, he looked toward the hills in the east. He never saw himself going back to Bill O'Brien's packing shed, not while his eyes sat upon his future like the Ford's headlamps might lie upon an open road of adventure. But he never saw himself not going back there either.

That crazy time warp meant that time never passed for Ed Kaspar, even as it passed.

Connections were forever lost, no matter what he thought or did.

The sun slipped back behind the flatness of cloud but not before it irradiated the Adelaide University campus and its students across North Terrace.

Ed tried to guess what went on inside those heads, inside those bright student minds, those clever minds that belonged to people from tree-lined streets in the genteel suburbs to the east of downtown Adelaide.

He thought about the movie "2001: A Space Odyssey," where Dave Bowman and Frank Poole were too smart to argue with each other while they journeyed to Jupiter.

Several levels below the car park, he visited Standard Books, the city's largest bookstore.

It was a community, a village. It was a business, sure, a

business like record stores and photo labs that would not weather the Internet-to-Come. But Standard Books was more than just a business. Book readers gathered there, and store assistants knew everything about books. Store assistants were really into books as if selling them not only paid their mortgages but paid their souls too. They knew that plenty book buyers finally felt normal while they hunted among the shelves of books spread throughout the multistory store.

"Want some help?" an assistant called to Ed.

With directions, he found the literary section and searched for God knew what. Henry Lawson stories were as close to literature as he got, and even they came to him by way of his mother.

Jean owned her own library back home on Main Street. Ed's father made her hardwood bookshelves and lined one wall of the jarrah-floored dining room with them beside the fireplace. Jean owned books by Charles Dickens and the Bronte sisters. She owned books by Tolstoy, such as "War and Peace," actually only "War and Peace," the tiny-print Signet Classics edition the size, shape, and weight of a brick. Ed devotedly read it serially in random snippets from the age of fourteen, uninhibited by the formality of bookmarks. Books by Hemingway, too, but not by Dostoyevsky, except for "Crime and Punishment." Also, she never got over how Hemingway was literary fashion when she was young, pushed down her throat, as it were. But she loved "The Old Man and the Sea." She loved how age was its own nobility. When she left Britain, her father gave her the pocketbook edition of "The Rubaiyat of Omar Khayyam" and nursing friends gave her a volume of O. Henry stories. She retained these in her library too. She owned books by Jacqueline Susann and John Steinbeck. And by Harold Robbins and Jackie Collins. She owned a whole collection of Catherine Cookson novels. She had a shelf of spy stories written by English writers, where spies were very patriotic and witty, but not always. Readers Digests books, though small in number, were mainstays. She owned books by Australian writers, but only if they cracked the international scene and the subject matter wasn't obscure or weepy. So she possessed books by Tom Keneally and Colleen McCulloch, and she owned one novel by Patrick White, "The Tree of Man," and plenty of books by John Cleary and Morris West.

While he ambled around Standard Books, Ed overheard a conversation between two men not much older than him. They sounded university educated. In Ed's mind, everyone in the store seemed university educated if they spoke well, if they dressed well, if they carried themselves well.

"He hadn't finished high school. Why let him in?" one of the men asked.

Ed took matters to heart, entirely out of context, and slunk back to his car in the rooftop bay.

Of course he knew the men hadn't talked about him. How could they have? But he thought they talked about men like him, and he let himself believe this. He encouraged himself to believe it. He wondered what signs betrayed him, what told the two men and the people of Adelaide, which included the clever students across North Terrace, that he, Ed Kaspar, hadn't belonged in a bookstore. He didn't belong in a community of educated readers.

He drove the Ford to Stepney, a nearby suburb within walking distance of the rooftop park. There his second brother, Gus, shared a house with his old school friend, Katherine McKechney.

The sun belted from the wet asphalt like sticks poking his eyes. He parked the green Ford two houses back from his second brother's tiny city cottage, unsure if he parked legally. After he knocked on the door of the cottage, he discovered that Gus was not home, but Katherine was.

"In town for long?" she asked.

Before he answered, she let the door swing wide and slipped along the corridor as quiet as a nun.

He knew Katherine for years, and he entered the worker's

cottage with a lean-to bedroom and outside toilet. The rental house passed for student accommodation and not much else.

His second brother finished with university midway through his degree and planned to become a paramedic. Ed wanted a box of his old university textbooks.

Near the top of the stack was a book about Australian history written from a socialistic perspective, "A New Britannia." Ed hadn't an idea where it fitted the Australian history canon. He rarely thought about things like socialism. When he did, he pictured feudal societies from TV, where dependent souls pleaded to their betters for sustenance or favors.

"Where's our share?" they might cry.

The thought of the new ideas in the box thrilled him. But good feeling only made him feel bad about the tiny cottage his brother lived in. In the country, houses were bigger and more settled. Drinking water was cleaner in the country.

He couldn't know this for sure, that drinking water was cleaner in country towns, or why he thought it now while he looked back from his Ford at the dark little cottage with a lean-to bedroom, and at the tight street of cottages without driveways or parking. But he thought it.

He thought that food was more plentiful in the country, and fresher, and better quality, and not so frozen or fatty or quick like fast city food.

Back home, in the country, was real work that paid well, and friendships and freedom. He needn't plead for sustenance or favors.

She lived here in the city during the workweek and worked here. She traveled home most weekends to her parent's dental business two towns east of Ed's hometown. Carmen. Not his second brother, Gus, not Katherine McKechney, but Carmen. Carmen had beautiful hair of a color he hadn't seen before. Or would see again.

She seemed different. All girls who boys fall for, especially for the first time, seemed different from other girls.

And now Ed wondered if neither Henry Lawson stories nor the wish for hard work in shearing sheds drove him to want to roam the outback. He wondered if she, Carmen, turned him away without meaning to, without knowing it. If he, Ed Kaspar, ran from her. From Carmen.

He broke it off with her on principle. He remained fixed about it, even if breaking it off with her almost killed him, and even if he couldn't recall why he did this, what his principle was about – and even if he hadn't considered her feelings.

"I don't get it," Twigs Rogers counseled. "Talk to her."

Twigs was a levelheaded guy.

Ed was defiant.

Sometimes he thought he broke it off with her after he heard that she made it with a mutual friend, Danny MacArthur, one of the MacArthur boys, the eldest, whose father ran one of the town pubs, the Woolshed Hotel. But he wasn't sure if this was what he heard, let alone if she actually made it with him. All he knew was that his love for her was sweet agony to him. He suffered sleepless nights and restless days while loving her.

He saw her now, as he pulled the Ford away from Gus's cottage with a trunk load of first-year university textbooks. He saw her as he drove home, and as he arrived at his hometown an hour later. He saw Carmen in every woman, and in every hope, and in every desire to reunite with her. And he would not stop seeing her for years, and even then he would not stop seeing her ever.

***

NEXT DAY, FRIDAY, Ed Kaspar awoke in a bedroom that he called his own since his eldest brother, BJ, five years his senior, fled the house following an argument with Zolli.

BJ fell in with radical 70s counterculture, and not the free love sort, but the anarchical sort that followed the free love sort. Flower power switched from tie-dyed chemises to purple

V8 muscle cars. Kids bought them straight out of school on hire purchase agreements, seen as evil in Ed's household, hire purchase agreements and purple muscle cars both. Newly licensed drivers span wheels from one end of Main Street to the other. Twin exhausts thundered and tire rubber burned.

"Hear that?" the All Tires manager said to twelve-year-old Ed and his dad one day while Zigs Werner laid burnouts on Main Street. "That rubber could have taken Zigs to Darwin and back."

Ed and his family lived on Main Street after all. Zigs Werner burned rubber in their front yard.

By the time Zigs tore up Main Street in his V8 muscle car, motorcycles entered BJ's life. Bikers were around in Australia for decades. Zolli rode an Ariel Square Four with his buddies during the 1950s. They strapped .22 caliber rifles to their backs and rode into the saltbush along the River Murray for target practice. Imagine it. Groups of motorcycling immigrants with rifles strapped to their backs?

During the 1970s, some bikers started riding not with their buddies, but in outlaw gangs. These bikers became "bikies," a distinction lost on most of the world, but not one lost on particular aspirational teenage boys and a few switched-on journalists. Outlaw gangs of "bikies" moved into criminal enterprises such as drug dealing and prostitution, even if their criminal prowess, like the engineering prowess of their motorcycles, had nothing on the sophisticated models to come. But bikie gangs were a presence in the 70s, and a helluva presence.

During the summer of 1976, smack bang in the middle of BJ's teenage formative years, bikie gangs from around Australia squatted in a nearby abandoned farmhouse. Town spokespeople, such as Jake Williams, made the national news.

"They're in the Warburton house. The Kerneckes lived in it before buying the Turner farm."

The Kaspar family sat around their brand new color TV to watch the grain storeowner appear on the screen rather than three blocks down from the Kaspar household where he lived.

Once he finished with town genealogy, he declaimed the mayhem that the bikies brought to Ed's town that summer.

Bikies stripped naked and urinated and fornicated in the swimming pool.

During the summer, the town swimming pool kept townsfolk sane.

They rode alongside Mao Dwight, and kicked him from his bicycle.

"Lucky the ground broke your fall," Rex Goodman said while he filled his truck at the Esso pumps.

Mao agreed. Lucky.

Bikies threw darts at bar patrons. They stole food from grocery stores. They trashed the remains of the farmhouse they inhabited.

They rode in wild packs of thunder and costume, wearing leather chaps, waistcoats, and Uncle Sam top hats (because bikies have always loved dress-up.)

The period was that of the "Vehicular Rumble."

The wildly engineered choppers scared young Ed. They thrilled BJ, then seventeen.

Fate was fate, and BJ walked his path to counterculture anyway. But seeing thunderous hordes of costumed outlaws overrun the town helped stir the pot.

BJ hung up his hiking boots for motorcycle boots. In the space of a single roll of Kodachrome, he left off campfire snaps and snapped customized motorcycles.

By the time he turned eighteen, which was a year after the bikies stormed the town, he saved enough money from his apprenticeship wages to buy a new Honda 750, the bee's knees of motorcycling in the day.

The 70s was where two rivers met. Zolli represented one of them, BJ the other. Life frothed wildly at this natural confluence.

When Zolli arrived in the family garage early one Sunday morning to discover BJ's friend, Sloop Davis, in the back of a panel van, or "shaggin-wagon," with Chantelle Barton, the out-of-town daughter of a reputed tough-guy, he took it as a sign that his eldest son walked a troubled path. What was he thinking to bring them here?

"Enough was enough," a favorite saying of the times.

Zolli confronted BJ as he tried to escape the house early to move the shaggin-wagon from the Kaspar household.

Later, Zolli claimed that BJ raised his fists to him, as in "raised his fists to his own father."

Probably he had. But if he had, he had done so lamely, and fearfully, and as a matter of saving whatever dignity he believed Zolli hadn't stripped him of.

That morning, BJ vacated the family home with the clothes on his back. He never returned, not to live anyway.

Truthfully, Zolli and BJ, the loving father and son pair, fell out of love years earlier. One was as hardheaded as the other. Zolli had his demons. BJ, too.

Though Zolli was the adult. He should have checked his demons.

After BJ left Main Street, Ed rearranged the two wardrobes that acted as a privacy wall between their single beds. To this day, the wardrobes lined the wall opposite, opening up the room.

But BJ's old bed remained. Its bedspread of abstract green circles fell to the shagpile carpet as if awaiting his return, and the return of the 1970s.

Ed gave up waiting for BJ when he left school to work at the local carriage plant. At that point, he had the financial means and the maturity to buy into his own life. But the bed held on for two years, until Ed needed room for a home gym.

Knowing that BJ was out there somewhere was never easy for Ed. BJ left Ed's childhood of Sunday mowed lawns, Christmas trees, and birthdays celebrated by sips of Minchinbury bubbly for the world of muscle cars and motorcycles after he raised his fists to his own father, so said.

Cut and blow hairstyles for men came and went too. They

hung around a little longer for women.

***

A MAN'S VOICE reached Ed while he reminisced in bed about his and BJ's history.

"Wally Stahr's son, Walter, crashed into the Hassold fence on Venecke Road a week ago…You didn't know?"

No. Jean didn't know.

"Terry Costello's fixing the car now, a '74 Fairlane."

The voice was not that of his father. A week ago, Zolli flew to the old country, Hungary, to comfort his aged mother. Zolli's father, the octogenarian grandfather Ed never met, passed a few months back. Zolli would be gone a while. On his return to Australia, he would visit relatives in the States.

The voice belonged to Barry Litz. Barry, black-haired, short, and thin ran the town's only restaurant. He employed several workers, mostly his relatives. Alternatively, he hired locals who were not smart enough to steal his business.

Employing people made you someone in a small town. Enough money stayed on Main Street to notice its absence were employers to close their businesses unexpectedly and their employees to leave town for work elsewhere.

Barry, entrepreneurial to his core, recently entered used car sales, and he knew cars. He knew people too. He cultivated contacts everywhere, in all walks of life. His business wouldn't have survived in such a small town selling crap.

Where he sold lower-priced vehicles with a few warts, he didn't cover anything up – he didn't cover everything up - and he priced the units accordingly.

Ed's first car was a cheapie. In fact, it belonged to Barry when he was a kid. Ed's green Ford was upmarket in comparison.

Barry's sales yard was at the other end of town. After test-driving it, even Zolli said that the Ford rode like a Mercedes.

At the point of sale, Barry told Ed they could fix things up

28

directly. He waved his hand. "Fix things up" meant "settle payment" and "directly" in country-speak meant "whenever."

Ed kept the cash with Jean for a couple of weeks. Now, this morning, Barry came to collect. He talked one million miles an hour. Ed loved having visitors in the Main Street house. Not grand entrance visitors that everyone, including the visitors, planned for and suffered over. But drop-in visitors, people Ed knew all his life, people who knocked at the front door and entered with news and business.

The truth was, visitors dropped by rarely. Zolli liked privacy. He expected formality.

Ed dressed quickly, ran to the kitchen, and greeted his mother and Barry Litz.

Jean chose this moment to tell him that she found him a job just that morning with the Doleman Brothers.

"Actually," she explained - more to Barry than to Ed – "the brothers are two cousins who bought the Doleman Brothers business."

They contracted shearing runs across much of the state and parts of the neighboring states, New South Wales, Queensland, and Victoria.

Ed was to start Monday, three days away.

"It fell into place," he said, relieved. Excited.

Listening in, the local squash champion, Barry, advised him to refrain from consuming too much alcohol while he traveled the outback away from family and friends.

"Shearers are big drinkers," he warned.

Barry Litz mentored Ed. The entire town mentored him. A century earlier, it surged into history as a global mining center. Enough money remained following the boom for local benefactors to brighten the streets with gaslight while the capital fifty miles away burned candles. The next generation of benefactors built the area's best sports ground with their own hands. They built a magnificent primary school too, and a hospital. Local marble was shipped to Adelaide to construct Parliament House. Sir Charles Peterson, the world's greatest turn-of-the-century pastoralist, made the town his home. He held the world's biggest horse markets at the railyards at a time when horse markets were pretty damn big affairs. He bequeathed his mansion to the education department. Ed roamed its halls, receiving his high schooling amid that degree of magnificence and history. For a century and a half, the local engineering plant manufactured and exported train carriages to the nation. It provided Ed with his first job. Colin Thiele and Geoffrey Dutton, literary luminaries, once lived nearby.

There was BJ to think about, though, while getting carried away with how supportive life in a small country town was.

And there was Zolli.

There was the way in which the town reacted to Zolli and the way in which BJ dealt with it.

The way in which all the Kaspar family members dealt with it.

In this small town, a resident might claim a relative three generations back who was a town mayor. Outsiders sort of had to not only know this but respect it too. And not just respect it but be obedient to it.

Here was Zolli, an immigrant with a strange accent. A suited reffo, a displaced person.

And "Hungarian" could be shortened to "Hun," couldn't it?

It mattered little that "Hun" as used during the first and second world wars referred to Germans, not Hungarians.

Or that Nazis occupied Hungary.

Jean's background didn't always go easy with townsfolk either. Because she was English and talked that way, superior, even if she was not English by upbringing, but Welsh, and was raised in Cardiff amid Second World War aerial bombings orchestrated by men whom Australian soldiers fought against too.

Were townsfolk Rotary Club members or Masons? Or Lions? Golfers or lawn bowlers? Were they Catholic, and if so, Irish Catholic or Italian Catholic? Were they Protestant and

30

if so, Church of England or Lutheran?

Or were they in the no man's land of Methodism?

Or were they Presbyterian, like Ed, and without a place of worship in town at all?

"What's Preptarian?" some kid asked at school.

Worse by far than to belong to the wrong church, or not to belong to any church, was to challenge local businesses. Twenty-two years earlier, in the 1960s, before Ed was born, Zolli moved his wife and two boys to town after he purchased a liquor license to a rundown wine store along Main Street. He planned to import fine liquor and sell it to corporate bulk buyers and restaurateurs back in Adelaide. Stand-alone liquor licenses were so rare during those days that he found one for sale only an hour's drive from the city. It helped that country life appealed to him.

He sourced domestically produced wine from the nation's vineyard – and soon that of the world - minutes away in the Valley. He sourced the beer from quality brewers in Adelaide.

Naturally enough, he sold grog to locals as well as to his Adelaide customers.

This meant going head-to-head with local publicans.

"It's not the way to make friends," a grizzled customer told Zolli.

The stranger never bought anything.

He told Zolli that he owned the building. He gave him and his family forty-eight hours to vacate.

Zolli left for his den and returned with the title deed.

The man grumbled, "What do you know, reffo?"

"There's the door," Zolli pointed.

The man grumbled some more, like losers do. He left the store and never returned.

A grocery store accompanied the liquor store. When Zolli introduced a new line of bakery products manufactured by a national conglomerate, Pip Pop, he went head-to-head with the local baker, Damper Chiffly.

Pip Pop bread lacked the personal touch in the streets of

small-town Australia, or at least it had back when Zolli introduced it. But locals wanted to try it, so he ordered it for them.

Town bakers were people of note. Tall, wizened Damper Chiffly was, at any rate.

And to be fair, like Barry Litz, who only sold quality used cars, Damper Chiffly baked serious quality goods, despite his nickname. And, like Barry, he employed people whose money stayed in town.

It came back to money, of course. It always did.

Unprotected by the church and by community organizations whose members wore funny fur hats, Zolli doggedly went up against the local traders. A damned outsider that he was, and a reffo to boot, a war of attrition set in.

Zolli was left to wonder which came first, the cause or the effect. But by then, it no longer mattered. He just had war, and he was in it. It continued long after he closed the grocery and liquor businesses and re-entered the building trades.

***

AFTER BARRY LITZ left with cash for the Ford, Ed went to the cellar and wandered into his father's study where he surveyed photos of his grandfather's grave. Zolli's cousin, Ilonka, sent them. One photo showed the tomb to be a big marble affair, maybe the biggest in the cemetery. Zolli's mother and his cousin Ilonka, along with other old women, congregated around the grave and laid flowers and wreaths.

Ed grew up believing that his paternal grandparents were dirt poor. He imagined that his father, Zolli, escaped war-torn poverty in Europe for the Lucky Country and enjoyed the latest motorcars, toasters, TVs, and triple fronted brick veneer homes upon his arrival while his folks back home – Ed's grandparents – rode wooden carts.

There was nothing to shake Ed from his thoughts. There was evidence, of course, evidence by way of family photos and Zolli's anecdotes. But evidence was not enough to sway his beliefs. Evidence might sway a dog's beliefs. But it would not always sway a man's beliefs.

In fact, Ed's grandfather died with a sort of wealth that no Australian could match. Ever. And it would always be this way. Because the horse had bolted. His grandpa died in the country of his origin, in the country of his clay. He died in the air and the sounds that his forebears called their own forever.

In Australia, Aborigines might claim that they would die in the country of their clay. But it was getting harder for them to do so. Experts proved that Aborigines arrived in Australia forty thousand years earlier, yes. Later, science would prove they arrived seventy thousand years earlier. Again, yes. Either way, modern Aborigines descended from a genius race of seafarers and explorers such as prehistory and history never saw.

Congratulations, it was a whole lot earlier than when Hungarians arrived in Hungary. But congratulations along these lines sent a message to the descendants of heroes that they were merely immigrants from an earlier time.

"Well done," the congratulations seemed to tell them. "You were first. You beat the Europeans and the Asians to Australia. But you make your claim in the same shiftless sands of immigration. You have the first chair at the table. But you eat from the same plate as everyone else, so follow the rules."

Australia was all about "following the rules." The whole-of-life rules that accompanied convict settlement, which *was* the community rather than merely a part of it, and the intensive colonial regulation that followed convictism, constituted the nation's true gestalt.

Later European Australia, being a settler nation, gutturally relied on rules to cohere peoples of disparate backgrounds.

By the 1980s, tall-poppy-programs proliferated everywhere.

Show-cause laws popped up everywhere.

In a melting pot of races and cultures such as the world

never saw, where one group might hold the ring that ruled them all, tall-poppy-programs and show-cause laws were voiced in increasingly acerbic tones. No one wanted to be chief when no one knew what that might mean. But no one wanted anyone else to be chief either.

As such, Australians hated being told what to do even if they believed it their right to tell other people what to do.

It ended with everyone feeling edgy and without their own clay.

It ended with everyone gripping the steering wheel too tightly. It ended with the shrinkage of one's heart and the eclipse of one's outlook.

Consequently, Ed Kaspar only ever breathed air that he borrowed, even if he was born to it, this air, even if it was the only air he ever knew.

"Go back where you came from."

He heard these words rarely in the town that birthed him. But he heard them. He heard them at intervals regular enough. And he asked himself, "Go back where?"

He arrived here from here, as had the stones that were quarried in the town quarry.

Rather odd when he thought about it. But evidence was for dogs, not men.

***

ED SLIPPED THE photo of his grandfather's tomb back into the leatherette album and left the study.

His mother's sewing room was to the other end of the cellar. To this end was a billiards room, replete with a competition-sized table that Zolli made, along with one of the entrances to the indoor swimming pool.

The swimming pool itself was a part of the cellar. Zolli reconstructed it from a subterranean water tank. Consistent cellar temperatures kept the water cold enough to make Ed gasp and wonder where his nuts went every time he stuck anything more than a toe in the water.

His dad would pull the mercury from the cellar wall. "Perfect room temperature," he would say.

Not by Ed's measure, not in the water anyway.

Zolli experimented with running black polly pipes along the roof of the garage and the workshop in a vain attempt to warm the water beneath the northerly sun and return it to the pool at slightly above freezing.

A lot of "hold this" and "hold that" eventuated. But nothing defeated the cold beast. Nothing except absolute desperation to escape late summer temperatures that rose well over a hundred on the old scale, and that barely dropped below that into the night.

Also tucked away in the cellar was the winery.

The winery was not a wine cellar stocked with exotic wonders or locally fermented specialties. No, the winery like everything in Ed's house on Main Street was far more functional. Zolli made his own booze. Of course he did. Mud-brown stuff, it bore a powerful kick. The family harvested small, sour grapes that ringed the backyard to make it. Vats of the stuff gurgled and bubbled away for most of the year, protected, as Zolli explained, by the same "consistent" cellar temperatures that iced the swimming pool.

***

THE LAWN WAS long and patchy. The late autumn sun shone. Apple, orange, lemon, and grapefruit trees lined the northern boundary. Weeds grew in the strawberry patch near the grapefruit tree. Toward the western boundary of the Kaspar backyard, plum, apricot, and nectarine trees grew together with a young walnut tree and another orange tree. An ancient walnut tree, reputedly a hundred and forty years old, grew in the southern corner of the yard. Beside the corrugated-iron fence to the unsealed side-road, clumps of dormant rhubarb awaited summer.

Grape vines edged the southern and western boundaries. Around back stood the compost bin. Two cubic meters in capacity, Zolli wired it together from framed galvanized sheets that he sourced somewhere years ago. Veggie scraps and garden cuttings went into it. Tins and bottles went to the tip. The workshop incinerator handled the rest of the household waste.

An earthen track led from the concrete path outside the workshop to the storage-shed, as big as half a house itself. Ed entered the shed now and collected the gardening tools.

Work was sweetest when no one reached for his back with a reminder of what he owed.

For as long as Ed remembered, Zolli made him and his brothers work an hour each Sunday morning in the garden. There was no church in Ed's young life, only the church of Zolli's work ethic. No excuses and start and finish times were strictly enforced, and penalties applied.

His dad made Gus put in an additional ten minutes one morning. Ed couldn't recall why. The injustice was serious enough to prompt him, six at the time, to sit down with his brother in sympathy and strike.

"Are you a martyr?" Zolli asked Ed while leaving the siblings to their punishment.

Years passed before Ed understood what a martyr was. Even then, he never really understood what the word meant. Understanding it proved as tricky as understanding who he was while he studied a reflection of himself in a mirror.

Sure, forcing his kids to work an hour in the garden once a week exhibited immensely good parenting skills on the part of Zolli. The chore comprised the primary task that underwrote the weekly allowance. Other chores included washing vehicles, wiping dishes, tidying his bedroom, stacking, chopping, and retrieving firewood, and running messages along Main Street, for example, paying bills, which meant Ed kept the coin-change, but not the notes. Zolli paid the allowance without fail each Tuesday morning, with yearly increases based on the all-important child indicia of age. But oh how Ed moaned to Gus and anyone else who listened. The weekly gardening ritual was so unfair, he told people. It proved that he indeed lived in a concentration camp.

As a kid, Ed began to believe the tales that ill-behaved children told about Zolli. They claimed he ran a concentration camp on Main Street. They secretly referred to him as "Adolf." You know, the whole confusion around the syllable "Hun" in the word "Hungarian." Hey, his dad spoke with a foreign accent, too, and he wasn't Italian, wasn't an "I-tie." He was another war enemy. "Adolf" fit the bill.

Billie Barton, an out-of-towner kid who stayed in town with his local uncle for a few years, led the assault.

He had a combatant father who encouraged him to fight and to be disrespectful to authority from an early age.

Billie, a sinewy teenager, once cornered Ed on the Saturday football coach, about the only time Ed caught it.

Still a kid, out on a big kid's expedition for his first time, Ed wore Billie's blows and spit until he confessed he was a "foreigner."

It was unfair. Ed, a little kid, didn't deserve to be met with that unconditional degree of ferocity.

He didn't deserve to be yanked from childhood so quickly.

But when it came to "foreigner" taunts, Billie said what plenty townsfolk said with their eyes. Not everyone despised "foreigners." And if Mr. Wittiger, the coach driver, saw Billie beating Ed, he would have stopped him, no question. But all townsfolk saw Ed and his family as foreigners.

Being interred in a concentration camp for displaced peoples at the end of the Second World War, himself a kid at the time, hadn't helped Zolli's case. The fact of his own internment befuddled his detractors even more.

Later, when he sold the liquor license and re-entered the building profession, he "persuaded" his children to work for him on his building sites. This compounded his image as a tyrant, even though plenty of kids worked for their dads, especially farm kids, and even though he paid his kids good money.

In reply, BJ, a teenage rebel with a cause, attitudinally aligned himself with the ill-behaved kids.

He fought back directly too. One day Zolli scolded him for the way he chiseled plaster from a wall.

"I'm not a builder, and I don't want to be one."

"While you live here, you follow my rules," Zolli said.

Unlike Ed, BJ was a talented and enthusiastic sportsman. He resented his father for making him work on Saturdays, in turn preventing him from playing town sport.

Certain schoolteachers and community leaders involved themselves.

Zolli was not a big man. But in his black and white world, he knew where he stood.

It was an awful circle. Like all circles, there was no beginning or end, but only unwarrantable accusations.

It wasn't easy for BJ. What kid, especially the eldest son, could find it easy siding with sniggering peers against his father?

And when schoolteachers and town notables involved themselves?

The teachers and notables were oblivious to the damage they caused the family. They didn't see that their intervention put BJ against his father. They didn't see that BJ ended up despising them also, and the rest of the town establishment. Or that it was a reason why he quietly cheered the bikies when they raised hell in town. And why they influenced him later.

Family dysfunction might never have taken hold had Zolli remained in the city of Adelaide, not a shining example of cultural diversity back when he left it in the early 60s, but by force of actuality a more diverse community than Ed's birthplace.

"We should've stayed there," Gus –city born - whispered.

"I wouldn't have been born," Ed – town born - replied.

"Yes, you would've," Gus said, to make him feel better.

BJ might have found avenues to explore in the city when teenage issues of cosmological stature entwined his heart. Jean and Zolli might have found ways out of their marital troubles. Ed and his second brother, solutions to their growing pains, too.

Instead, when dissension entered the home on Main Street, Zolli didn't get it. When Jean and the kids took sides against him, he became conflicted. He knuckled down in a forbidding fashion.

All-in-all, the family - fragmented rather than whole – made choices it shouldn't have had to.

***

JEAN INTERRUPTED ED as he worked in the garden that Friday with the news that his Uncle Robert and Auntie Anne planned to visit in the evening. They wanted to take their new Nissan Skyline for a drive.

Jean also explained that BJ phoned her.

"He promised to visit Sunday before you leave for the sheep farm," she explained.

Ed never knew with BJ. He dropped by from time to time, although never when Zolli was home.

Including Barry Litz, four people chose to visit Jean so far while Zolli was in the country of his birth belatedly attending to the entombment of his father in a fashion that spoke of a people who knew their clay in a way that Australians could not.

Like Ed, Zolli's home was here, in a place where he wasn't always wanted.

***

ED MOWED THE lawn. He plowed the garden beds with the motorized rotary hoe. He enjoyed being a good son. He wanted to be good on equal footing, to partake and to contribute. To be part of, which was to be not less than.

Perhaps he felt guilty that his mother hosted visitors while Zolli was in another country. Maybe he enjoyed hard work and the fat reduction that came with it.

Perhaps he worked for Carmen, imagining that she saw him working hard in his parents' garden.

During late autumn, May, and during the very thick of an Australian winter, June and July, fields everywhere erupted green with weeds and grasses.

Ed walked the motorized rotary hoe over the garden beds. He raked the bigger weeds to the top of the soil and carried them off for composting. They weren't noxious, dreaded couch grass aside.

Some of the uprooted grasses remained beneath the turned dirt, now brown, rich, level, and clean of them on the surface. Their roots or seeds would sprout later this winter or early summer. They took hold after every rain.

"The rotary hoe makes a big difference," Ed told Jean while she hung washing.

He meant because it was motorized.

As little as a year ago, hand implements, hoes and forks, were all Ed and his father worked with.

The possum trap was empty of apple-bait, and the door was jammed wide open, which was the case for a year. Originally, Ed trapped the possums and released them at a nature reserve out of town. But they always made their way back to his Main Street house, or to someone else's house, or other possums moved in. In the end, he learned to compete with them for the summer stone fruit.

The house was between dogs. Old Blackie, after nineteen years, born in Ed's own year, lay some twelve months beneath the orange tree beside the western fence. Rusty the cat joined him, scarred to the bone in-rest after a long life of resolving neighborhood disputes of the tomcat variety. A nameless budgie from second grade lay there, too.

Before leaving for Bill O'Brien's packing shed last week,

Ed chopped down the peach tree that grew beside the ancient walnut tree. Today, he grubbed out the roots.

"I'll plant sweetcorn here," Zolli told him before leaving for Europe.

It would be odd seeing sweetcorn here, but times changed. The peach tree was old too, not as old as the ancient walnut tree. Yet, it stopped bearing fruit long ago. Yearly it struggled even to leaf.

Ed dug the roots with a mission, with purpose, because everything in his life was filled with mission and purpose.

He wished that Carmen were here to see him now.

***

ED WASHED HIS hands with Solvol soap in the laundry tub. He brought in a box of firewood earlier, even though the season remained touch-and-go as far as needing additional evening warmth went.

"When's Uncle Robert and Auntie Anne getting here?" he asked his mother while drying his hands.

"Six o'clock."

"For tea?"

"Yes."

"I'm hungry."

"Can you wait for tea?"

"No." It was one of the rewards of hard work, food. "I'm going out tonight," he said.

"Will you see your girlfriend?" Ed's mother waited.

Eventually, she switched subjects and explained that she was okay with Ed heading to the outback provided he was home in time to collect his father from the train station when he returned in a couple of months.

The cost of international flights dropped sufficiently enough to allow a man such as Zolli to fly overseas. Adelaide had an international airport from 1982. But, flights to Munich departed from Melbourne, which meant that Zolli trained-it to

Melbourne first. He would train-it back home to Adelaide later. (He also trained-it from Munich to Budapest and then coached-it to Szeged.)

The cost of domestic flights locally was prohibitive, with two airlines sucking Australians dry for all they were worth. Once competition arrived fifteen-years away, local air carriers would try to rally national pride to save themselves. But before then, they stuck their hands so deeply in their countrymen's pockets that they felt their knees ache and wondered where their body parts went.

"As long as you don't forget him," Ed's mother said.

"I won't forget him," he said.

She told him that she worried about him leaving home again.

What could he say to that?

Then he made a concession to his mother's question about his girlfriend.

"I want to see the boys tonight before I head north."

He said it like a man, like a character heading to the great Australian bush or a romantic war in a movie staged in a previous era.

Actually, the golden summer of mateship in Ed's young life had passed. Between school and adulthood, everyone his age and a year either side commingled in a fantastic adventure. But already most of his friends moved to the city or other towns. Or they entered steady relationships with girls whom they mistook for objects of domesticity. Other kids looked for the meaning of life in sports. Some wanted rock band fame. Those kids, the ones who wanted rock band fame, left their betrotheds and their trades and were never seen or heard of again.

***

UNCLE ROBERT AND Auntie Anne hadn't arrived by six o'clock, so Ed went to the Woolshed Hotel two blocks up and off Main Street.

As he walked the quiet street, a big, affable, woolly-headed young Scotsman, Scottish Nick, who once worked with Ed, rode past on the back of a truck.

"Olympic swimmer, Chester, have a drink for me," he yelled as he flew by.

Riding the back of a truck meant gluing your bum to the deck, perching for purchase, and throwing your head to the wind. It also meant you hadn't made cab class.

And there Scottish Nick rode, a great, affable man riding the back of a truck, his head to the wind, like a happy, dumb dog.

***

THE WOOLSHED HOTEL was just off Main Street, more or less opposite the Ambulance Station. Ed detoured past the North Town Hotel and the relatively new Australia Post building. Rafati's land sales was on one side of Decker's Deli. Decker's was an epicenter of local information, great steak sandwiches, confectionary, fruit and veggies, ice creams in summer, and newspapers after hours and on the weekends.

Beside Decker's farther up was the old council chambers, now the town library. The building was a drop-in youth center after the council removed its offices to new digs across the side street from Ed's house, down near the cream-brick police station. Inside, teenagers painted brilliantly original murals of magic mushrooms and acid-dreams.

"Dropout center, more like," some locals said.

The center hadn't stayed open long before the library took over. Kids just stopped going. But the town made an effort.

Many buildings along Main Street were a hundred and twenty years old. They were built to last during prosperous times, and they were well maintained. Ed walked among them since he knew how to walk. He explored the rooms and long, high hallways in most of them.

The interior of the magnificent Woolshed Hotel was off-limits to him until an out-of-town boy, Bradly, moved there and joined Ed in class. Eventually, Ed got an inside tour.

"You can't go there," Bradly panicked during the tour.

Ed went anyway.

The long halls, high ceilings, large, heavy doors with brass nobs, and Bakelite electricals intrigued him because of the moment alone. Otherwise, he saw the pattern repeated in every old building in town, including in his own home.

The previous publican of the Woolshed Hotel ran a gambling ring for years, during which the local police turned a blind eye. Don't think mafia. Don't think seedy haunts. Think Big Daddy when you picture an SP bookie in this lower mid-northern country town.

Tall and rangy beyond belief, people called him "The Boss."

One Saturday while a kid, Ed walked to a home game of football wearing BJ's pullover. The Boss stopped in his limo and offered him a ride.

"I thought you were BJ," he said.

Which was to say that BJ was cool, and Ed wasn't, because The Boss would never stop for Ed. His tone said so.

The new owner of the Woolshed Hotel, not the SP bookie owner, fathered a brood of children, the MacArthur boys and girls, all black haired. Ed befriended them warmly. The eldest son, Danny MacArthur, was a definite lure of the ladies. He was the one who reputedly made it with Carmen during relationship downtime between her and Ed.

The thought of this betrayal was something Ed would live with forever, even if he lived with it in the absence of knowing the facts. But who needed facts? Suspicion sank the boat a whole lot quicker.

Ed and his friends met and caroused at the Woolshed Hotel as well as at other town pubs after they graduated from the local pizza bar and Space Invaders and pinball. Frankie Demir, the bald and bearded pizza shop proprietor who challenged teenagers to consume hits of Ouzo and hot chili straight, though not together, eventually accumulated enough money to return to his native Turkey with his wife and young children. So the pizza bar wasn't the same anyway.

Plenty of townsfolk met at the local pubs. Barflies haunted them during the day. Men who valued companionship, not of the TV variety, met out of work hours over one or two ponies, short glasses of beer. Ladies of the Catholic faith enjoyed counter meals at sit-down tables following Saturday mass. Counter meals, although limited to a chalkboard menu, passed for restaurant meals by any standards. On hot summer nights, young people met in wild gatherings of dance and gossip that spilled from front bars onto the streets outside.

***

AROUND SIX YEARS ago, Zolli renovated a farmhouse for his client, a retired chemical engineer, and the father of the high school science teacher, and handsome local football star, Mr. James. Ed worked there on the weekends and during the school holidays. The farmhouse was one of three houses on the big hobby farm. Once Zolli restored it, it would be perfect for Mr. James and his bride-to-be.

While alone together at the site, the father of the young woman asked Ed what people did around here.

"For entertainment?" he clarified in his French accent.

He didn't need to clarify what he meant by "here." Naturally, he meant Ed's hometown. But he also meant everywhere in Australia outside its coast-hugging cities.

The man and his daughter hailed from Salisbury, one of Adelaide's oldest suburbs. Twenty minutes' drive north of downtown, part of it was redeveloped during the 50s and 60s to accommodate voluminous waves of immigrants.

The Frenchman was pale and thin. He sucked on his cancer stick and pulled his head back quizzically as he asked his question, genuinely wanting an answer given that his daughter was his focus. He called Mr. James "Craig," which sounded odd to Ed's student ears.

Actually, he was quite a nice man in a city-folk way. He hadn't talked down to Ed, really still just a kid at the time.

While he awaited an answer, he looked around helplessly, and Ed couldn't blame him. Dry grass and blowflies surrounded them. Wheat and weeds filled the four-mile terrain between the hobby farm and town. In the eyes of the father of the betrothed, there was nothing "here" except summer dust and winter mud.

Then Ed replied enthusiastically, "There's everything to do around here."

The eyes of the father of the bride-to-be lit up and smiled warmly at him.

Football and netball in winter, tennis and cricket in summer. The municipal swimming pool. The new fitness center, with biannual squash pennants and a modern gym, which included a spa, a sauna, and a plunge-pool. Entrants at annual show day exhibited conserves, pies, bulls, wool, hogs, chooks, and incredible cakes, while equestrians contested in full regalia as a brass band played. Carnival rides arrived on show day along with the Jehovah Witnesses' stall, the cheap bling-ring man and his matchbook-decks of cheesy playing cards, and military recruiters in their massive army tanks. Main Street was busy every Saturday morning. Toby Alans brought his disco to town Friday nights. Once the police organized a "blue light disco" for under-sixteen-year-olds, "blue" because of "police blue." Not many kids went. Someone was always building a new house. The hospital got an upgrade and a helipad. An outlying road was finally sealed. Everyone attended funerals. Long lines of single-lane traffic trailed the hearse, which Damper Chiffly's uncle drove. There were dirt roads and mineshafts to explore. Swimming and fishing holes on the river bend. Old men's hats to aim your chewy wrappers at. Always something going on with friends. Occasionally, a local identity made the area newspaper.

46

Sometimes, local personalities such as Jake Williams made the national news. One man made national TV because of his whacky singing voice. True. Ed was amazed when a couple had a baby. Just think, the new mother was a few years ahead of him at school. When not-very-old town elders blocked Main Street at Christmas, and a street-party followed sundown, Ed knew what "special" was. He felt the heartbeat of "special" in a way that he wouldn't have felt it had something been on offer every day of the year, such as in the city. More than anything, he knew people in ways he wouldn't have known them in the city. He knew them across time, place, and community. And it wasn't about being nosy. Because privacy existed where people wanted it.

The town accommodated newcomers, especially if they brought football talent with them. City baggage was forgiven immediately if a football age son cut his ponytail, donned a guernsey, and took to Saturday playing fields. If he exhibited flair, not only would his current story be written for him in glowing terms, but his history too, and it would be a fine one, despite his ponytail days.

People were real even where their realities were fabricated.

Trouble started for Ed when he wanted to discover who he was and where he fit in and what the town wanted from him.

After kids graduated from school, the town assigned roles according to their backgrounds, and not necessarily in a negative sense. Why shouldn't a boy follow his father's trade? That sort of thing.

On the other hand, and it hadn't directly applied to Ed, and it wasn't everything, but, Ed didn't want to kowtow to an ex-classmate who ran his dad's company simply because that was how things turned out.

He never related the downside of town life to Mr. James's soon-to-be father-in-law. Fourteen-years-old at the time, he didn't know it. He couldn't have expressed it.

Rather, these thoughts crossed his mind as he walked to the Woolshed Hotel tonight, three days out from departing for an outback shearing shed.

He could have tried harder at football. One day he might have made A-grade.

He could have become a respectable tradesperson.

Maybe he could have run a local business.

Zolli always reinforced what it meant to be a part of town life.

"You contribute," he told Ed. "You make a difference."

The point was that Ed no longer felt this way.

Nowadays, he pounded his chest before the mirror when the blues got him.

He avoided riding the backs of trucks with his labrador snout to the wind.

***

ALL ED NEEDED to prove that his hang-ups were real was to recall how he mistreated other marginalized townspeople while he, himself, grew up.

At school, Ed teased one of his best friends, Mark Georgiou, because he was a second-generation Greek. In fact, he was an exceptional intellect and a very balanced boy.

He berated a kid a grade above him who came from the home of a deserted wife. The term "deserted wife" was not really used during Ed's childhood. But he heard the older generations use it, so he adopted it as a matter of nasty-minded convenience.

He teased another kid of part Fijian descent because he was the high school administrator's adopted son, even if he liked this observant, humorous kid considerably.

Outside of school, he ridiculed a town drunk.

"Bernie Alckie," Ed shouted when he knew he could cycle away fast enough.

Bernie's surname was "Malckie." Later he escaped to the city to lead a reformed life.

Ed joked with his friends about a man in a wheelchair who

self-medicated with alcohol and yelled obscenities on Main Street.

He whispered about the shoe store's family, which practiced an unorthodox religion, the nicest, smartest, best adjusted, and most giving family around.

"Words hurt as much as blows," Miss Kenny, his teacher, told him.

He grinned foolishly.

Other times he did nothing when he should have done something.

"Stump," the Thurston boys yelled. "Get over here."

Ed knew it unfair for the older boys to call Scottie Stamp, his Aboriginal friend, "stump" – capitalization unwarranted. The only thing holding the nickname back from serious insult was the pun, you know, "Stamp" and "stump...black stump...beyond the black stump."

Actually, nothing held it back from serious insult.

It was a un-PC era, and kids never knew the exact repercussions of what they said, not when it came to the offensive business of name-calling. But everyone, including kids, knew what went too far.

So why had Ed mistreated vulnerable people while knowing how bad he felt when others mistreated him?

Had he transferred the burden he lived with to someone else?

Was it misery loving company?

An inability to deal with things?

Had he reached for a light switch in the wrong place?

Self-hatred?

Or – excuses aside – was he bad to the bone?

***

ED'S MOTHER AND father emigrated from ways of life that their forebears claimed for a thousand years. They had roots. Though she never knew it, Jean's British lineage was traceable back to the 1300s, and it was eminent. Admittedly, she shared it with thousands of contemporaries around the globe. Little of its eminence remained during her formative years, except for a slightly plum way of speaking, confidence, and a willingness to pass on the drudgery of everyday work for a somewhat elevated life influenced by literature, the pianoforte, and sojourns to the other side of the world, namely Australia. But her lineage belonged to her.

In fact, Jean never sought Australian naturalization, ever, and died that way eventually, even if she rose early every Anzac Day to watch the Anzac Parade on TV and hum along with the march tunes and weep at the sight of the honorable humility of the returned soldiers.

Ed's parents were always going to be "new" Australians who spoke funny.

But Zolli and Jean knew who they were. They knew where they came from, and where they were.

They especially drove this point home while opposing the government's attempts to foster multiculturalism during the late 1970s.

"But you know where you came from," Ed told them.

He couldn't elaborate.

He wanted to say that they had roots, and he didn't.

His roots were "where he came from," a place where – on occasion - he "should return to."

He couldn't even poke that place with a stick. It didn't exist.

***

DURING HIS LATE teens, Ed Kaspar began reinventing himself as someone other than someone with an odd sounding name. He didn't want to originate in a non-existent place. He wanted to be included without being excluded at the same time.

A year ago, when he was nineteen, he purchased an

Australian made V-neck pullover with a small Southern Cross embroidered on it. He purchased a football club pullover too, cut a similar way, which bore its own insignia, a little clock (which symbolized "it's time to win.")

Likely, the same company manufactured both pullovers.

The club insignia, a little clock, and the little embroidered Southern Cross on the other pullover were close to heart.

"Ralph Lauren sits his polo player there," Bruce Brigham, Matt's older brother, pointed out. "Looking good," he said in a rare show of respect toward Ed.

Town respect was a tooth and nail affair.

With a propensity to shrink in the wash, and not entirely weaved to a European standard, on the heavy side as they were, the pullovers were nevertheless neat. They fit Ed's trim, muscular figure just right.

He wore the club pullover to the Woolshed Hotel tonight. He didn't play football anymore. Playing in the rain last year on a muddy field in an outlying town that hadn't afforded ground upkeep helped decide things for him. That, and his opponent running to the field with a storm of belly blows rather than a handshake. His motivation slipped too, as in, he lost interest in playing.

The game still thrilled him as a spectator, though. Almost. Team loyalty still thrilled him, almost. Club membership still made him proud, almost.

In fact, he was over it. Everything. Apprentice, sportsman, drinker, inexpert lover, half-hearted fighter and half-hearted peacemaker, bar patron in the way that only bar patrons of small country towns knew. Everything, anything. He was over it. Club pullovers and southern-hemispherical-constellations stitched in yellow thread could not help him.

At times, he beat his chest.

He wanted something else.

To be someone else.

***

AUSTRALIA WAS OUT there. It was reachable.

Peter Allen's tribute to a country that never gave him the fame and freedom that America gave him remained all the rage. A few years earlier, the movie "Picnic at Hanging Rock" reinvented the Australian bush as something globally palatable even if somewhat eerie. With backing from the Port Pirie impresario, Robert Stigwood, Olivia Newton-John introduced a modern world audience to the compressed vowels of an Australian accent while playing Sandy in "Grease." Movies such as "Breaker Morant," "Gallipoli," the first installment of the Australian revenge story, "Mad Max," renamed "The Road Warrior" in Mel's homeland, and "The Man from Snowy River," re-written with an American lead, Kirk Douglas, made tremendous impacts in the box office and in Australian life. "The Lighthorsemen" film and the TV miniseries "Anzacs" were around the corner. "Crocodile Dundee," which would bust Australian and American blocks, was around the corner after that. Novelist, Colleen McCullough, became a household name when "The Thorn Birds" rated second only to "Roots" on US TV. Pride in Australia's win in the America's Cup endured. Greg Norman controlled the globe from a golf tee. Australian cricket and rugby teams dominated world sport. John Newcombe just retired from the tennis world stage, and Dawn Fraser and Shane Gould remained universal darlings. Melbournian Helen Reddy was a decade past her knee-slapping, toe-tapping international chart-topper and endured as a US favorite. The Bee Gees originally cast their music magic from Australian shores and continued to mesmerize the planet. Redgum, Men at Work, Aussie Crawl, Chisel, the Oils, and Goanna painted Australian streetscapes in song.

Between letting go of Britain and reaching out to America, Australia sort of existed.

In recent months, Ed boisterously looked for partners late at night to play two-up – a gambling game involving two coins and popularly associated with "diggers."

"Diggers" referred to nineteenth-century gold diggers and

World War I soldiers. The meaning in both cases suggested a rebellious streak, resourcefulness, and a willful sense of egalitarianism and machismo on the part of its heroes.

In Ed's hometown, men played Australian rules footy, yes, which was sort of diggerish. But they sang in eagerly anticipated, locally produced Gilbert and Sullivan musicals, too, which wasn't diggerish at all.

Also, Ed's hometown historically surged as a mining center. "Miners" rather than "diggers" ruled in local history. Town dignitaries were a year from commissioning a marble statue of a "miner," not a "digger."

Returned soldiers, particularly Vietnam vets, were quietly respected by townsfolk, undoubtedly. But they weren't seen as "diggers" in the popularized sense.

As such, Ed Kaspar was the only "digger" in town, and he existed as one in his imagination alone.

Ed hadn't even known how to play two-up. He knew he was meant to throw two coins into the air and call out "come in spinner" in a nasally, flatly intoned voice, in syllables drier than deserts, as the coins fell to the floor.

"What now?" Dog Wilson asked late at night.

Ed pretended that gross inebriation caused his weird behavior as well as, conveniently, his total ignorance as to the rules.

Beer, meat, something about spinners, still "calling Australia home," these were the tools at hand when Australia startled Ed most into being Australian, but not "huzzahs," because "huzzahs" were something he read about in Russian, not Australian novels. But something like "huzzahs." Maybe a "you bet" in an Australian drawl. In a nasal intonation. "You bet," which was the Australian "huzzah."

He hated Englishmen of course. They sat around lardy-dah drinking cups of tea while they drove innocent Australians into Peter Weir's and David Williamson's Gallipoli slaughterhouse.

Englishmen hadn't helped Peter Allen establish his

songwriting career either, and you could almost argue that Hugh Keays Byrne stressed his English accent as Toecutter as a clear stamp of evil Downunder. Certainly, the English weren't friends of the "Breaker," bloody bastards. But Ed hated them in a "you're all right" inclusive sense. Because that was what it was to be an Australian.

He had no right to do this, to hate English people. His mother, Jean, though raised in Cardiff, was born in Colchester. All around him, English immigrants brought unique ways of seeing things to the antipodean table. Contemporary English immigrants weren't arrogant. They were articulate.

In 1984, the real issue in Australia was whether to hang onto British standards or follow American standards.

Even when Australia was culturally at its freest, it feared Britain looking down on it, and it feared America overlooking it.

Its demand for independence and its reality of dependence confused everyone, including Ed Kaspar.

In fact, Australians drove Australians into the real Gallipoli slaughterhouse. More English soldiers died there than Australian soldiers. But the movie "Gallipoli" wasn't about the truth. It was about 1980s Australia peeling away from the UK, willingly and unwillingly.

As it eventuated, feeble resistance aside, America became Australia's true cultural leader. Locally made movies with scenes of the outback were etched in Hollywood celluloid. Australian pop songs drove with American backbeats. Local pride in authors and actors who made the scene was pride in authors and actors who made the American scene. Australians loved athletes who stormed the waters off Rhode Island and overran the greens of Maryland. News of America and news of American leaders, and of Americans, became more every day than Australian daily news.

"The police shot someone."

"In Sydney?"

"Nope, Alabama."

Even a desire for a republic wasn't a desire for independence. It aimed for an acceptably American way of life. Though it was no sillier than remaining subservient to a head of state that broke from Australia in trade and citizenship.

In the end, Australia dismissed anything new as inconsequential unless America explained it first. Abba was the exception. One of the three global pillars of New Wave Rock, the Brisbane band, The Saints, wasn't.

Australia wanted to feel not so alone. It needed this level of assurance, and Britain no longer provided it. A culturally provincial nation (not always to be confused with a derivative one,) Australia exhibited unparalleled skill in selectively appropriating the best that the world offered and bringing it home rebadged as local product. Its corollary kryptonite, however, was its inability to understand or even recognize originality among its own. Consequently, it lacked the means to center itself and grow on its own terms. Australia headed to the end of the century a suburb.

As such, Ed had little to no real Australian culture to reach to. Tall poppy eradication programs didn't inspire him. Nor adherence to unwarrantable claims of egalitarianism. Saying it didn't make it so. A readjustment of the Marmite recipe, Vegemite, didn't grab him, not really, not as a national icon, despite its superior taste and life sustaining qualities. Nor misplaced adoration for murderous bushrangers of bygone eras. Pointless us-and-them rebellion and dummy spitting didn't grab him. Leftist, centrist, and rightist political elitism rallying around the same old mulberry bush didn't cut it. Ockers, in reality, were chip-on-the-shoulder thugs who exhibited pathological reverse-snobbery and got away with it.

"Fuck off."

"No. You fuck off."

Why don't you both fuck off!

Newly minted fair-go legislation hadn't any more backend in Ed's life than one drunk's promise to another. Collective trigger-wire defensiveness around national identity revealed mass insecurity more than durable national tropes. Ultimately, these indicia went the wrong way. They drew negative energy. They narrowed Ed's heart when he wanted to open his heart.

In the circumstances, the prospect of a shearing career became Ed's sole path to follow, the way of the iconic Aussie who competed and collaborated with other Australians on his way to making an income for cockie and country. The beer, the sweat, the laughs, the raw tobacco. The yarns, oh the yarns. To give, to be, which was the aim of all young men, not least Ed.

The life of the shearer appealed to a young man who couldn't or wouldn't keep a good job, save money, date girls, marry, and buy a home.

Instead, Henry Lawson's romance of the swag filled Ed's head and colored his world.

The shearing industry would save his soul from second-generation purgatory.

Once he established himself in the shearing industry and brought home tall-tales to prove it, his parents could hold their heads high. It would be as if Ed returned home from a socially acceptable war or as if the local newspaper wrote him up following Saturday football, even if, in reality, his parents never understood why he left steady work for the Australian outback.

But what would they know?

Like Australia, Ed wanted saving.

***

DANNY MACARTHUR, THE publican's eldest son, worked one end of the bar tonight. Thankfully, his brother Stew MacArthur worked this end of the bar, where Ed entered. Nevertheless, Ed gave Danny a "how could you have done this to me?" look.

With his departure for the north of the state close, Ed's

chances of fate reconnecting him here with Carmen, the place they first met by luck alone, were running out. His behavior toward Danny had something to do with this.

Anyway, he had a right to be here.

As it was, Danny went on doing what he was doing, which was drying a beer glass with a short towel.

Stew MacArthur was another matter. He idealized Ed, and Ed took what he could get. Men idealized men one-step ahead of them. It was pointless for Stew to idealize his brother Danny because Danny was two, maybe three steps ahead of him. He represented an unattainable standard. It was how it worked. Ed watched him pour a schooner of beer.

"Up ta much?" Stew asked when he returned with the beer.

Ed collected his thoughts. "Heading north for work. Sunday. Start Monday."

Two women passed to the other side of the frosted windowpane to the hotel lounge.

Ed turned from Stew to look.

He couldn't make out the faces through the frosted glass.

The women had jet-black hair.

After they walked by, he revised what he saw in his mind's eye, but came no closer to identifying the women.

He felt Stew's eyes on him, and he thought that Danny glanced his way, too, and he didn't want to appear strange. But he continued to look toward the hotel lounge.

The word "Ladies" was removed from the lounge door in these enlightened years. The word "Lounge" remained. Largely, though, women still inhabited the lounge and stayed away from the front bar when they patronized the hotel. The front bar was a place where men must feel at liberty to curse and fart. Progressive times or not, the front bar was no place for ladies, the publican's wife excepted. In reply, men rarely frequented the lounge. When they did, they sat down to a meal with their wives in washed collars, and they behaved. Unmarried men needed a reason to be there, too, which was the same as that of married men, visiting their women.

One Sunday afternoon Ed and his friends watched football on the big screen TV in the lounge. The hotel was closed that day, and they were there at Stew's personal invitation.

The only other times he visited the lounge was when the disco was in town. Every few Friday nights, chairs and tables were cleared from the room. Toby Alans arrived.

Fast-forward a decade to the mid-80s and, yes, Toby Alans' discos involved the sort of thing Ed saw in "Saturday Night Fever," though only in the first part of the movie, which depicted mirror balls and amateurishly attended dancefloors. Silk blouses only ever appeared later in the film, and they never appeared at Toby's discos.

Also, forget the strippers. No strippers attended Toby Alans' discos as they had in the opening scenes of "Saturday Night Fever." And his discos were a whole lot more crowded than the first part of the movie. They drew kids, boys and girls in equal number, from the lower north of South Australia, and from the Valley, although the Valley had its own entertainment for the most part.

His discos were magical experiences for eighteen to twenty-year-olds and some illegal seventeen-year-olds.

Toby Alans, the DJ, never spoke during his shows, except maybe to announce the last song, but he was inimitable. A shockingly white haired Dane by birth but not upbringing, with a heavily bearded jaw, he knew dance floor moods, and he knew dance floor moves, a highly skilled dancer himself.

By any standards, his ex-wife was stunning. Danny MacArthur, the dark Casanova, made short work of her, apparently, one night after a show. He was just too pretty for his own good. And he nearly always kissed and told.

But he never talked about Carmen, at least not as far as Ed was aware.

He loved Toby Alans' discos. He loved having a reason to dress up in tight scrub denim jeans and a tight V-neck pullover with just a T-shirt beneath, like Andy Gibb. Unlike Andy Gibb, Ed wore cowboy boots, or the direct opposites to cowboy boots, a soft 80s shoe named the "kayak," something popular at the time and quite unlike the kayak shoe been and to come.

Ed loved meeting his friends at the discos and drinking beer with them.

Sometimes fights broke out, especially among kids from rival towns, and even between kids from rival groups within Ed's town. Booze nearly always played a role in these dust-ups. Opponents threw roundhouse punches and they bear-wrestled each other outside until someone broke them up. Toby Alans hired bouncers, and they were decent guys, locals, not meatheads.

"I like you boys. You don't cause trouble," Tim Schmidt droned to Ed and his friends. "Don't prove me wrong."

Other kids were brutal fighters. Booze never figured with them. They jabbed with the left just-so and threw the occasional right straight, which was all they needed.

Two boys, in particular, used their fists to carve up their victims' faces and leave them bloody, bruised, and swollen. They left the parents of the pulped victims pushing for answers and police action.

Billie Barton was one of the fighters. In school – primary school! - he threw the son of a Justice of the Peace to the ground and straddled him from behind. He wrenched at his shoulders and repeatedly slammed his face into the asphalt while he yelled, "Dirty thief." (The kid's dad had fined Billie's uncle for public drunkenness.)

This hadn't been fun to witness. The boy's face was a mess afterward. It was one of those things that Ed watched as a child that just wasn't right.

As an adult, Billie Barton had no middle gears. He was violent to win, to destroy, to expunge.

The other so-called "natural" was in Ed's school class. He was a churchgoing, piano playing boy from a hardworking, prosperous family that sold farm machinery. He had drop shoulders, which meant quick fists and long, low reach.

Someone trained him to fight, no doubt. But the will to fight was his. He harbored a vicious streak, a predatory streak. Sometimes it got the better of him.

For this kid, fighting was a sport, though a brutal one. He scheduled bouts with his opponents. His victims chose to fight or not, if only nominally, given the inherent teenage bravado around saving-face. He waited for his opponents to raise their fists. Then the bouts began. Ed's friend planted his feet, leaned back at his narrow waist, and let fly out-fighter style, like a pugilist from the 1800s, one who knew his business.

Only occasionally someone wanted to fight Ed for real at one of Toby Alans' discos. They were fighters of the roundhouse punch and bear wrestling variety. A couple of them actually told Ed that they wanted to fight him because he was a "poser." That he thought he was "better than everyone else." Believing you were "better than everyone else" was a massively heinous crime. Yet, it was true enough. Ed was a poser (though he didn't think he was better than everyone else.) He enjoyed dressing in tight jeans, laughing, and finding unattached girls to make friends with on the dance floor, which involved a sort of clumsy bear wrestling of its own.

Ed took his challengers' accusations as compliments. They were two, possibly three steps below him. He talked them around and sometimes stood them beer. He practiced playing peacemaker all his life while intuitively sorting out rows between his mother and father.

Mostly the Friday night discos were safe, familiar places in which to explore adolescence. Without them, a generation would not have become what it eventually became. Ed would not be who he was. He might not have met Carmen.

Toby Alans' discos were not the only songs playing in Ed's two-year-long Summer of Fun. But they provided the lighting and character set. Thanks, Toby.

He looked away from the frosted windowpane.

Three days out from his new shearing career, there would be no disco at the Woolshed Hotel tonight.

He wondered why the strangers – the two women – were here if they weren't here for a disco.

Then he knew it in his heart, even if he knew it was plain impossible.

It would be too coincidental for her to be here on the night he needed to see her most.

The night before he prepared to leave for a faraway place.

He remained transfixed on his barstool.

It had to be her.

His body ached as he blinked with disbelief.

He sipped a beer he could not taste let alone appreciate.

Stew stood opposite him, waiting, watching, bar towel over his shoulder. His slender, soft hands pushed on the bar counter for support. He asked, "So how long you going for? Up north? Is that where you said?"

Ed shrugged in reply to Stew's question.

He realized he hadn't paid for the beer.

He jolted to life, grabbed his wallet, and pulled out two bucks.

Stew announced, "On the house."

Ed couldn't figure why.

He thought it was because he was leaving town, and he was right. He nodded his thanks to Stew.

And that was it. The whole conversation that night regarding his departure from the town where he was born and lived.

He was about to embark on his first significant journey in life. Sunday, he would leave for the far north of the state to work in the last Australian occupation, shearing. No one knew or cared.

Stew accepted that Ed was leaving town to pursue work in the Australian outback. But he hadn't understood that he planned to seek employment at one with the national ethos.

"Don't you get what I'm doing?" he wanted to tell him.

"Do you?" he might have replied.

Everyone except Ed wanted modern, urban lives. Nobody

cared for bush life for the sake of an ethos.

Even Bill O'Brien admitted that no one respected farmers anymore, which was his reason for wanting to sell to property developers rather than another farmer.

If agricultural work involved Ed's only chance to make a livelihood, so be it. But why choose it otherwise?

Dust, risk, flies, and cow and sheep shit.

But the ethos, that validation of being at one with a national way of life was important now.

Being someone, being real, was all the more important with everything telling him Carmen was here tonight.

Ed needed to talk with Philip Wagner. He saw him at the bar earlier. A year older than Ed, Philip Wagner was an independently proclaimed "gun" shearer who regularly shore more than two hundred sheep daily. He was nuggety and tough. He rolled when he walked. His body was perfect for shearing, like Elle Macpherson's was for modeling.

He purchased his own house with his earnings. As in, he paid it off! Admittedly, the house belonged to his great uncle who moved to assisted living on the sale proceeds. But it was a known fact that Philip Wagner paid close to market value for the nicely decorated timber-clad cottage.

Philip Wagner left school when he was fifteen as fast as he could. Ed was close buddies with his brother, Tom, and Ed once thought about dating his sister, Marion, after he broke up with Carmen, and would have if not for other reasons. Blessed with incredibly excellent natures, and without bad bones in their bodies, none of the Wagner kids were rocket scientists. Also, Marion, nuggety like her brothers, showed signs of becoming a likeness of her mother, a lovely woman, but rather a dumpling of a woman too.

Marion couldn't give him what he wanted anyway.

Dating other women was a way to date Carmen again.

Ed needed to talk with Philip.

He needed to tell him that he made it, that he was going to be a shearer too. On Monday. Up north.

Philip would get why shearers were important, why shearing was important to Ed tonight of all nights.

But Philip Wagner was busy at the bar talking to someone else. Perhaps it was for the better. Nowadays, he was aloof, a sort of king-of-the-heap, even if his back was almost ruined as a result of overwork in the labor that made him king-of-the-heap at such a young age, and owner of his own home.

Ed drank his beer in a gulp that hurt his throat.

He continued to look away from the lounge window.

Instead, he looked down the long bar. Barflies and itinerants. Maybe a few locals. He hardly knew anyone.

The gang was nowhere and was no more. Tim Griegson, who loved fishing, found welding work in Port Lincoln, and relocated there, where he met a girl and played footy.

Brent Edwards spent most of his time training for the state cricket league.

Cerebral classmates, Mark, Michael, and Russell, left town the day school cut out years ago, or earlier in the case of Michael, who attended a private high school in the city. A supremely talented mathematician and writer, a combination hardly seen, Michael drifted, without finding his place.

Mark, the boy of Greek descent whom Ed teased at school in some psychologically projected fashion, was just too smart for the town. He had no interest in it, and his intellect and winning attitude took him elsewhere to exciting work in aeronautical engineering.

Russell left for Brisbane to study and then he moved to Sydney. Anyway, he hated the town. He accused it of mocking him for being gay. He had a heavy, powerful frame, heavier and more powerful than Ed's. He came from four generations of pig farmers.

Gay people lived in town, and the town didn't hold it against them. The inhabitants of towns not too big and not too small tolerated each other to a point because they worked and socialized together in some form or fashion. But, true, townsfolk, including Ed, sniggered at Russell's dyed green hair and leather pants. Though Ed thought his outfit pretty cool too.

Another of Ed's old school friends, Ronald, not super cerebral, but not dumb either, and definitely a hard-working basketballer and a profoundly thoughtful individual, left town for city work. He stopped returning home weekends because he thought "basketball wasn't everything." Funny. Even where lauded by the town, some kids felt constrained by it.

Ed alienated other friends when he dated Carmen.

He alienated others again when he broke it off with her.

Matt Brigham confessed a month back that his older brother, Bruce, the guy who complimented Ed on his neat pullovers a year ago, warned Matt to steer clear of him.

Bruce was married and paying the mortgage on his first home. According to him, one day Ed Kaspar would swing from a rope. Whenever old-timers, or in this case a young-timer, wanted to finally and indubitably trash someone, they did so in whispers of someone who would "one day swing from a rope."

To be fair, Bruce had preliminary material to work with in denouncing Ed in such terms.

Although it hadn't stopped him helping Ed from the gutter one night recently, when Ed, in tailspin, was vile and drunk.

That was what big brothers were for, even someone else's big brother.

Ed's moment in history in this town was already like a little dance on the beach as he watched waves roll back. New waves rolled in. Something new was at his feet, and it looked just the same as before, but it wasn't what he calibrated his life around. Something different moved him forward, and it was all the lesson he had, just this insistence to move forward, to meet something new, to have something new meet him, nothing else by way of preparation.

He might have sensed the changes. But in raising his nose to the wind, he would have breathed in Stewie MacArthur's fart, which the proud man claimed as his own every time. His face brightened into a broad unrestrained smile on this occasion while he tended front bar.

It was time to leave the Woolshed Hotel. Ed would get an early night and all that. Think back to the yard work he completed today. The garden looked fresh and well cared for, and that hadn't occurred while sitting on his backside.

Gathering his senses, he forced himself to accept that he hadn't seen Carmen through the frosted pane after all.

That she hadn't come to see him on the night that he came to see her with no pre-planning other than what fate alone might have served up.

He was stupid to think it.

As he turned to step into the chilly night, someone called out, "I thought you were working at the winery. All the grog you can drink. Why go shearing? It's a mug's game."

This was Hugh Hutchinson. He must have overheard Ed's conversation with Stew. Likely he wasn't playing football tomorrow because he wouldn't be in the bar the night before a game. He pointed to his ankle and smiled, saying, "Problem," and then pointed to his beer, saying, "solution."

Ed shook his hand. Hugh was four years older than him and a great guy in a million ways. He had thick, messy, yellow-blonde hair and tanned skin, even in winter.

He wore rubber-framed spectacles when he played football and gold-rimmed specs for the rest of the time, like now.

So it went, one night Hugh Hutchinson joined the James brothers, one being the high school science teacher who married the woman whose father hadn't seen the point of living here several years earlier, and together they beat up a gang of hooligans in another town. The hooligans had the temerity to insult the cousin of the James brothers, the woman who was soon to be Hugh's wife and mother of his children.

Hugh should have inherited one hundred and fifty years of history by way of the train carriage plant. The plant indentured Ed as an apprentice. Hugh always gave him time. Sadly and undeservedly, Hugh inherited a plant closure and went looking for work with everyone else after the new owner absconded interstate with the plant name but not the plant or the workers.

Ed liked Hugh too because he never talked down to Zolli. Having married the niece of the retired chemical engineer who provided his science teacher son with fixable digs on his expansive hobby farm, Hugh was likewise housed. Ed's father, Zolli, got the reconstruction contract on that building too.

"What about what's-her-face?" Hugh asked Ed from the barstool.

What's-her-face was Carmen.

Danny MacArthur was nowhere to be seen. Stew MacArthur looked away.

Hugh Hutchinson dropped the subject. "Well, best of luck," he said, and held out his hand again.

Worry marked Hugh's brow. Straight after it marked Ed's.

Now Ed thought about the women behind the frosted pane again as he returned Hugh's handshake.

Funny thing, he was sure one of the women was Carmen, because he was sure he saw her friend too, Tanya, and they always traveled together. Their jet-black hair made them unmissable.

Suddenly, he became paranoid that Hugh knew something he didn't. That everyone in the Woolshed Hotel tonight knew something he didn't know.

And where was Danny MacArthur?

He slipped his hand from Hugh's and left the hotel. Immediately.

He could have walked next door and exited from the lounge room. But if he had, he would have set the record straight. Setting the record straight would prove that Carmen wasn't here. Or if she was here, she hadn't come to see him.

In turn, that would mean he could not win back her love by pretending to himself that, in ignoring her, he hurt her in a way that told her how much she hurt him.

***

AS ED WALKED home from the Woolshed Hotel, the town ambulance raced from the station and then north up Main Street.

It was a road crash; he knew it for sure.

One night a couple of years ago, Steve Donaldson killed himself on an out-of-town sweeper. He flipped his car nose-to-tail into Peterson's lucerne crop totally sober.

That very night, he offered Ed and his friend, Matt Brigham, a last-minute ride with him.

"Coming or not?"

Ed and Matt decided not.

Like clockwork, townsfolk fed the enormous, gaping hole of the road-death monster a victim a year, which was twice the tithe of the national average per the town's population.

Ed's first experience with losing someone close to him in age was when Chappy Lauder died. Ed was hanging out at the pizza bar playing Space Invaders when Spud Richards arrived and asked if he heard the news. Ed walked straight home and locked himself in his bedroom.

"What's the matter?" Jean asked through the door.

Later Zolli tried the handle. Eventually, he walked away too.

Ed remained in his room until morning.

Road victims were not all young. Old Miss Billings, a perennial pedestrian, died while she returned home from the Gawler train station with elderly relatives. She was sleeping upright in the back seat when the Holden FX gently hit a bump and snapped her aged neck.

Other victims wandered the town lonely, drunk, and mad upon medical grade wheelchairs until someone removed them to urine stained beds in old folk's homes in the city years before their time.

Others faced the change that disablement brought better, usually with the dedicated support of close family members

67

and friends. And with a verve that the road crash hadn't killed.

During the recent years, Ed rode fast, crowded cars excited about everything in life, and with an ear for ambulance sirens. He experienced rollovers, collisions, high-speed departures into fences and furrowed fields. A car struck him at dusk, a pedestrian. He fell from motorcycles too often to tally.

A beer too many on the part of the driver, a joke told ill or well by a passenger, a breath held or released too soon, loose pebbles on the road hit or missed, or crazy, mixed-up driving for kicks gone wrong, these happenstance factors separated him and his friends from the disaster of death and disablement. Or delivered them to it.

Leaving the Woolshed Hotel tonight, Ed worried that Scottish Nick fell from the truck and hurt himself or worse.

He couldn't bring himself to know the truth.

He did what he hadn't done since high school. He walked the nighttime streets unnoticed while thinking deeply about everything.

He thought about why he hadn't checked the lounge room before leaving the Woolshed Hotel tonight too.

And why neglecting to do so seemed like a road death itself.

***

NEXT MORNING, SATURDAY, Jean told him that Uncle Robert and Auntie Anne hadn't visited after all. Ed suspected this when, rather late, he returned home from his solitary nighttime walk to a quiet house. The usual telltale signs of semi-formal visits hadn't been apparent - emptied chip bowls and the good china and the silver tea service airing on the draining board. Auntie Anne hurt her ankle tap dancing. So they were coming today, the day before Ed planned to leave for the northern sheep station to begin his life anew and finally for real come Monday.

He remembered the ambulance siren.

"Did you hear it last night?" he asked Jean.

"No. What time was it?"

Ed put the matter out of mind, intending to look into it later.

Uncle Robert and Auntie Anne arrived for lunch and stayed for a light dinner, which was the way of things. On past occasions, the oldies – including Zolli – sat around the record player singing along with "It's a Long Way to Tipperary" and other memorable wartime classics while the kids exhausted flashlight batteries and themselves in afterhours games of hide-and-seek. Not tonight. Ed's Uncle and Aunt returned home to the northern suburbs of Adelaide forty minutes' drive away in the early evening.

Waiting on the street beside the new Nissan Skyline, Auntie Anne told Jean about the sort of girl she thought Ed should date, someone nice with shoulder-length hair.

Jean hinted the topic was off limits, which annoyed Ed. It wasn't his mother's job to guard his feelings on these matters.

Meanwhile, with motorcars the conversational topic between the males, Uncle Robert asked Ed whether he knew the man who died in last night's road crash. He heard about the crash on his car radio as he and Auntie Anne drove here this morning.

"Where was he from?" Ed asked.

As in, what town had he lived in?

His heart sank, and his voice was weak.

Everything local mattered according to where someone lived. He was sure Scottish Nick died.

His Auntie Anne always referred to his sixth sense as something that belonged to the Welsh.

Presently, the thought of Scottish Nick dying mixed with the thought of Ed not seeing Carmen again.

Another death of sorts.

The only thing Uncle Robert knew for sure was that the man wasn't from Ed's hometown. This meant Scottish Nick hadn't died.

Knowing this was a relief, but Ed felt deeply for the road victim of last night, whoever he was. He considered the man's family.

***

THE NEXT DAY, Sunday, Ed felt better. A night's rest helped.

It also helped that he acknowledged that he missed his last chance to meet with Carmen on Friday night, whether or not she actually attended the Woolshed Hotel. Challenging fate, or wanting more from it, was one thing, accepting it, another.

He rose early and jogged along the metal road opposite his front door. Crushed foundry slag covered the road, hence the word "metal." The road twisted past the disused mines, the old convent, and the rifle butts to the wheat and sheep land beyond.

He reached the River Light, a river that sometimes flooded in winter and almost dried up every summer.

"I like running distances," he once told his neighbor Cynthia when she asked him why he ran.

He liked what he saw and what he heard while he ran. He loved the life around him that no house or man disturbed.

It was a life that was still, quiet, and everywhere.

Perhaps God lived out here past the rifle butts.

Sometimes he thought this while he jogged to the River Light, that this was where God lived.

Of course, God was everywhere, not just here.

Perhaps this was where Ed knew God then.

He never told Cynthia this.

***

MID-MORNING, BJ arrived in a twenty-year-old EJ Holden station wagon with a vintage motorcycle, an Indian, tied to a box-trailer. He wanted to store the motorcycle at Main Street.

70

"Little man, how do?" he announced to Ed.

Ed last saw BJ two years ago when he advanced him nine hundred dollars to buy a brand new trail bike, a sweetly motored Honda XR200, the conventionally sprung model. Nine hundred dollars was an enormous sum. Ed dutifully paid it back a few months later by mailing BJ a postal order, a type of check drawn on Australia Post in return for a cash payment over the counter in the required amount together with a small drawing fee. Now BJ appeared alien to Ed.

Sure, his nose remained broad and manly, especially when he smiled, which was often. His body was burly in a warm, secure way. His wide-set brown eyes continued to take Ed's measure without finding him wanting. His open smile revealed inherent confidence and intellect as well as the front tooth he chipped as a boy. He wore the same goatee beard, which was before those future times when office men wore them as a means to get in touch with their essential manliness. He wore his trademarked indigo Levis and a sky blue windcheater. His hands were still strong. They were capable. BJ hadn't been a kid for a while now. Why should he have been? Ed was no longer a kid, and BJ was five years Ed's senior.

But unlike two years ago, tattoos covered his arms. He tattooed his fingers. He boasted that tatts covered his legs.

"Check this out."

He lifted his windcheater to reveal a massive bunny rabbit tattooed on his chest and abdomen.

In 1984, extensive tattooing marred people with a subculture status, as in seriously marred them with a subculture status. Zolli would hit the roof if he knew.

Mostly, though, Ed witnessed a sort of sadness around BJ. It lay beneath his smile and brown eyes but showed as much.

Maybe BJ realized he was a stranger in the house where he grew up.

But maybe it was the other way around. Ed and Jean were strange to him now, and this saddened him.

In twelve months, the police would knock on Zolli's door

to inform him that the vintage Indian was stolen property. BJ never knew when he purchased it. After talking with him, the police would believe his story. But it was the sort of strife he brought the family even though he long moved away from Main Street.

Today, there he was, sitting in Zolli's chair at the head of the jarrah table in the formal dining room behind silver candelabra and scented candles.

Sunday lunch - Sunday roast - was always a formal affair.

Ed left for the north of the state before Jean finished setting the table.

"Stay out of trouble, little man," BJ called when Ed steered the green Ford from the garage.

Ed was pleased to see his brother. He loved him dearly, and his heart always burned for him.

Though it broke for him too, dreading the day when he would hear the news that other families heard, that the life of a cherished family member was lost in some awful road crash or other misadventure.

***

OUTSIDERS RARELY BELIEVED Ed Kaspar when he told them he worked on building sites from the age of four. It was as true as his being born.

"Weren't there laws against it?" people asked.

Sure. There were laws against everything. Still are.

Before leaving Adelaide in the 1960s, Zolli constructed commercial buildings such as the Hindley Street ice skating rink. He built plenty of residential buildings, too, including his home in the inner-suburb of Ashford. He and Polish George employed builders from non-English speaking backgrounds. Back then, people from non-English-speaking backgrounds – continental Europeans, all - were "New Australians." Britons were "poms," just so there wasn't any confusion.

Zolli's extended family in Hungary was famous as

72

builders, though his father served as a police officer, and Zolli himself passed the national post office exams, a critical career step. Nazi occupation and postwar Europe changed his plans.

His first building job in Ed's hometown involved patching a laundry at the Hansburgh farm. Possibly as a form of respite for Jean, he took the children with him some days.

Gus, three years Ed's senior, and BJ, five years his senior, worked eight hour days. They started on site at seven thirty and finished at four o'clock, packed and ready to leave for home. At ten o'clock, the workers broke paid for a piece of fruit and, at noon, they broke unpaid for a thirty-minute lunchbreak, normal in the building industry.

Ed, four years of age, worked seven and a half hour days at the Hansburgh site. He qualified for an extra thirty minutes at lunch, rounding his unpaid break to an hour. He ate a sandwich with the others and a quartered-apple and drank weak tea from the Thermos out of a plastic cup, mixed with milk powder from a tin. Then he napped for twenty minutes in the cab of the Ford, which seemed to do the trick.

For the remainder of his break, he joined the Hansburgh girls, who kept horses at the farm.

"Their tongues are thick. Like rubber," he added while he watched the horses lick sugar cubes from his hand.

"Give 'em more," the eldest girl, ten, ordered.

Jean provided the box of sugar cubes, which was more expensive than packet sugar, courtesy of the general store.

Then Ed worked through the afternoon. He held Zolli's tape measure or the survey-cross. He swept up. He ran to the canopied pickup for tools, a hammer, or for fixings, a nail. There was plenty for a four-year-old kid to do on a building site.

Hard to believe in a world where some twenty-four-year-olds haven't worked a single day.

At the day's end, Zolli drove home to Main Street in the canopied Ford, three kids in a row up front on the bench seat with him. Once home, he prepared for the next day's work. If he had time, he exercised before dinner.

It couldn't have been easy for him, ringleading three little kids while trying to make his name in town as a builder.

Jean served dinner at six. In those days, she still ran the store with the help of a paid assistant, Dianna, and the store closed at six o'clock.

Ed saved his wages. Together with his weekly allowance, he purchased a Timex wristwatch for $11.65. Or $11.85. It was a long time ago.

He worked for his father many weekends into the future and during school break, as did Gus and BJ.

He purchased pup tents, cricket bats, long trousers, flashlights, radios, radio-cassette players, travel souvenirs, and books, among other things.

When he was fourteen, he purchased a 125cc twin cylinder Suzuki Stinger with his wages.

Ed accepted work responsibilities at the local train carriage plant effortlessly when he commenced working there as an apprentice a week after he turned sixteen. He experienced nothing as exciting as signing the oversized indenture papers, parchment really, which Zolli co-signed, Ed not legally an adult at the time.

But he took liberties at the plant that he hadn't taken while working for Zolli. Because the plant, while work, was a little like school, and he always took liberties at school.

What saved him was that he knew how to work hard when he had to work hard. It also helped that he remained affable when his long-suffering, good-natured boss, Martin Standish, tried to talk sense into him. Over and over.

"Guess how much this cost to make?" Stando asked one day. He held a milled pin. "You should know. You made it."

"Two bucks," Ed offered.

"A hundred and three with your labor. I wonder how much of it involved skylarking with these guys," he pointed to the apprentice welders, Ed's age.

Ed reddened.

"Anyway, just so you understand," Stando finished.

Ed knew all the men who worked at the engineering plant. His relationship extended to the plant manager, old cigarette-puffing, port-drinking Landy, whose grand home he first visited as a toddler while attending the birthday party of Mistress Landy, who was a year Ed's junior. Working at the carriage plant was as close as Ed was ever going to get to a "not what you know but who you know" career.

But work at the engineering plant, eight-to-five employment, the sheer routine of it, also bored Ed terribly, almost to the point of annoying him into some sort of psychosis. He longed for the freedom to walk in the afternoon sunlight and to play.

He justified his internment with the thought of the little yellow envelope of bills and coins with his name penned on it, delivered directly from the paymaster's wooden tray every second Friday.

That, and an absolute fear of losing his job, and being unable to complete his apprenticeship, and being thrown into life unqualified at such a young age, which inevitably must result in penury and lifelong disrespectability.

Then, two years into his four-year-long apprenticeship at the carriage plant, the old mogul who owned the place - Hugh Hutchinson's childless great uncle - sold it to a young woman and her father from the economically stronger state of Victoria, and the doors closed anyway.

The paymaster, actually the company secretary, and a far more efficient version of what later evolved into that corporate treasure, the "human resources manager," told Ed that the apprenticeship commission refused to sign his trade papers. His apprenticeship was cut short, and there was nothing he or the plant could do about it. Meanwhile, the other boys who completed three of the four years of their apprenticeships obtained special dispensations from the apprenticeship commission. They qualified as tradespeople without a stick of training more. Ed was the youngest. He was the last apprentice the plant ever employed, and it employed thousands of apprentices over the century and a half it operated. But he was not going to be the last apprentice to qualify for a trade.

"Sorry about that," the paymaster offered.

"What's my old man gonna say?"

The paymaster shuffled his feet.

In other ways, the day the carriage plant closed became the happiest in Ed Kaspar's young work life. He wouldn't walk earthen floors in an ancient factory any longer. He wouldn't endure summer heat and winter cold and cut his hand on sharp steel while watching machinery go around and around all day, day after day, week after week.

He wouldn't have to risk his neck.

But freedom from employment brought tremendous uncertainty of another sort and, along with it, awful anxiety.

The streets were weirdly quiet during work hours. Definitely, Ed saw no other men around except for the men who lost their jobs after the plant closed.

By way of concession, Zolli agreed to employ Ed full-time and train him to be a master-builder.

"You'll have to work hard," Zolli commanded.

Ed promised he would.

Building work was a really honest occupation that Ed would revel in. He experienced an enormous amount of relief and excitement when Zolli offered him a job. But, although Zolli and Ed got along okay outside of work, Ed knew they would kill each other if they worked together full-time. And Zolli wasn't the sort of man who eagerly took to the responsibility of hiring a five-year master-builder apprentice.

Ed wrote dense, long letters to prospective employers in neighboring towns and in the city. He received three incredibly great job offers in real go-ahead organizations. The prospective employers explained to Jean - and Zolli in one instance - that Ed's earnest letters persuaded them to offer him work.

He chose to continue with his apprenticeship nearby at

Reynolds, a global winery in the Valley. The other two offers came from companies too far to commute to. One was city-based. Ed would have to relocate. He didn't want to leave home when he really thought about it. At age-almost-eighteen, his town and everyone in it was his life.

The engineering manager at the winery, Doug, a tall, red-haired athletic type, actually lived in Ed's hometown, and, like Ed's mother, he was Welsh.

"Ed?"

"Yup?"

"When are you going to give away those tight shorts of the Australian rules game and play a real man's football, rugger-bee?"

And, "Ed?"

"Yup?"

"Don't tell me you can't hold a tune. All Welshmen can hold a tune."

(The "who you know, not what you know" aspect of his life was still on a roll.)

Working at the winery was as good as it got for an apprentice. Hundreds of people worked there, and the job came with plenty of overtime. Work clothes and boots were included.

Don't picture the movie "Metropolis." Picture a tightly knit, affluent community with all the diversity that the old, young, male and female, and varying skill sets and degrees of intellect brought to it.

Men worked as coopers. Ed hadn't known what one was before he started working at the winery. They made huge, wooden wine barrels banded with steel from scratch – hogsheads.

Old cellar hands still spoke German or accented Australian with roundabout German grammar out of a Colin Thiele novel. "That's we do it the way."

University degreed engineers engaged the eager but distracted boy in highly technical conversation. Back at the carriage plant, on the other hand, the head foreman, Mr. Hawker, a sort of barely-balanced prodigy, told Ed things like, "Nothing like a hot bowl of soup for lunch."

Winemakers swaggered like rock stars, some reputed to be touched with genius, or to be the great-grandchild of a winemaking luminary.

Old men carried plastic tubes in their pockets and not so secretly siphoned the top shelf stuff from wine barrels, that is, from the hogsheads.

No one fired them. Firing them would kill them because without keeping busy, they would drink themselves to death. That was what people said, anyway.

And Ed got lost in quiet places and explored them. He went off-site to farms and other wine cellars owned by the company.

The administration building, styled like a Prussian castle, had a massive function area and private restaurant beneath the building. Often the bosses laid out cheese and crackers while they announced their boss-stuff to the staff.

The industry was fertile, organic, as in Ed worked with sweat-soaked farmers while they unloaded their trucks of fruit. Around Easter, he smelled the grape lees after the massive crushers crushed the grapes. He touched and held the finished product, the wine, which was shipped proudly around the country and the world.

And, yes, he did get free booze. A dozen quality bottles every two months.

But Ed gave it away before his time, working at the winery for only eighteen months instead of the twenty-four months he needed to qualify for his trade.

Remember, this was a time when intelligent young people entered apprenticeships in the absence of opportunities to study at universities. And the economy had actual purpose; people made useful things; people valued trades. Ed's peers in the maintenance workshop were enlightened, chess playing, politically inclined, book-reading, worldly men of substance.

They contributed to the reality of things, the real reality of things. Urbane people, humorous people. Women – a woman – just entered the engineering fold. Ed might have modeled himself after his workmates in a genuinely positive, life-affirming fashion.

But he left the organization before his apprenticeship was up, even if he managed to qualify for his trade after all. He wrote the apprenticeship commission and argued that the winery imbued him with a tradesperson's responsibility during the recent months. The commission bought it. It was true. Two tradespeople were required to cover night shift during the hectic few weeks of the winery-vintage, which was when the grapes came off the vines and the winery crushed and processed them in huge volume twenty-four-seven. Ed was one of those two tradespeople, even if technically he remained a final year apprentice.

The romance of the swag gripped him. Ed wanted to travel the outback in a quintessentially Australian way, and he couldn't wait.

Perhaps his impulsiveness grew from childishness. Perhaps it grew from self-doubt – if not now, then never. Because sure enough, another carrot would catch his eye. Deep down he knew it. Perhaps he led a generational charge, even if blindly, choosing a life of other than lifelong mortgages.

Ed wanted adventure and fun, a never-ending series of first awakenings, like Christmas gifts that re-wrapped themselves with each new day and re-created themselves with each new unwrapping.

Adding fuel to flame, he remained playful and anarchic.

His intellect, energy, and ability should have hunkered him into a productive work life at the winery. They should have hunkered him into a steady relationship. Instead, these qualities manipulated his personalized version of the work ethic into something that validated him chasing rainbows.

***

HERE ARRIVED ONE now, a rainbow, sitting on the horizon of green hills two hours' drive from Main Street. Ed Kaspar drove toward it on wet roads Sunday afternoon after leaving BJ and Jean to their formal luncheon of roast beef, delicious plate-licking gravy, and tremendous baked desserts. His spiritual pot of gold awaited him at a sheep station near Wilcannia where, tomorrow morning, Monday, he would commence his new shearing career.

True responsibilities such as steady work and mortgages felt dull in comparison.

"Try to make this job last, won't you," Jean counseled as he drove from the Main Street garage.

***

FOR EIGHT MONTHS, the upper mid-north of South Australia, which was a couple of hours' drive from Ed's home on Main Street, was sunburned fields of yellow grass. For a few months of the year, the late autumn and winter months, which was now, the landscape resembled that antipodean yardstick, England in spring.

Three hours from home, the rolling green hills became flatter. The soil turned red, and the earth became fine like dust. The grass was not green or yellow anymore, but dull blue.

Four hours into Ed's journey, terse clumps of blue, stilted, desert-like grass grew meters one from another.

Back at the plant, old Dreyssig told Ed how he once upon a time delivered rolling stock to World's End.

"Dirt roads all the way."

That was a different era from the one Ed lived in, and occurred on Mars for all he knew, along with cross-ply tires.

Now the pavement threaded into the Australian desert as fast as his eyes saw, a place of isolated Aboriginal communities, ex-nuclear bombsites, current rocket launch sites, and farms the size of countries.

Out here drought held sway even as mud gathered at the

edges of the long road and grass grew in sprinkles. Kangaroos ate the only grass for miles at the road verges. They died by the score, hit by cars and quadruple-length road-trains. They were left in red, gray furry lumps as carrion for Australian-ravens.

Flatness stretched from the highway either side.

Trees, where they appeared, were broken, stunted, wretched things.

The ruins of one-room farmhouses appeared sporadically. A century ago, settlers saw the harsh outback for the first time during periods of higher than average rainfall. These good times lasted several years, just long enough to trick them into thinking that God invited them to move in.

"A bountiful land."

"And no competing legal claims, thank God."

They cleared the few trees and built cottages of mud and rock. Some industrious souls erected fences as if they caught the outback in a bottle. Then drought arrived. Drought was the actual reality of this terrain. Broken and bloody, the settlers headed - likely enough - back to where they came from.

Towns still survived, towns where flies buzzed louder and longer than words were spoken. Ed passed through them now, barely blips on the landscape. The government hadn't even bothered to regulate highway speed through them.

Five hours after leaving Main Street, he arrived at the inland city of Broken Hill.

Broken Hill was the work of Charlie Rasp, a Saxon (German) who fled the nineteenth century Franco-Prussian War for the far ends of the world, Australia. By the by, he tripped over silver while looking for tin in the area. His legacy became the now globally relevant mining giant BHP, Broken Hill Proprietary.

The desert city of Broken Hill was in New South Wales, not South Australia. Ed crossed the state line some ways back on the roadkill-strewn highway. But South Australians felt connected to Broken Hill, just as they felt connected to

Mildura, a Victorian border town. Even the Silver King, Charlie Rasp, retired to his Medindie mansion in Adelaide with his barmaid wife after making his fortune in Broken Hill.

Built grand with wide streets, Ed wanted to believe that the city of Broken Hill – a rural one - meant more to him than the city of Adelaide. But he was alien to Broken Hill and remained alien to it, like everyone not born to it.

***

SUNDAY PUB TRADING didn't exist in 1984, not unless patrons knew the publican, entered through the back door, and risked the local constabulary raiding them. Australia was barely a decade out of six o'clock pub closings.

However, hotels across the nation did provide for "bona fide travelers." This legal loophole encouraged car drivers to consume alcohol on Sundays. Of course it did. Ed pulled up outside a hotel along the city's main street and entered.

Patrons eyed him suspiciously.

He ordered a toasted ham and cheese sandwich, generally a prelude to ordering beer as a bona fide traveler.

Then, "Southwark, thanks." (The South Australian beer.)

The locals looked away and went on with their business, which was not very much, aside from drinking alcohol on Sunday while avoiding detection as "non" bona fide travelers.

In those days of economic downturn, Broken Hillians were seriously dyed-in-blue working class folk and fully unionized to boot. Ed, for all his workingman ethos, never really fit in with dinky-di, ridgy-didge workers.

This had nothing to do with Zolli and Jean, foreigners though they were. The boys and girls he grew up with, third, fourth, fifth generation Australians, were as middle-class in outlook as him. Wit, insightful observation, local arts, playfulness, tall yarns, sports, reading, experiencing life, an aspiration for more and a willingness to give more, these were the things that obsessed him and his cohort while the town

82

back home raised them.

"Nup" and "fuck-orf" weren't badges of honor where Ed spent his youth.

After eating his ham and cheese toasted sandwich and drinking his beer, Ed escaped outside and consulted his roadhouse foldout map on the hood of the Ford.

He followed the road out of town with his index finger along the large map. Then he hopped into his Ford and followed the road to Wilcannia for real.

***

A FEW MILES this side of Wilcannia, maybe forty miles this side of Wilcannia, which passed for a few miles in the outback, Ed turned left from the tar onto an unsealed road that likely would remain unsealed were it to run to the northwest edge of the continent fifty hours' drive and several deserts away.

At dusk, he rumbled the Ford across a sheep grate into the outer territories of the expansive sheep station.

"Tell him to follow the dirt track to the shearer's quarters," the shearing contractor told Jean last Friday.

Red dust, gray shrubs, and white rocks led him there, a modern community of buildings nowhere near the actual station owner's homestead. He pulled up next to one other car.

Inside, he discovered the recreational room, kitchen, and mess, with chairs, laminated tables, and a lounge suite, and a TV and video player in the corner.

Long-life video tapes of forgettable movies made on million dollar budgets caught dust in the corner too.

A spotless bookcase with enduring Australian classics, books by Marcus Clarke, Rolf Boldrewood, CJ Dennis, Henry Lawson, Banjo Paterson, Ruth Park, Miles Franklin, Joan Lindsay, Henry Handel Richardson, Joseph Furphy, Norman Lindsay, Frank Hardy, Thomas Keneally, George Johnston, Colleen McCullough, and Patrick White held pride of place against the wall.

Enormously popular Readers Digests also occupied shelf space, along with a few bestsellers, and that global immensity of compact, rural storytelling, "Of Mice and Men."

Later, Ed learned that modern farmer hospitality was measured in how, usually, the farmer's wife, stocked the bookcase. Books were "civilizing" agents.

A firewood cooking-oven and kerosene icebox held back the present.

**

THE MAN IN the shearers' mess reclined in a threadbare, well-padded armchair while he ravaged a bestseller.

Ben was Ed's age. He wore Levis and a blue checked flannel shirt. He had thick, curly hair, a pronounced chin, and large blue eyes.

In later weeks, come one Monday, Ben would relate how he romanced his girlfriend all day Sunday following an all-night interlude with someone else's girlfriend.

Like Danny MacArthur, Ben would stand witness to his own claims, sure enough, but Ed would have every reason to believe him, given the wow factor.

More immediately, Ed witnessed another of Ben's astonishing attributes. He flicked through the final pages of the bestseller, checked that no more pages sprang from inside, and pressed the book closed.

Ed knew a sexagenarian at the winery, Reginald, who read novels like Ben read them. The old Englishman devoured them in noisy lunchtime environments and looked up later with soft, open, vulnerable, keen eyes, and asked, "Is that the time?"

Ben had the same look now, the look of a man whose mind was rested and at work. Like a Tibetan monk after an hour or a lifetime of meditation. Reading freed him.

Jean, Ed's mother, did not emerge from reading with

beatific expressions. But she put away her novels, one or two a day, depending.

Mick Williams, son of Jake Williams, who owned and ran the town grain store, an epicenter of information on Main Street, read unencumbered in entirely encumbered places also. Unsurprisingly, Williams Senior, Jake, was a big reader. Ed's second brother, Gus, read voluminously too.

Ben stretched his legs, leaned forward and returned the book to the tiny but magnificently well-represented library beside him. He noticed Ed for the first time. He pulled his long body from the worn armchair, his chin dimpling as he smiled, his crooked, perfectly white teeth showing, and offered Ed his hand.

Ed met a man as tall as himself, but leaner, with an angular strength. They could have been brothers.

Flattening his tone and ripping vowels lengthwise into something resembling consonants, as Australian strangers do while first meeting, Ed asked, "Dija ya brng tha bk?"

"Nup," Ben said. "Mistimed things. Got here hours ago. Hadda do something." He nodded to the bookshelf. As if to explain things, he said, "Farmer let me in."

A prodigious reader he might be, he spoke in four-word sentences.

Later that night in his sleeping quarters, Ed pulled the box of books he borrowed from his second brother, Gus, from the trunk of his green Ford and looked them over.

They were valuable to him primarily because he could not, and could not ever, rip through them and digest them as he witnessed Ben rip through the farmer's bestseller.

***

THE NEXT MORNING Ed rose with Walt Foreman, the wool classer.

Walt slipped into the single bed against the opposite wall late last night.

85

The room contained two single beds.

A considerate man, he let Ed sleep.

But he woke him at four-thirty with a measured, articulate, intelligent voice, a truer standard of the Australian accent.

"Are you Ed?"

Ed blinked thinking someone woke him in the middle of the night.

Someone sorta had.

"I'll show you the generator and donkey."

Walt meant the diesel electricity generator and the wood-fueled hot water heater.

He subtly notified Ed that his workday had begun.

***

BREAKFAST WAS ENORMOUS. It was just massive. Cereal of every type covered the sideboard. Hot toast. Freshly baked buns. Plates of fried eggs. English split muffins. Grilled chops. Who ate grilled chops for breakfast? There was plenty of bacon. Grilled tomatoes, fried mushrooms. Butter, jam, honey, milk. Apples, bananas. Coffee. And tea! There were desserts for afterward. Desserts for breakfast!

No one really wanted to meet the new roustabout, because that was how shed hierarchy worked. People did not ignore Ed. They just stuck to one another and caught up with the news. Ed preferred it to forced introductions. Nevertheless, he felt silent eyes on him.

Eventually Trev, the smiling shed cook, introduced himself.

"What you don't eat, I throw away," he told Ed. "So eat up."

Some shed cooks might just well be the best cooks in the universe, and they had to be. Rain fell on the sheep in the outside pens. Farmers returned them to the fields if drying took too long. It could take days or even weeks for the sheep to dry again, depending on the wind and the humidity. And they had to dry again because shearers refused to shear wet or damp sheep. The cost to the farmer in monetary and labor terms and the frustration on the part of the livestock was significant.

Contractors couldn't help bad weather. But they could, and often did, choose the right cook, because shearers stopped work rather than eat lousy food. They stopped work just as if the rain wet the sheep and made them unshearable.

As well as being a fantastic cook, Trev was a fantastic man. Nearly always, the two go together, being fantastic at something, and being a fantastic person.

He finished introducing himself to Ed with a song and dance.

"Later I'll show you the foxtrot," he laughed.

A lifelong bachelor, he explained to Ed that he danced ballroom with the older ladies his age. In 1984, in rural areas, he still found plenty of dance halls with regular ballroom events.

Trev combed his thick, black hair under the perfect weight of Californian Poppy hair oil, a grand old favorite before the days of hair gel and bad taste haircuts.

He grinned big with dentures, a showman smile. He was the sort of man for whom lemons never existed, except in fish dishes and sweet tarts.

Ed entertained his lifelong demons by eating all the food in sight during his first shed breakfast. As a kid, he often ran afoul of adults (not Jean or Zolli) for eating everything in sight at public functions and school functions.

This was the first real shed he worked in. Small things like the enormous size of meals, and their frequency, caught him off guard.

In contrast, the farmer's wife at the first of the two small farms near his home where he began shearing – crutching, actually – provided a cookie and a cup of watery tea for morning break.

"I was told to give you this," she said with a twenty-past-seven mouth. She pointed to the broken cookie.

Thankfully, Ed and his mentor brought packed lunches.

(The second of the two small sheds near home was a pleasanter, memorable experience.)

Crutching – which was not mulesing - involved giving the sheep a double-zero haircut around their backsides, hocks (lower legs,) and muzzles in an attempt to prevent flystrike, which occurred when flies laid their eggs in damp, dirty wool, and later maggots hatched and burrowed into the sheep's skin.

After crutching, with no harm to the sheep, wool grew back as might be expected. So shearers crutched annually.

Actually, sheep were cleaned up every six months because they were shorn once a year too, and that occurred at the polar axis, calendar-wise, to when they were crutched.

Crutching around Ed's hometown was a good way for young men to introduce themselves to shearing, and a good way for old men to earn money without traveling too far from their homes and families.

Here at his first real shed, in outback Wilcannia, which ran ten thousand sheep, everything was the same but different. Ed wasn't totally without a clue. But he had to learn fast, especially when it came to restraining himself from overeating Trev's great food.

∗∗∗

THE FIRST SHEARER in the shed was Warwick Apotherick. He made sure that Ed heard him right. "Apotherick," not "Apothrick."

"The 'Apothricks,'" he explained, "live in Spalding, which is near Gladstone, where my family lives. People confuse us. I'm not saying you will. Just to let you know."

He was a few years older than Ed. He was a whole lot thinner. His face was longer than that of the guy in the "Scream" painting. He even had a little, tiny o-mouth that gave him a concerned look, if his face, taken as a whole,

88

hadn't existed on the verge of something like irony and humor. He had sparse, shoulder-length hair, carrot-red in color, which he parted in the middle and swept back, and cut high above his ears.

As a mullet, it rocked.

As a standalone, it was slightly in-bred.

He sipped delicately from an enamel mug of hot tea that he carried from the mess.

He wore shearers' dungarees, double lined denim pants that tapered narrowly at the ankles to prevent the cuffs from entangling with the mechanized shearing cutters.

He wore a blue shearers' singlet, also double lined in places, and shearers' moccasins.

He wore a thick woolen wrap-around cardigan to keep out the cold of early morning.

As the months rolled by, and as the team moved from shed to shed, Ed would watch Warwick sip early morning drafts, not from mugs of hot tea, but from bottles of beer, warm or cold it would not matter.

Warwick's nickname was "Whip."

Old Larry occupied a stand, a man in his sixties, like the cook, Trev, a confirmed bachelor, a quiet man of wry humor, who rolled cigarettes from tins of tightly packed raw tobacco.

Ned Ding, in his fifties, occupied another stand. Ned was taciturn, which Ed, a hypersensitive youth in many ways, took personally. Also, he sniffed every time Ed walked by. Ned looked out for Ben, whose father he was friends with.

Rick Bell, an Aboriginal man in his forties, occupied the fourth stand.

Later, Ed befriended Rick and shared rooms with him, and traveled to sheds with him in his Ford. He told greats stories, and he knew people from Ed's hometown. He was a mild, friendly soul. Warwick sometimes joined the pair.

The wool classer, Walt Foreman, a slightly built, erudite, crisply attired, bald, chain-smoking, middle-aged man, would class the fleeces when the day got going. He would hold the shorn wool to the light and gauge its fineness and tensile strength as well as assess its general condition.

Under-class the wool and the farmer lost money. Over-class it and the wool board lost money. Either way, the role would test Walt's reputation.

"We're down one roustabout," he told Ed as the day was about to begin. "He's coming on the weekend. It's you and me for now."

Walt would skirt (clean) the fleeces of the yellow, straggly wool and remove the edge dags – that is, the grease (lanolin) and dirt balls that gathered around the rim of the fleeces. Ed would help where he could.

Ben, the wool presser, would also help Walt skirt the fleeces when possible. But his job was to bundle the clean fleeces into the correct classing bins under Walt's direction, and when enough wool accumulated, press it into condensed bales in the hydraulic wool press ready for transport.

Ed's main job was to clear the fleeces from the boards as the shearers finished shearing each animal. He would organize the sheep inside the shed too. Roustabouts were all-rounders.

The team was a small "four-stand" team, which meant that four shearers would shear here. However, the shed itself accommodated twelve shearers.

Things would not get real busy in this shed, not with four stands running, not this year, and not for a few years to come, not before rain returned to the area with some regularity. It wouldn't take much rain to sprout the grass needed to feed an additional thirty thousand sheep on the surrounding plains. But it would require some rain, and that rain had to be regular if things were to pick up again.

Late autumn showers offered hope. Ed heard it in the shearers' voices, as few as the men were this year.

***

ZOLLI WAS A great lover of photography even before he

departed the European port of Marseille for Australia in the late 1940s on the refurbished American supply ship, the "General M. L. Hersey." Barely an inch square, the photos he took in Marseille were iconic in their own way. They caught something of the age. They expressed something of the photographer, something of Zolli.

He continued his interest in photography into his marriage with Jean, all the way to early fatherhood. At that point, when he became a father, he started taking family snaps, quite good ones, but family snaps all the same.

The family snaps exhibited moments when conspiratorial petulance on the part of his three children ought to have worn him down.

"Hold the picture of your grandparents when I photograph you," he told Ed, but not Gus or BJ, who sat beside him.

"Why?"

"It shows them that you think about them."

"Why?"

The family snaps remained, like his more serious photos, expressions of the photographer, of who he was while he clicked the shutter, as if he blinked his eyes and recorded the images there among his thoughts and feelings, and then shared them with the world.

Zolli made a photo enlarger from the slide projector, something that hummed with the intensity of a regional power station and weighed a ton, its housing cast in iron. He dragged his workshop drill press inside and elaborately mounted the projector to it. He constructed a makeshift darkroom, essentially his study with a red light replacing the white light, and with the door closed and sealed with a draft-snake. He purchased development paper and solutions from a Valley photography store.

He and Ed became excited as pictures formed like ghosts from nowhere on the special photographic paper.

Zolli included Ed in activities other schoolchildren wouldn't experience in a million years. But Ed never appreciated his father's efforts. He already drew from the poison well of sibling disdain for anything Zolli did that directly or indirectly affected him. Also, he wanted to watch TV.

A decade following the darkroom experiments, a year ago, Ed debated with him about what sort of camera to buy. Ed wanted a pocket-sized snapshot camera. The art of photography was less relevant to him than a record of places and people. But, on Zolli's advice, he purchased a Pentax SLR with auto shot technology and an interchangeable lens. Zolli owned a Pentax SLR, though an earlier model without auto shot technology.

An SLR camera (single lens reflex) with an interchangeable lens was a big thing to Zolli. His photography experiences spanned the period in which lenses moved from fixed to interchangeable lenses. He couldn't overstate the freedom to choose and change lenses, whether with screw or bayonet fittings. He lectured Ed, "Remember, the lens' fitting has to be compatible with the camera body."

"And we watch the subject through the lens," Ed said, catching up.

Ed never figured where Zolli obtained his photography knowledge. He was far too no-nonsense to waste money on magazines. TV, a bog standard medium in those days, despite its ability to cohere family members into functional units during dysfunctional moments, hadn't provided him with a regular source of photography tips either. He did own a reference book or two about photography.

Whatever, because of Zolli, Ed, and BJ for that matter, but not Gus, shared at least some interest in photography during their formative years.

***

ED THOUGHT ABOUT photography while herding sheep into pens ready for shearers. How to capture what he saw?

How could he record his experience and later study it in a way that permitted him to rise from the mire of daily concern and appreciate just how valuable and unique his life once was?

How could he share his experiences?

How could he capture the white wood of dead and living trees that existed hereabouts beneath wind and sun for centuries? The undulating, lazy caw of a raven? The dog yapping at the heels of sheep while it pushed them into the shed beneath an infinitely domed blue sky?

Come the weekend, he would photograph the shearers' quarters with his Pentax SLR, and the shed, and the surrounding area, and the red-yellow dirt as fine as dust, and the flat expanse stretching out into the forever world of the Australian outback, and the blue-gray shrubs no higher than his knees.

At best – at the very, very best - he would be left with a photo that reminded him of an image from a calendar.

"Sell them," Harry Deane once told him.

Ed photographed motorcycle races his friends entered.

Harry Deane had a point. Pinup calendars with glossy pictures for each month were a sort of poor man's window into art, travel, and soft porn. Perhaps they were all-pervasive since before Ed was born. He wouldn't know. As a tour de force in everyday life, they would die in twenty years, when digital devices would populate the world a hip pocket at a time.

The truth was that no photo could genuinely capture what Ed felt on his first morning in a commercial shearing shed, limited to four stands as it was rather than its full twelve-stand majesty.

***

SHEARERS DRIPPED WITH sweat thirty minutes into the workday. Their first shed of the season, they suffered like footballers undergoing preseason training.

Ed sweated with them. Like the shearers, he wore a shearing singlet, double lined, he wore shearing dungarees, double lined, and he thought nothing of it. Roustabouts could wear what they liked, as long as they moved like wingmen on a sports field. Ed, wearing his catalog bought shearer's outfit, must have left the men wondering whether he was a shearer waiting for his next shed or his first shed.

The classer, Walt, was run off his feet while single-handedly cleaning fleeces and picking, flicking, and straining strands of wool against the light. Ed and Ben helped where they could. But even inexperienced Ed knew when the team was down a shedhand.

Very quickly, the day was like a big hill. Other jobs let Ed daydream. Not shearing. Time slowed painfully while his tasks multiplied at the speed of light.

Warwick moaned, "Another three runs to go."

"We haven't finished this one yet," Ed offered.

"Thanks for reminding me," he snapped.

A day in the shearing shed involved four work sessions. The first commenced at seven-thirty and the last ended at five-thirty. Each was two hours apiece, timed precisely with a brass bell. The sessions were known as "runs." The word "run" also described the shearing season or a geographical area as in "the contractor managed the far northern run."

The workers had a half-hour break between the two morning runs, nine-thirty to ten o'clock, and between the two afternoon runs, three o'clock to three-thirty. They had an hour break at lunchtime, twelve to one o'clock. They took lunch in the mess and morning and afternoon breaks in the shed.

The shed fell silent at nine-thirty with the end of the first run, with the end of the first two-hour session. The men toweled off their sweat.

"Hand me that," Warwick told Ed. "Please."

Ed handed him the clean singlet that he brought to the shed earlier, and he changed into it.

The other shearers cloaked themselves in their favorite

94

coats and pullovers to stave away the chills on what remained a cold, bright, late autumn, desert morning.

Warwick draped his coat over his shoulders like a shawl after he changed singlets.

Ed pulled the last fleece from the shearing boards and threw it to the classer's table, a ribbed table similar to a slatted bed base, though with thinner slats and wider gaps. He returned to the stands and swept up.

Trev, with Ben's help, carried the morning smoko to the shed in wicker baskets.

In bigger sheds, a fulltime kitchenhand, or one of the roustabouts, helped the cook carry the smoko to the shed.

"Smoko" was an Australian and New Zealand term that meant "breaking from work for a cigarette."

By Ed's day, it just meant a recess or the food and beverages that went with the recess, as in, "What's for smoko?" which Ned Ding asked now.

Trev prepared everything, sandwiches, cake, scones. He whipped cream for the scones.

Yes, butter, jam, and sliced bread were store-bought. But the idea of providing the team with pre-packaged cookies or pre-packaged bakery products (aside from the sliced bread – even the bread buns were baked) or breakfast leftovers was outrageously unthinkable.

The shearers ate five meals a day, namely, breakfast, morning and afternoon teas, lunch, and, of course, dinner. Each meal was bigger than what most people in regular occupations consumed as their main meal of the day.

The contractor deducted the cost of the food and the hire of the cook from the shearers' checks at the end of the shed, at "cutout." The pays of the roustabouts and wool-pressers were unaffected. This would lead to some quiet discussion among the men around Ed's appetite.

Even this morning, Ed's first among the men, Rick Bell defended him at the other end of the boards after Ned Ding, a top shearer, but a sour man, offhandedly criticized his appetite.

"He's a growing boy," Ed heard Rick joke.

Hypersensitive in so many other ways, Ed would be too obtuse to absorb the meaning of all but the most direct comments on this topic. He was always a big eater, and he was a big eater now, especially after he worked two hard hours in his first busy shed. Sandwiches, scones, jam, cream, back for seconds, again for thirds. And he grew up at a time in Australia, and he lived at a time in Australia, when nothing prompted him to connect the consumption of actual food with cost. As a child, he knew that icy poles came cheap, ice creams on a stick for a little more, and choc-coated ice creams, sundaes, and banana-splits were, because of their cost, left to rare occasions indeed. But he never connected real food, the food he lived by, with money.

The fact that shearers paid for food became an industrial issue in a shed down the track. There the contractor, Harvey Harvey, would believe he picked up a bargain in hiring an ex-pastry chef husband-and-wife team who wanted an exciting way to see the country together. Money-conscious shearers as well as shearers with trim figures and vanity issues - it was to be a big and diverse shed – would complain about the richness of the food and its expense. By the next shed, the husband and wife team would be gone.

The breaks were not only for eating. The shearers sharpened their cutters during the breaks. In bigger sheds, a special team member entitled the "expert" sharpened the cutters through the day as well as managed the shed.

The farmer and the farm workers had time to catch up with their jobs during the breaks. This was especially the case where shearers – paid by the fleece - wanted the sheep kept in the races until the end of the run when they could count them. This prevented the farm workers from getting on with things until the breaks, at which moment they dipped the animals in liquid insecticide, wormed them, tallied them, branded them with paint, and one way or another released them back into the vast outback.

After Ed finished eating his smoko, and before the second run commenced, he went outside to check the sheep. He had to restock the inside pens, so it didn't hurt to see what was outside first.

The outside pens held thousands of sheep ready for the days of shearing ahead. The farmer and his workers managed the sheep in these pens.

Noticing Ed, a farmhand joked familiarly, pointing to an uninterrupted blue sky. "Hope the weather holds."

"Me too," Ed noted, probably a little too seriously.

Farmers always shared a few words with shearers, even though they wouldn't recognize them in the nearest two-car town next day. Some farmers, especially in the outback, craved companionship and took a genuine but limited interest in the itinerant workers. But all farmers wanted the shearers off their land quickly. Shearing time was hectic for farmers and significantly disrupted the animals and the routine of farming life. And farmers wanted their wool checks too, and understandably so.

Back inside, Ed overheard old Larry say, "He has the shoulders for it."

Later, Ben told Ed that Larry referred to Ed's physique, and its suitability for shearing. The remainder of Larry's brief investigation was into how Ed became interested in shearing. What was he doing before? Was he the son of farmers? Was he sent into the world for experience? Was he a student on a sabbatical? That sort of thing.

Moments before the second run commenced, Walt Foreman called him over.

Walt was with the cockie's wife and the cockie, a trim couple in their thirties. The word "cockie" meant "farmer," specifically the farm owner, likely because farmers "sat on the land" in a representatively similar fashion to the way in which Australian cockatoos - cockies - sat on the land while eating the seed.

The cockie's wife managed the homestead year round, and much of the business, and worked with the men in busy periods like now during the shearing season. She discovered that Ed used her bedsheets as sun protectors for his Ford.

Last night, Ed followed Ben's directions and chose any room he wanted. Without knowing it, he picked the room that was reserved for the classer. The classer's room came with laundered bedding. It explained why Walt bunked with him when vacant rooms were available.

Desert nights froze water in pipes by midnight. But winter days were glaringly bright. Ed didn't want the sun to damage the interior of his brand-new-used Ford. Barry Litz, the man who sold him the car, would not have wanted it either.

"I assumed they were your sheets," Walt now told Ed.

Ed's face turned red. He thought the sheets were castoffs or that a previous shearing team left them behind. He was still young enough to not know better. His honest apology and his fulsome gushing explained the rest. He ran to his car. The wind and early sun dried the sheets of heavy frost. He removed them, folded them, and returned them to the cockie's wife, who met him as he headed back to the shed.

He had one more idea to make amends.

"I'll wash them," he told the cockie's wife.

But she had what she wanted, explicit knowledge that one of the shearing team had not abused his stay here. She almost apologized to Ed as she took the sheets from him. The farmer looked pleased, knowing that his wife bore no slight.

***

ED ARRIVED BACK at the shed a few minutes late.

"Where've you been?" Ben asked dramatically. He pulled the first fleece from the floor. It came off Larry's shears.

He continued to help Ed while waiting for the wool to pile up enough to press into tightly packed bales.

In four word sentences, he explained to Ed that his father

shore sheep before he retired to a fruit block in the Riverland, the aim of many hard working shearers.

"Now he grows oranges. Thirty acres of 'em."

Throughout his childhood, Ben and his mother and sister joined him regularly at shearing camps.

"Like a second home," he said.

Ed saw it, the way Ben moved around the place with ease.

Ten minutes later, Ben checked the wool-bins for wool to press and helped Walt where he could.

Ed resumed his roustie duties alone.

The cardinal sin was to leave the fleece on the floor as the shearer returned from the pen with the next sheep. Timing mattered. At the very worst, Ed pushed the wool against the wooden pen-rails opposite the shearing stand. Otherwise, the shearer could not shear his next sheep without messing the previous fleece to smithereens. Paid by the sheep, shearers didn't like to wait.

Sometimes shearers, old and young, dropped their cutters together and raced each other to the pen for their next animal, eyeing each other askance to see who shore fastest, which occurred quite a lot because it made the day more interesting for them. On these occasions, it was almost impossible for Ed, or anyone, to do a proper job. So he flicked the fleeces and dags back to the pen-rails and waited to clean up better when he could.

Mostly Ed scooped the fleeces cleanly from the boards with flicks of his wrists, gathered them against the length of his body, and ran them straight to the classer's table. He unfurled the fleeces like he unfurled a bedsheet across a bed, or like he unfurled a bedsheet across the windscreen of his green Ford. He hot-footed it back to the boards to sweep up before the shearer returned with his next sheep.

Things became busier for Ed when Warwick started acting out. This was his first shed of the season. Some lean guys appear as if they are always in condition. Others do it tough. Warwick did it tough. He looked ready to expire halfway through the second run.

He put on a turn when Ed failed to sweep away the dags from the base of his stand immediately. He claimed that he could not work in such extreme conditions. Once or twice, Walt grabbed the broom and swept the boards. Classers never carried out such menial duties. But circumstances called for it, and Walt was a good man. And everybody, Ed included, saw that Warwick looked for excuses to take a break.

Shearers needed an excuse to break mid-session. It just wasn't one of those jobs where workers caught their breath whenever they liked. When the work was on, the work was on.

At other times, Warwick said that his mechanized cutter was not working right. Then he said he ran out of drinking water. On another occasion, he asked Ed to rub his back. When Ed declined, he accused him of filling his pen with what he claimed to be the farm's meanest ram, the horned, male sheep.

"Pull him to the boards. I'm not. I didn't put him there," Warwick whined.

Some sheep were as big as lions, especially the big rams. But they hadn't fangs or claws or a predatory will. They were stubborn but relatively docile.

While catching a sheep, Ed braced its side with his knees. He grabbed its muzzle, twisted its head back, and reached down and grabbed a foreleg. He released his knees and tipped the animal back on its bum while he controlled it by the foreleg. Then he dragged it by both its forelegs from the pen backward, him and the sheep, keeping its hind hooves from the ground. If the sheep's hooves touched the ground, it kicked and fought to free itself.

The object was to keep the animal calm. The catching method was tried and tested for centuries. It might sound as if there was a lot of twisting, grabbing, and pulling. But done right, the technique led to a sort of wrong-footing that was totally low stress for the animal and for Ed.

Handlers who stressed animals applied incorrect catching

100

technique. Handlers who used strength and force to catch sheep proved their incompetence. Handlers who chased sheep and grabbed their rear legs on the run explained to the world in big headlines that they were dangerous. People who intentionally hurt the animals while they caught them needed to be investigated.

Appropriate catching methods were not only about the animal's welfare. Shearers and roustabouts couldn't waste valuable energy fighting animals all day.

Then there was the cockie. The cockie might not treat his animals like pets. But they still represented money to him. So did the stuff he used to pay expensive vet bills. Shearers pushed the cockie around on almost every score - like how builders excluded homeowners from building sites to get on with their work - except where they mishandled the animals.

The same catching process applied to the rams, except that the rams were bigger, they had horns, and they possessed something of a superior attitude to the ewes, the female sheep.

Ed stepped cleanly out the way as the ram came at him. He grabbed it, braced it, wrong-footed it, tipped it on its bum, and handled it in the way he handled any sheep. He dragged it to Warwick's stand. Warwick watched with an admiring grin. Warwick was a big baby, but not a big mean baby. Not yet.

"You can shear him if you want," he said.

He was a smart-aleck, but with little, if any, meanness in him.

Ed took the handpiece from Warwick and pulled the ignition string that engaged the cutters with the overhead drive shaft. He sheared the belly wool, the pisel wool, the back-leg wool, and the wool around the ram's backside. He clipped the forelegs and the muzzle. Effectively, he crutched the ram as he had the sheep in the two sheds at home.

He was about to shear the throat wool in preparation for the long stroke on the ram's side. He didn't want to betray the fact that he would be uncomfortable going forward, and thankfully he didn't have to. Warwick stepped in and worked hard all that day.

Once again, Ben picked up fleeces during the entertainment. Walt Foreman looked on with a smile.

The men treated Ed differently, seeing that he not only knew how to handle a big ram, but also a big baby, Warwick.

Even Ned treated him better. If not directly engaging with him, at least he no longer strategically disregarded him. He no longer sniffed noisily whenever Ed walked by.

After that, Ed collected every fleece and left no dags on the floor. Confidence played the greater part in his success for the remainder of that first day.

By now Walt was busy as part of his one-person show at the classer's table, skirting the fleeces and classing the wool.

Ben, the all-rounder, and always at home in a shed, helped Walt. But Ben's stockpile of wool increased, and soon he pressed bales regularly.

With that, the first day passed. The shed fell quiet except for the bleating sheep. They bleated through the night and filled Ed's sleep, which came early. He wrapped himself in blankets in the freezing dark, ready for a four-thirty start next day.

***

ED WAS ENVIOUS of BJ and Gus when they left for school each morning. He suspected he missed something wonderful and grand. They left him with Jean to watch Humphrey B Bear on TV and to break for a suitably endorsed honey sandwich late morning on his non-kindy days, which were many.

He was glad when the measles kept them home. Unable to actually read, he "read" the patients stories from picture books. They watched him from behind dark glasses.

He created the tales as he flicked from page to page, trying to recapture the cadence of "T'was the Night Before Christmas," whose rhythms he loved, and not only at

102

Christmas time. He conjured themes from Little Golden Book seven-inch records. He ad-libbed the rest. Stories moved him deeply in those days, even to tears.

Then he contracted the measles himself and his brothers returned to school and left him alone in bed.

When he recovered, Jean introduced him to kindergarten.

Kindy was about finger-painting and cutting patterns from colored paper.

Ed walked the two and a half blocks there, which involved four street corners and two street crossings. Car traffic was light, if traffic at all. The sound of dogs barking and flies buzzing kept him company.

On his way home, he harvested monkey nuts from fallen pinecones.

"Why collect them?" Jean asked.

He stared at them as if they were a form a currency, the exact value of which he was unable to figure out. But other kids collected them, including older kids. So who knew?

Ed feared little while out on his own. A bad-tempered dog maybe. But even at the tender age of four, he knew which homes angry dogs belonged in, and how to avoid them.

BJ, of an entirely different temperament to Ed, did the opposite one day when, eight years old, he entered the Smith's yard, and goaded a chained dog, Blue.

"Watch me," BJ reputedly told Pete Koontz, his school friend.

For his efforts, the dog bit him, and he carried the scar for all time. Next day Mr. Smith called the veterinarian to euthanize Blue, the done thing in those days for any dog that bit someone, despite a kid having provoked the hapless animal first.

Ed's dog, Blackie, followed him to kindy once. He didn't bite anyone, though Mrs. Brennett, the kindy instructor, was understandably concerned for the other kids.

There he was, running around the playground like a loon.

The event caused Ed a considerable embarrassment. He

hadn't wanted anyone knowing he had a home.

The kindy playground was small and cool. Big Norfolk pines shaded it; pine needles matted the ground sweetly.

Next door was the public playground where Ed spent many days during the following years. The roundabout span so fast that he flung unsuspecting kids from it. They flung him from it. Sprinkle a little dry sand on the big slippery dip, and he got airborne as he flew from the end of it. Swings went so high the chains slackened at the very, very top, giving that zero gravity moment. Seesaws, with a four-foot drop to the compacted dirt, were all about trust and breaking trust when the bottom kid – Ed or his partner –bailed without any warning except for a sort of devious superiority reflected from the eye at the very last moment.

In time, Ed graduated to the decommissioned locomotive coalbin, where he and his teenage friends smoked cigarettes, mostly smelly, used, hand around stubs.

"Amanda Brinkley gave them to me. She got them from Julian. He got them from his old girl's ashtray."

Later again, he experienced his first fumbling encounters with girls in the locomotive cabin, an educational rite of its own.

As a fifteen-year-old, he abandoned the public playground for the pizza bar and Space Invaders.

But school interceded long before then.

Ed purposefully hustled his mother out the front door on his first day, not wanting to be late, so eager was he to attend class and learn. He hustled her so much that she wore her dress back to front and didn't know it until she returned home.

School pleased Ed while it promised new educational experiences. It pleased him not so much when it proved to be a form of dull restraint and peer-group pressure. He saw no point to school sports, which stifled the fun of outdoor games, and told him that physical activity needed to be competitive, disciplined, and serious if it was to qualify as physical activity at all. He lived for the occasional pat on the head, jellybean,

104

and gold star.

The term "child of the 70s" generally referred to people born in the 1940s and the 1950s. However, Ed and his cohort were truly children of the 1970s, schooled during these actual times. Ed's early schooling involved singing the national anthem, namely, "God Save the Queen," sitting with forty-five kids in classroom rows, and marching to military tunes in the expansive school grounds. By year five, the anything-goes flower power experiment in education came to town. Prescriptive grammar was abandoned in favor of "universal grammar." Guitar strumming teachers traded "God Save the Queen" for "Blowin' in the Wind." Garden Studies (growing beans and chasing cabbage moth) and Craft Studies (making leather dilly-bags and clay pots) entered the curriculum. Normality caved altogether when select kids from two age groups – including Ed - shared the very same classroom as part of an educational experiment using live bait.

Otherwise, life at school – high school, especially – was a drag. At best, high school provided a venue in which to test authority, that is, a place in which to act up and show off. Along with puberty, it got in the way of adulthood and freedom, or freedom as defined by a teenager's expectations of it.

Glad to be done with classes, because it meant being done with childhood, Ed strode boldly into his first job at the local engineering plant.

"Are you sure you're doing the right thing?" his history teacher asked.

How could Ed really know?

Within a year, he hankered after something more than a trade qualification.

He suspected that his apprenticeship was a day off from another life that he really ought to get back to now.

He found himself admiring Jean's library.

He admired Mick Williams, who was BJ's age. Mick read bestsellers like Ed drank beer while trying to prove his manhood. Mick did the very adult thing and discussed the books he read with his father, Jake, and with Jean.

As a seventeen-year-old boy, Ed took counsel from his best friend, Brent Edwards.

"I read a novel for thirty minutes every day," Brent explained. "Mum tells me to."

Brent's mum was very refined.

Ed held the advice in mind like a seed with the power to change his life.

Brent attended Year 12 at a city Marist college. Ed visited him and his friends in the city some weekends. He was amazed to discover gentlemanly boys who did not despise education or give each other wedgies over it.

One of Brent's friends – a second-generation Indian kid in gold-rimmed spectacles – was sprawled on the carpet over a portable typewriter.

"What are you writing," Ed asked, "a job application?"

"A play."

A goddamn play! What an incredible world!

During his apprenticeship, Ed completed three years of trade schooling, comprised of a weekly study day at a technical college in the northern Adelaide suburb of Ellaville. He commuted each week on his motorcycle, the sweetly motored Honda XR200 with conventional suspension.

Just a few years earlier, apprentices billeted all the way across the metropolitan area and studied in two-week blocks.

A decade before that, masters schooled apprentices in the Institute building off Main Street during the evenings as they had for the previous century.

After completing trade school, Ed purchased a correspondence course in diesel mechanics from Stott's College, which sounded a lot like the eminent "Scotch" College if he said it fast. He blitzed his initial units, distinctions everywhere.

One night at home on Main Street, Ed showed Brent Edwards the correspondence course while they shared a plate of fish fingers. This was three years after Brent confessed his daily reading ritual.

"You're good at learning," he told Ed.

By then a hard-working cricketer at state-level, Brent believed that all his friends had special qualities. He was Catholic, which helped.

At that point, Ed suspected that his path to self-improvement might involve education.

It seemed like the right thing, the proper thing.

***

COME SATURDAY MORNING, his first in a commercial shed, Ed closed his car trunk on the correspondence course in diesel mechanics. He trucked the ring binders to the Wilcannia shed intending to complete an assignment or two.

Now he didn't like where the course headed, which was back to engine grease, overalls, Solvol soap, and, worse than anything, employment of a humdrum nature.

Shearing was hard work. But it was romantic, hard work, romantic in the tradition of Australian bush culture.

Shearing was romantic in the tradition of Australian literature, in the tradition of Australian yarns.

Ed was not just reading a Henry Lawson story. He was living one. It was all the education he wanted.

Back in his quarters, he kicked the box of his brother's university textbooks beneath his bunk too.

Brawn was all he needed in the sheds.

Because of his extracurricular activities, that is, stoking the donkey (fueling the hot water service that ran on wood,) and cranking the diesel electricity generator, Ed still rose early. But today, Saturday morning, that meant sleeping until six o'clock.

Walt helped him with the diesel electricity generator most mornings, including this morning. The thing was a beast. It started with a crank, just like an old motorcar. Walt told stories of how generator cranks broke men's arms. Not here, of course, but elsewhere, like in all good bush stories involving amazing facts.

Walt, a lightly built man, had no problems. He didn't even disturb the ash from his cigarette while swinging the crank.

"From your hips, see," he said. "Keep your elbows in and swing from your hips."

To fill in time, afterward Ed read a Morris West novel, "The World is Made of Glass," which Jake Williams gave Jean to read, and Jean gave to Ed. Jake read plenty of Morris West books because of the papist themes and because Morris West studied to be a priest. Ed was new to that sort of novel.

He returned to it after he closed his trunk on the correspondence course and kicked the university textbooks beneath his bunk. But he decided that reading a novel wasn't for him either, not with life going on around him.

Halfway through a chapter, Warwick walked past his room to the mess. Ed joined him.

A late breakfast – a help yourself affair - was available Saturdays. Trev left the shed last night in readiness for ballroom dancing and Californian Poppy hair oil.

Walt ate alone with his paperwork at a small clean table. Later in the morning, he would drive to Broken Hill for the weekend to meet with the Doleman Brothers, the contractors. Between sips of black coffee, he told Ed that the Doleman Brothers ran several sheds at the same time.

"They're on the road a lot," he said, "especially Harvey Harvey. He's the younger of the cousins."

"I hope to meet him one day," Ed said.

"You will." Walt continued checking numbers.

Warwick wandered around picking up boxes of cereal, shaking them, testing volume.

"Think I'll stick to a liquid diet," he said, and left.

Ed finished his bowl of Kellogg's Nutri-Grain. Then he wandered back to his bunk, grabbed his dirty singlets and dungarees, and headed to the laundry, which was tacked to the amenities block with sheets of rusted corrugated iron and heavily weathered, roughly hewn hardwood.

Come weekends, the "have-nots" began their unpaid work. Irritability suddenly bled from every exhausted limb.

Ed wanted to collapse with fatigue. He wanted to watch movies, smoke cigarettes, dream, stuff his face silly with food, the richer, the better, and carouse later that night.

***

THE BRUCE LEE cult was prominent into the early 80s, so Ed learned to tolerate the movie phenomenon of words spoken long after mouths stopped working. Back home, he replayed video scenes in slo-mo with the VCR corded remote to catch the action (because Bruce moved so damn quick.)

He and his friends availed themselves of an unprecedented opportunity to take up karate when a black-belt trainer moved to town, Ken Kendersen.

"Fourth Dan," some kid said.

That was very important to acknowledge, apparently, fourth Dan.

Routine, akin to dance routine without music, put Ed off karate in the end. Self-inflicted injury by way of hardening his knuckles (by punching wood) and callousing his forearms (by whacking them with bottles,) and inculcating a willingness to hurt people, and to be hurt by people, put him off too.

"Punch him like you mean it," Ken Kendersen yelled at Ed.

Okay. But the "him" was a kid two years younger than Ed. They hung in the same gang. The kid's talents lay in making wisecracks and playing softball. It wasn't easy punching him like Ed "meant it," especially while seeing the look on his face, which bordered on fear.

But not being violent in this regard didn't make Ed an angel.

He suffered ill temper toward people, and toward things,

mainly when he was dog-tired, and when life wasn't going his way. Or when people needled him. He was like this since he was a kid.

His family understood his outbursts. That is, they realized he was prone to them.

Many of his friends understood them (that he was prone to them), and worked them to their advantage. They had a human fireworks display at the ready with the push of just a couple of the right buttons.

Some schoolteachers knew of them.

Ed knew of them, though he couldn't control them.

Strangers such as the men Ed now shared his new life with at the sheds never knew of his hotheaded tendencies. But had they watched him during the previous week, and not carefully, they would have caught glimpses of them when pressure piled on him and inexperience undid him.

Presently, Ed walked to the quarter's laundry, irritable at the thought of work on his day off. An unanticipated breeze might trigger a nasty outburst.

Therefore, watching mild-mannered Ben spit the dummy over a portable washing tub surprised him. Ben danced around the tub, kicking it hard and cursing it brutally. He purchased it used a day before he arrived at the shed, and brought it with him in the trunk of his car. All week he talked about how it would improve his life.

The thing started spinning after several more kicks to its belly. It choked, it shuddered, it swished, it span. It was tiny.

"You can use it after me," he told Ed hopefully.

Meanwhile, Warwick had his own meltdown. It started when he decided to forgo breakfast cereal for beer. It was the weekend, after all. Trying and failing to hand-wring double weight dungarees over a washbasin of barely warm water, and tired of it, he yanked them by their cuffs and walked outside, making a watery mess everywhere. He claimed he knew a better way to wring them dry.

"This is how you do it." He was South Australian. So he

spoke with word endings.

He swung the soaking wet dungarees by their cuffs like a rope around his head. On the second rotation, ultra-heavy with water and slippery with the residue of unrinsed suds, they left his hand and flew into the red dirt a few feet away.

"Fuck this for a joke," he said. With word endings.

He was in no great physical shape. A cigarette hung from his lips.

To be fair, a big job lay before him. Almost by law, shearers changed their dungarees and singlets daily. Otherwise, sheep lanolin mixed with sweat excreted by the gallon led to skin lesions and premature arthritis.

He announced he was driving to the small rural city of Wilcannia, an hour away. He wanted a laundromat.

"Coming?" he asked Ed. He asked like a mate.

He asked Ben too, but sorta from a distance, going through the motions.

Ben said he wanted to rest. Less convincingly, he said he had his laundry under control.

This was when the serious-minded, unionized, long-haired kid from New Zealand, Sam, introduced himself to Ed. He arrived late last night, and now he approached the group in hammering strides. Sam would join Ed as a roustabout next week. He should have started a few days ago, but something personal held him back.

The best thing about the sheds, where support workers were concerned, was that workmates couldn't rank each other against their respective experience and skills, as much as they might want to, as was natural in any workplace. After as little as a week of shed work, Ed already weathered himself to the roustabout's life. So the far more experienced Sam, a serious and formal guy, met him on equal terms.

They shook hands, shared a few "yeah, rights," and then Ed ran water into a washbasin that his donkey heated to lukewarm earlier. He soaped his dungarees. He found the energy to pummel his oil-packed, wool fiber threaded, double weight jeans and blue singlets.

Once the reality of the task set in, he washed his clothes with gusto. He understood somewhere in him that this was how he lived: he took care of himself, maintained his things, kept his clothes clean, kept himself going, worthy things to do. He found satisfaction in his responsibilities. Later, he even washed the Ford.

By now, Ben's machine clapped itself out again, and he began a fresh round of kicking it in the bowels.

**

AN HOUR LATER, Ed joined Warwick in his '73 Monaro, the four-door version. This was his everyday car. He said he wouldn't bother owning a car if he lived in the city. Cars were too much trouble and they cost too much money. Instead, he would catch buses, and cycle and walk places. Nevertheless, he explained that he owned a two-door version of the same model car that was "immaculate." He would show it to Ed one day when driving to the sheds no longer involved traveling along dirt roads with red dust that wheedled its way into every crevice of the car and became rust after returning to wet climates. He owned a backup of the same model for parts.

Rick, Rick Bell, joined the men too.

"Notice I'm not drinking," Warwick said as they headed to the tar.

He decided to forgo cereal *and* liquid diets.

Ed hadn't noticed, but he nodded anyway.

At later sheds, Ed would come to realize it was an enormously significant thing for Warwick to decline beer in the morning, weekend or weekday.

Maybe it was too early in the shearing season to drink alcohol to excess. Maybe this sheep station was too far from town pubs. Arriving at a new outback shed with a trunk load of beer would be a dead giveaway.

Ed himself enjoyed a two-year-summer of drunken sprees

with his friends back home. Twenty-four hours of solid drinking was ultimately achieved on several occasions. But post-adolescence provided many forks in the road, and a life without party sized thirsts was one of those forks in the road that Ed wanted to take. Most of his friends, intelligent, responsible kids with the lights on, walked it. Ed wanted to walk it. Youth was a great time to party like there was no tomorrow. Or like there were endless tomorrows. So why budget, sort of thing. But it was a great time to lay foundations in life too.

Barry Litz and his excellent advice remained with Ed.

And there was money to think about. Ed wanted to save some of it, which he couldn't do if he made a life of drinking beer without a thing in the wide world to celebrate except for the need to get pissed.

But that would be tomorrow. Today "Whip" Apotherick was at the wheel. He brought a cooler of beer along with ice from Cook-Trev's kerosene icebox.

"I'll show you the outback," he told Ed.

**

LIFE AS A kid revolved around food, glorious food. Oliver Twist, starving, couldn't get enough of it. Ed couldn't get enough of it. Downy sideburns demarcated then and now, but an insatiable appetite for food cut across both periods.

While other kids polished their football boots before Saturday morning football games, Ed polished off packets of low priced, cream-filled cookies. Not only had he run sluggish to mud soaked fields an hour later, but he also felt dizzy, lightheaded, that is. Racy, too. Racy in the wrong way. Not in a Speedy Gonzales way.

"What's wrong with that kid?" he overheard a retired player ask when he ran to the field one day.

Ed's chubby legs flashed brilliant white beneath the low cloud.

The football club secretary, Jack Jenner, a man in his sixties, drove Ed to away-games in his pale green Holden. He was the town train stationmaster. During the week, he wore a commander's hat and a black suit with red braiding and brass buttons. Those were the days. He wrote up the football news for the local paper. He called the announcements over the P.A. at home games. He had been an association champion.

Other boys whose fathers couldn't or wouldn't drive them to away-games rode with Ed in the backseat of the pale green Holden.

Other kids, again, caught the specially chartered Saturday football coach.

The advantage of traveling with old Jack was that Ed and his one or two traveling mates, not the best of buddies outside of Saturday morning, remained in the car after the junior colts game with old Jack's wife to watch the senior colts and B and A games from the boundary carpark.

Mrs. Stationmaster packed sandwiches for the boys, and she always brought home-baked cookies.

Now, when Ed added these viands (food) to the cheap cream cookies that he ate before leaving home, and throw in a canteen-bought sausage roll and cream bun for lunch too, and maybe some potato chips later, a pattern emerged.

And this was a sports day, where physical activity, not watching cartoons, was required.

On Saturday night, theoretically Jean's night off, the family purchased steak sandwiches or fish and chips from Decker's Deli. Frankie Demir hadn't arrived in town with his pizza bar, and Zolli hadn't instituted his Saturday evening barbecue ritual. Or when practice overwhelmed theory, which was often, Jean cooked French toast or stacks of crêpes or Welsh rarebits. Or whatever, as long as it was quick, unordinary, and tasty.

For school lunch, Ed supplemented his Vegemite and cheese sandwiches with prepacked bags of sweets that he purchased from Damper Chiffly, the baker, who visited the

114

school – high school, anyway - under contract in his tiny, little, yellow bug-eyed van.

"Yep?" Damper Chiffly asked without looking up.

Then he looked up, saw Ed, and reached for a pre-packed bag of sweets.

The contents filled Ed's pubescent hands. The delectables included jelly babies, bananas (candy bananas,) teeth (great to practice with were his actual teeth to ever rot out from overeating sweets,) raspberries, raspberry creams, cobbers (mates – chewy choc-coated caramel to work those jaw muscles,) jaffas (orange coated choc-balls,) bullets, crown mints, choo-choo bars, clinkers, fizzes, mint leaves, caramel buds, snakes, musk sticks, freckles, aniseed rings, fags (candy cigarettes,) and jersey caramels. Cobbers, clinkers, and jersey caramels were always limited.

Having the cash to purchase bags of sweets – as in, not having the cash – limited things somewhat too.

On Sundays, Ed's mother roasted beef, chicken, lamb, or pork for lunch. She baked an incredible selection of pies, tarts, and puddings to consume that day as well as frosted slab-cakes destined for school lunchboxes. Often that very Sunday night, Ed scraped thick, creamy chocolate or lemon butter frosting from the slab-cakes and ladled the stuff into his greedy little fat mouth. He carefully plastered what was left of the frosting back into something that resembled its original form, hoping to avoid detection. What a dirty hope!

Then there was the regular weekday evening meal, "tea" as Ed's household and all Australian households called it. It consisted of pot roasts, toads-in-the-hole, shepherd's pies, steak and kidney pies, stews, chops, casseroles, thick soup, sometimes T-bone steaks, spaghetti bolognese, sometimes goulash (every ten years,) flour dumplings the size of tennis balls, crumbed Wiener schnitzel, chicken from the Chisholm's chook run at Walkers Flat, creamy mashed potato, and very occasionally fish (because Ed lived in an inland town and because Salmon from Holland came only in cans.) Even boiled carrots and peas tasted good because there was always gravy. Roasted carrots and gravy, even better.

The main course of any meal was only ever a precursor to dessert. Sauced chocolate puddings, bread-and-butter puddings, walnut and raisin crêpes, Welsh cakes, apple pies, fruit puddings, jam tarts, baked cheesecakes. These were just a few of Ed's favorite foods.

Birthdays brought out the really tremendous desserts, tremendous sponges made from a dozen eggs and walnut cream filling, a unique Hungarian delicacy, or the Dobos, another Hungarian treat that had to be experienced to be believed, and only then if it was homemade, and a million other preparations, including stinky-cheese shortbread, boiled fruitcake layered in marzipan frosting, and the occasional dishes of homemade raisin chocolate.

"You'll make yourself sick if you keep eating," Jean warned.

Let Ed be the judge of that.

Oliver Twist couldn't get enough food, and he walked around starved. Ed couldn't get enough food, and he walked around stuffed.

BJ dubbed him "Chub" as in "Chubby Checker."

Yet even if his performance on Saturday morning sports fields was sluggish, Ed at least played Saturday morning sports. Which meant weeknight training. Which, in turn, meant walking to and from the sports ground at the edge of town. Additionally, he walked two miles to and from school every day. Or he rode to school on the Dragster that Zolli worked overtime to buy for his ninth birthday, bringing the momentous gift forward a year relative to when Ed's brothers received their first new bicycles.

School lunchtimes and recesses always involved yard games from chasey to red rover to brandy to formal games such as basketball and tennis. His after-school visits to the homes of his friends involved treks across town. Many activities with friends involved wandering dirt roads out of

116

town, especially if the gang was building a clubhouse from objects of infinite description somewhere that parents, other adults, and rival kids couldn't see.

If he wanted to swim in early summer, before the town pool opened for chlorinated, Twin Choc, wet towel whipping fun, he and his friends walked a couple of miles to the river like "Lord of the Flies" tribes comprised of not just crazy boys, but crazy girls too.

Then there was work with Zolli on his building sites.

And growing up! Which involved its own expenditure of energy and in no small amount.

Ed's love of food porked him out through most of his childhood. Most definitely, he was porked out in comparison to his classmates, except for his good friend, Jenny Sampson, the daughter of a local mogul and town mayor, Mr. Sampson, another in the ranks of kindly and colorful men who heralded from town establishment.

But here was the thing. Chubby though both Ed and his tennis-mad friend little Jenny Sampson were relative to their classmates, their body burdens would have nothing - nothing! - on those carried by the overweight kids of the future.

Still, Ed was a fatty, and he was vain enough to do something about it when he hit seventeen. Out of school by then, and apprenticed at the local engineering plant, Ed nevertheless chose his former high school science teacher, and local football legend, Mr. James, as his role model. Craig James was a stud too, and, truthfully, this was what it was all about. He broke ahead of Rocky, he of movie fame, as Ed's ideal role model, because he was a stud, and because it was all about girls, Ed being seventeen.

Zolli was a reliable role model too. (As regards physical exercise, not being a stud.) As a kid back in Hungary, Zolli boxed competitively, and he played football (soccer.) He continued to play football in Adelaide when he arrived in 1949. Lifelong he devoted himself to some form of physical fitness, however inconsistently his devotion to physical activity resided with his contrary love of Seppelts claret, Coopers stout, and St Agnes brandy. He hung a hessian sack from his workshop rafters on Main Street and filled it with sand. A punching bag. Construction worker gloves – dilapidated ones – were all he needed to work it.

"Extend your arm," he counseled Ed.

Ed never struck the heavy bag right, not as Zolli did. But he used the padded sit-up board in Zolli's study okay. Zolli engineered it to hang on various inclines from the bookshelves. It was fun to use as a kid, more fun than striking a sand-filled sack with dilapidated construction gloves because it doubled as a homemade slippery dip.

Later, Zolli fabricated a high jump bar in the backyard. The Fosbury Flop was popular around the globe, corrupted to the "fosby-flop" in Ed's household.

There they were, the three kids and their friends – and Zolli - taking turns to jump over the bar, complete with new-age metric measures on the side supports.

Extra lawn clippings comprised the landing mat. Despite the global popularity of the "fosby-flop," the "scissors" jump was the method of choice at Ed's home. Lawn clippings provided only so much matting and the "fosby," which involved a "body" landing, called for serious matting.

For as long as Ed knew, Zolli practiced yoga. This was no new age hippie activity for him. Under the force of law, the kids kept the noise level down while he went through his daily ritual of bending and breathing himself into a variety of spiritually inspired Y-front clad positions.

"Keep the noise down. Your father's exercising."

This was Jean's late afternoon refrain for the better part of two decades.

The practice deterred Ed from bringing friends home after school. They would have had another reason to suspect Zolli a lunatic.

Many years away, toward the end of his life, when he would suffer a paralyzing stroke, Zolli would surprise city nursing-home staff with his remaining dexterity. They would respond by roping him to a chair and pushing him somewhere dark.

Imagine what this would mean to him, by then an old, dying man with stroke-induced dementia. His postwar internment and everything it implied would revisit him after he built businesses, houses, and a family, and after he paid his taxes on it all.

Admittedly, it wouldn't be easy caring for Zolli in those future times. Or at any time. Carers might have wanted to push him somewhere dark and leave him there. Doesn't mean they should have, though.

***

JEAN OBJECTED SORELY to Ed's late-teen weight loss program.

"You're still growing," she argued. "You need to eat."

Ed replied quietly during dinner that it just wasn't natural for a seventeen-year-old boy to be so fat. Zolli agreed. And that was that. Ed morphed into a paragon of fitness that would have tempted the eye of Michelangelo, had Michelangelo lived in late twentieth century Australia, which would be hard to imagine him ever doing.

Ed got svelte, and he got all misaligned in his way of seeing life.

Trying to manage his weight was like balancing on a floating plank in rough water. But he did become a man.

Other young men in the bear pit of youth gave him space. Not his friends, of course; they knew him too well, even if self-image issues gave rise to mental health issues that tested even the closest friendships.

Before he commenced his weight-reduction diet, he was a freckled, chubby, haystack-headed, red-haired, party-boy with big appetites for beer and pizza and zero-hope with girls. Now, svelte and toned, he "eyed-off" girls at Toby Alans' discos. He almost fell over backward when they "eyed" him in return.

Before the engineering plant doors closed forever, he fabricated a set of barbells and dumbbells and a weightlifting bench, complete with a padded backrest and an adjustable incline. His best friend, Tim Griegson, who was an apprentice welder at the plant, helped him make everything.

When the plant closed, and gym membership became an impossible expense, Ed removed BJ's bed from his room, appropriated the table tennis table from the cellar and, upside down, used it as a second floorboard in his bedroom, so as not to destroy the shagpile carpet with his gym equipment.

Though lonelier than working out in the town gym, and without an audience to show off to, he worked out every second night. He earned his "guns."

While he worked at the winery in the Valley, he occasionally cycled to and fro, a twenty-mile round trip.

He jogged, he jogged up and down steep hills.

When he jogged, especially up steep hills, yes, indeed, Rocky Balboa, and the tune from "Rocky," inspired him.

He played senior footy (giving up pre-game cream cookies,) and he played the venerated game of squash.

"He has a long way to go," his football coach announced at the end-of-year dinner while awarding him a trophy for "Most Improved."

Ed hoped his coach meant that "he has potential" rather than "he has a long way to go."

True, self-image motivated him. But sport also immersed him in the local community like never before.

Because Ed turned his life around, the judicious local cop, Uncle Pete, let him and his whole gang off with a warning after they illicitly entered the old-folks-home. They thought they entered the nurses' quarters (because, had they got it right, had they illicitly entered the nurses' quarters (on the pretext of visiting a friend of a friend,) then that would have been okay. Actually, no. But at least they would have

120

appeared to be over spirited young men rather than just weird.)

In time, friends forgot the "Chubby" aspect to his nickname, and the spelling rules as regards the remainder of it, and simply called him "Cheka." Staggeringly, they then convinced themselves that the nickname had something to do with his father being Czechoslovakian.

Confusion over his ancestry, and European geography, and maybe twentieth-century Russian history, led them to believe that he hailed from the Russian salt mines, a place to which, on occasion, he should return.

Oh, how they hummed the salt mines tune (da-da-da-daaah) from old jalopies whenever they drove by the saltpans along the northern Adelaide Plains. (Everything was fair game, and Ed was no saint in this regard, either.)

The Solo Man TV ad, that is, the macho hero's ride down whitewater rapids and his satisfying slurp of soda at the end, became Ed's refrain. He really wanted the beard but had to wait another few years. Some he-man facial scarring would help too. Though, he avoided the actual soda due to its high sugar content.

He felt guilty when he ate one salty cracker too many.

He took out his food deprived moods on Jean, something he would never attempt with Zolli.

Weight loss proved to be a yo-yo lifestyle and a never-ending battle, just as his friend, Harry Deane, economically predicted while Ed tried on a pair of unforgiving motorcycling leathers in a city motorcycle store one Friday night.

"What about when chubby-Ed returns?" Harry asked.

Three years after he commenced his diet program, Zolli could not be said to be wrong while sitting around the dinner table acceding to Ed's declared intent to lose weight. But was Jean wrong in wanting to stop him?

***

ED GLIDED ALONG unsealed roads to Wilcannia in the

front seat of Warwick's '73 Monaro, Warwick at the wheel, Rick Bell reclined in the back seat with the ice box.

"Beer?" Rick Bell maitre d'd.

"Please and thank you," Warwick replied.

Ed took one.

He was hungry too.

He could eat what he wanted. Laboring in the shearing shed stopped him getting fat.

But, the demons wouldn't let him go completely.

Why was he currently so damn hungry in spite of Trev's great food?

Would he lose control and eat to surfeit, to sickness?

On the other hand, could he go one step further?

Could he use shed work to attain the truly impossible? An incredibly athletic figure that trumped that even of his local role model and erstwhile science teacher, Mr. James?

Would that make him more of a stud than Mr. James?

More of a stud than Danny MacArthur?

Would Carmen come running to him?

***

HE AVOIDED CARMEN during the daylight when he was stone cold sober, a condition – sobriety – that he experienced more and more while he dated her, but rarely, if ever, while actually with her.

They met at a bar. Not a "front" bar. Not a barfly bar. Not a place with vomit-stained nylon carpet patterned in crimson diamonds and cigarette burns. But a Toby-Alans-disco-type-of-bar. Toby's disco, most likely.

A bar alive with mirror balls, a world governed by a midnight council ordinance.

Straight into alcohol upon his arrival, a sip or a gulp, it had not mattered, Ed danced and lied his way through the night with booze-induced courage.

Else, see, it would never have worked even in the

122

beginning, not even for the duration of that quantum-like erratic moment that characterized his and Carmen's relationship.

Without alcohol or its doppelganger of disassociation, he would have been just him, which would have been a disaster.

Love is seeing. Love is light, and mirror balls hadn't produced enough of it or the right kind of it to illuminate his and Carmen's way for real. But mirror balls achieved what he wanted. Together with alcohol, they concealed him from himself. He foolishly hoped that he concealed himself from others too. From Carmen.

He convinced himself it had to be this way. The alternative was unimaginable.

Ed feared to reveal who he really was. He feared to see this truth reflected from her eyes.

He was the son of immigrants, the son of a father with a foreign accent too fixed in his ways to see reason, a brother of siblings with odd sounding names, and with his own name – his full name - spelled strangely.

A similar stigma affected his brothers, no matter what they said, and Ed knew it for sure. The constant explaining of oneself, and explaining the spelling of one's name, and explaining away Zolli to strangers.

However hard Ed worked, however much he perfected his bushman's drawl, however many Australianisms he slipped into his conversations, however many footballs he kicked, outback terrains he traveled, Australiana clothes he wore, movies about brumbies – wild horses – he watched, no matter his diet-induced bushman's figure, Ed Kaspar watched his image of himself crumble whenever he heard a stranger read his name for the first time and pull his nose at its spelling.

"How do you spell it again?"

"It" being his name.

He was one of those others.

A body snatcher from another planet.

He found himself hanging back in shadow.

He suspected that the most he could ever hope to be was an all right bloke for someone who never belonged.

He doubted Carmen's ability to deal with this "truth." It was all he knew to give her.

While riding with Warwick in his '73 Monaro, he imagined overcoming all that and winning her back with a muscular physique earned from hard work at the sheds.

It wasn't the sort of strength he needed now or while he dated her.

***

THE NAME "WILCANNIA" in the language of the original people had something to do with dogs or rivers. No Europeans knew for sure when they named the place. With the historically swift decimation of the linguistic source that spoke the word, likely no one would ever know.

Likewise, the Aboriginal name of Ed's town. Might mean something. Or not. Which sort of broadened the etymological range.

Ed grew up forty-five minutes' drive from South Australia's capital city of Adelaide. Capital cities across the nation were the same in the quality of services and experiences they offered to residents on a greater or lesser scale, depending on the actual size of the city. The idea of a "regional" Australian capital city was an oxymoron. Also, barring the nation's capital, Canberra, they were all coastal cities.

Wilcannia was nine hours' drive from Adelaide, eleven hours' drive from Melbourne, and likely just as far from Sydney, the capital city of the state in which it was situated. Modern Europeans traveled a twentieth of the time to neighboring countries.

By Australian standards, the entire UK was a big city with parks. In America, a similar national expanse to Australia, even small towns were near somewhere.

124

Wilcannia was miles from anywhere.

Dust, red dust, islanded the outback town.

The rain had not touched this place in a long time. Tumbleweeds blew across the highway.

It was a sophisticated town, simply because of this, it being there, miles from anywhere, where spinifex grew.

Ed's elation was short-lived, though. Buildings were boarded up.

"Lookey there," Warwick said, slowing the car to a crawl.

Around the corner, the laundromat was closed, and might have been for years.

"Guess I'll just have to make do with the clothes I got until next week."

He planned to go home next weekend. He could wash his clothes then.

Anyway, the shed would be three-weeks long, possibly less than three weeks, if the rain held off, which likely it would.

"Should find me a gin for the night," he said, reassessing matters.

He asked Rick for his thoughts, whose women he discussed.

Rick laughed self-effacingly from his long neck beer, reclined in the back seat of the '73 Monaro, and said nothing.

When Ed looked up shocked at Warwick's comment, but with his own guilty passions stirred, Warwick grinned, and Rick laughed some more. Ed saw that Warwick was joking. He saw that Rick saw it too, but without seeing the funny side.

Ahead of them, a group of around thirty people gathered outside the one store that Ed saw open, a general store on the main street, which the eclipse of outback life relegated to the town center.

It hadn't surprised Ed to see thirty people congregate outside a town store. It happened in rural life. However, it surprised him to see a sizeable store open on Saturday afternoon. Not even stores in Adelaide opened for business

Saturday afternoons, not downtown. Some suburban malls opened Saturday afternoons. Anyway, suburban malls didn't belong to any city. Suburban malls arrived from someplace Ed didn't know.

Here in Wilcannia, teenagers raced tumbleweeds across the street to see what one car with its three occupants might bring them.

"Know anyone?" Warwick asked Rick.

"Can't say I do," Rick replied.

"Me either," Warwick said.

Before reaching the crowd, he hit the brakes, u-turned, and headed back out the long road from town.

"Law doesn't like you messing with people around here," he said.

***

OUT OF WILCANNIA, Warwick took an early turn from the asphalt. "The Darling's near here," he explained.

He asked Rick if he ever saw it, which he had, but not in a few years.

"You seen it?" he asked Ed.

Ed had not. The outback river caught water from Queensland and New South Wales and ran to the Victorian border, a few hours' drive south. There, it met the River Murray, Australia's longest river, slow and low in volume.

Messy displays of river hierarchy by those who depended on the waterways for farming, sports, ecology, and drinking plagued both rivers along their journeys, with inhabitants upstream resisting rules, while those downstream wanting them enforced, same-old-same-old, the length of history.

Warwick pushed the baby-blue '73 Monaro along the unsealed road. Plenty of roads like this existed around Ed's hometown. Back home, the local council maintained them, usually grading them once or twice a year, and backfilling bigger potholes with road base, that is, quarried gravel. The

126

roads, out of the way as they were, nevertheless carried considerable traffic, including semi-trailers and farm machinery such as harvesters and six-wheeled tractors. Invariably, transverse corrugations rutted long stretches of them in next to no time, like on the road they drove along now.

Ed did what he did as a kid, all of a couple of years earlier when he rode the cars of his friends. He opened his mouth and made vibrating sounds with his throat.

The last of his beer shook inside the bottle.

The travelers pulled up on a dirt track in a cloud of white and red dust that soon cleared in an undetectable breeze. They got out the car.

Outside was cold and the sky was bright and blue and very, very high.

Warwick pulled his wraparound cardigan around him and buried his hands in his pockets.

"Listen," he said to Ed, "will you wash my car like you did yours this morning when we get back to the sheds?"

"No," Ed replied.

"Oh," Warwick said. "That's nice considering you've been riding in it all day long."

They walked through the low, dry shrub of the Australian outback to the river with new long neck beers apiece.

They were at one with the most written about rivers in the country, the Darling.

The river was dry rock, with tiny pools of stagnant water. Ed saw from the faces of the older men that this was not expected.

Something like thunder rumbled across the other side of the dry, white riverbanks. Dust flew.

"Wild pigs," Warwick said.

Rick nodded.

"Hopefully, they're too stupid to know they can walk across the river bed and eat us if they wanted," Warwick said.

Ed watched the passing dust but did not see the pigs among

it.

The fatigue he experienced earlier in the day returned and brought him low. He wanted to sleep. Desperately.

***

BACK IN HIS quarters alone, the four large bottles of beer that Ed consumed while riding with Rick and Warwick in Warwick's '73 Monaro released him from their forty-minute highs and lows and dropped him where alcohol always dropped him, somewhere dismal.

Booze-induced guilt about God-knew-what triggered the blues. Ed wanted to clear his system with push-ups, squats, and sit-ups. A jog would be okay if he had a path through the red dust and saltbush to run along, and a pair of running shoes to run in. He only had excuses.

Fatigue from a week of seriously hard work invaded his bones. Sleeping in late this morning still saw him rise from bed at six o'clock. He washed three sets of heavy-twill work clothes by hand. Later, he cleaned the Ford. He felt like dead meat afterward.

Riding beneath the bright sun in Warwick's car while drinking beer made him inordinately sleepy.

Now, so late in the day and alone in his room, he was left with isolation and twilight.

"If I sleep now," he told Warwick earlier when they pulled to a stop outside his room, "I'll wake by midnight."

"Easy fix. Keep drinking."

"Don't think so."

He could not work in the sheds unevenly like this, without proper sleep. He had to perform at work like a worker, like an athlete, not drag his feet like a pathetic, sleep deprived loser.

Alone, he experienced a supreme willingness to implode, to beat himself, if only it would make sense for him to do so.

If he walked to the recreational room and watched a video - there was no TV reception in the outback - he would find the

128

whole experience a mess of discordant noises and flashes. He would question why in the hell movie characters did what they did. He would dismiss the movie as a show for idiots.

He wanted something that explained his life. Something to connect with. Something to reach to. But that was the world of books, not films.

He sat on his bunk and resumed reading "The World is Made of Glass."

Affected by alcohol as he was, the words were as discordant to him as would be a movie were he to watch one in the recreation room.

He thought he remembered bringing a notepad with him and went to the green Ford to look for it, something the size of a lecture pad.

Even as a kid, he periodically experienced sleepless nights and erratic days. Scribbling his thoughts on a page or in a journal eased things. The exercise wasn't therapeutic. It was creative.

True feelings were separated from ordinarily spoken words by something mere microns thick. But that thing microns thick kept him ignorant of not only his life but also of the world. Writing a few words allowed him to bypass the veil, to see things.

He didn't know why he thought he brought a lecture pad with him to the sheds. The assignments in his diesel mechanics course were pro forma. In the end, he couldn't find a pen in his car, let alone a writing pad.

And, he had to face it, he would be at a loss as to what to write. Feelings and thoughts raced for words in his head. Then, pen in hand, blankness would meet him given his present state of mind.

He returned to his room tired and techy with booze.

The bare light globe swung from the rafter. It hardly glowed in the new night.

The new night was the worst time to be alone because not even birds sang nearby.

He lay back on his bunk, cold.

He would remain in this biochemical state for the next twelve hours and even the next day if the hangover chased away sleep later tonight too.

He decided to go one step further than what Barry Litz advised him.

He vowed to give away booze altogether while he worked the sheds.

***

TWO AND A half weeks later, the team cutout from the Wilcannia shed. Ed pulled the green Ford over in Broken Hill as he headed back south. The idea of a counter meal and beer never entered his head.

A weekday, he angle parked his Ford along the busy main street of the mining city and walked to a newsagent. In country towns, newsagencies doubled as stationery stores and bookstores.

He wanted to read his brother's university books. And he flicked through his favorite Henry Lawson stories regularly. So he merely glanced at what this particular newsagency displayed by way of reading material.

Today he spent time with stationery. Eventually, he chose an A4 lecture pad.

"Need a hand?" a woman asked.

He smiled and purchased a Pentel pen along with the pad, a rollerball covered in green plastic.

He purchased a clipboard and a broadsheet newspaper.

Newsagencies, and later city bookstores, always calmed Ed. They provided him with a refuge of an undefinable sort.

Rick Bell waited in the Ford. Ed agreed to drop him at Peterborough along his way to the next sheep station in the Flinders Ranges, north of Port Augusta. There, Rick would find his way to the township of Laura, where he had family and friends. Laura was a tiny rural village and once home to the Australian poet, C.J. Dennis.

Nothing stopped Ed from returning home for a couple of days. He had the time. But he didn't want that. He wanted to explore a new world. Or explore his old world as a new adult.

Rick watched him slide into the car with the items. Seeing the writing pad and pen, he smiled and asked, "Book work?"

"Book work," Ed replied.

They headed south, and Ed dropped Rick at Peterborough before looping around back to Port Augusta.

***

FROM OLD PHOTOS, Ed saw that Zolli and Jean were tourists in the 1950s before he and his siblings arrived.

Later, Zolli and Jean introduced them to the geomorphically curious and archeologically significant Flinders Ranges as well as to many places around the state and neighboring states. The 70s was Australia's caravanning and camping golden age. The Kaspar family, with dog and cat in tow, which always made for lively times at busy campsites, camped and caravanned two, three, or four times a year.

Now Ed revisited the Flinders Ranges, namely Alligator Gorge, while driving to Port Augusta.

He visited as if for the first time, though he was here as a kid five years earlier.

He walked the gorge, contemplatively losing himself in its dry belly and narrow trail.

"You okay?" a couple asked.

"I'm okay," he replied

Walking bush-trails alone was always about losing himself contemplatively.

Ironically, without the mayhem of family, the site meant little to him. Experiences that he immediately shared with his parents and siblings in the ex-army canvas tent over a dinner prepared on a gas bottle stove, with five-card poker, buttered campfire damper, and corn tobacco pipes awaiting him no longer filled it. Now the site was lonely, empty.

***

UPON ARRIVING IN the Gulf City, Ed quickly toured its bigger streets in his Ford, eager to see this and that. He felt adult and free of small town holds over him. The sense of freedom had little to do with his hometown's real hold over him, and more to do with growing away from childhood and wanting to experience adulthood. He was in a supreme rush to "get there" and to "be somewhere."

No one knew him in Port Augusta, which was liberating. He had money from his last shed. He was anyone, traveling anywhere for whatever reason. He photographed the wharf and the flying doctor station. He read the flying doctor station signage carefully.

Flying doctors were just that. A pilot flew medical workers in a small plane to remote villages and outback farms when people needed urgent medical care.

Overwhelmingly, suddenly, Ed wanted to be a pilot for the flying doctor service. He recalled that his mother owned a novel about flying doctors, "Back of Sunset" by Jon Cleary, and Ed had read it.

But Ed also imagined himself as a photographic journalist while he drove around the place.

He never fantasized about being a writer. Journaling from when he was a kid was how he tumbled bound and free through life. It was the seeing and the being. It kept Ed Kaspar here, even while he ran from and to everything.

He parked the Ford outside a hotel in the town center. Regional cities like Port Augusta were prosperous places in the 80s. It showed in this hotel, built a hundred years earlier, and maintained and modernized in the simple style of the times.

He checked in, dumped his things to make the dinner period, and ordered a plate at the restaurant counter.

The manageress took an interest in him. Several years his senior, her bright eyes danced, and she smiled at him generously.

She was elegant compared to the women in his hometown. She had a sort of presence about her.

She shuffled closer to him while he ate his evening meal – an enormous fisherman's basket, namely, fries, crumbed stuff, and ketchup, Ed's favorite on eat-out special occasions.

They said hellos, and after Ed explained a little about himself, she offered him work at the hotel.

Odd things happened from time to time, like receiving job offers unexpectedly. But he couldn't see a point working here. He didn't even know exactly what she had in mind for him.

Also the barman, whether her husband or not, squinted at them from a rock.

Ed decided to leave it with him posing at the bar counter.

He went to his room. He was tired anyway.

Perhaps his ego got the better of him. He believed he could never live up to the image he wanted to project.

Earlier, worried he might miss the hotel dinner timeslot, he raced downstairs to eat his meal before he showered. So now, he showered.

The bathroom was along the hall. A hall bathroom, as opposed to an in-room suite, didn't detract from the amenity of the hotel, not a grand, old hotel like this one.

Ed looked both ways and tiptoed the hallway in a towel.

After he showered, a man in his sixties with a thin fringe of black, gray hair approached him in the hall and told him he could accurately guess Ed's weight by lifting him.

He lunged at Ed and reached around him front-on and lifted him from the floor, or attempted to. Ed pushed back while managing to keep hold of his bath towel. The man stepped away, wiping goop from his mouth.

Ed recalled seeing him while he ate his evening meal in the bar downstairs. He must have followed him.

Ed chose to treat the whole thing as a harmless mistake.

In the morning, the man waited in the hallway again, this time holding a grubby, day old newspaper as a sort of offering.

Ed nodded, said nothing, and continued to the bathroom. Afterward, the man waited in the hall.

"I heard you worked at the sheds," he said anxiously. "I do too. Tell me where."

Ed felt obligated to talk to the man, to say a few words. But again, the man, sweating, lunged at him.

Ed dodged him and kept walking.

***

A DIFFERENT WOOL classer oversaw the Port Augusta shed, a young bearded guy named Mark Johnson. He drove a new F-150 four-wheel-drive pickup. His female sheepdog joined him, Pixie, a bright, yellow-eyed, red kelpie. She helped Ed yard sheep later.

Mark completed his first shed as a qualified wool classer a few months back. As coincidence had it, he replaced the man Ed met in the Port Augusta hotel, the man who groped him and got all sweaty on the pretext of guessing his weight. The man, Blue Ridges, or some such name, left the shed those months back "of his own volition" after the younger roustabouts ganged-up and complained about him. He drifted now, desperately, unable to find work at his age and with his history.

Mark had little to say on the issue. He had little to say to Ed. He was a nuts-and-bolts guy.

Ed picked him for an in-group guy, for all his blokeishness, and Ed wasn't in his group.

Warwick was at the Flinders Ranges shed when Ed arrived, and Ben, reading as usual.

This was a ten-stand shed, which meant six more shearers than at Ed's first shed, as well as a full contingent of roustabouts. It was to be a short one, though, maybe six days.

Another cook, Betty, joined the team, replacing Trev, who

remained up north in the last of the northern sheds.

Harvey Harvey, the cousin-contractor, entered the cozy farmhouse kitchen and made himself a tomato sandwich. He was in his forties and lean and brown-haired. An unpretentious and welcoming air surrounded him, helpful even. He forewent margarine and butter on his sandwich.

"My wife," he smiled to a few of the guys, "runs a fat-free house back in Adelaide."

He parked outside in an impressive new Toyota Landcruiser built for bush work, unadorned by the chrome cosmetics of the four-runners that were beginning to swarm city life in emulation of a stereotypical English country doctor's Range Rover, along with an attempt to emulate the imaginary doctor's wealth and hubris.

Neither Ed nor Warwick met Harvey Harvey before this moment.

After the contractor finished making his tomato sandwich, he noticed the two men sitting in the lounge area to the side of the kitchen. He humbly apologized for not introducing himself earlier. He wiped his long fingers in his tan moleskin trousers and greeted them, offering his hand.

More than anything else that disturbed Ed at the sheds that year –and not in a bad way - was that Harvey Harvey, the contractor, mistook him for Warwick (that is, he mistook him for a professional shearer.)

People mistook him a lot that year. Some property owners even mistook him as "one of us," that is, as a fellow property owner, or as the son of a fellow property owner.

***

FOLLOWING THE SHORT Port Augusta shed, Ben headed to a learner-stand south of Jamestown.

Unions encouraged contractors to reserve learner-stands in big sheds. Learner-stands slowed things down economically. But they were in the interests of long-term, business-minded contractors, men such as the Doleman Brothers, who managed several teams throughout South Australia and the surrounding states, New South Wales, Queensland, and Victoria. Workers retired, fell ill, and moved between bosses. Wise contractors invited young people into the shearing industry. The Doleman Brothers saw an excellent prospect in Ben.

Learner-stands did not involve teaching or studying. Experienced shearers offered a few pointers to the new recruits where they felt so inclined. But mostly learners brought enough know-how to get them through their first day and keep them moving in the ensuing weeks. The chief ingredient for success was commitment, which meant wanting – or needing – to be a shearer.

Practical occupations, whether plied with wrench or pen, proceeded best on a monkey-see-monkey-do basis. Shearing fitted this category.

Patience with the animals helped because it led to expending less energy on them.

A sense of machinery helped, too, knowing how to let the cutters cut rather than push or drag through the wool.

Often the new recruits interspersed their learner-sheds with rousting or pressing wool.

A couple of shearing seasons weathered them to the role and let them know what they were in for. They earned their tips and tricks over a lifetime.

Ben's good fortune led to Ed's own. He filled the void created by Ben's departure from wool pressing by commencing to press wool at a small four-stander near Orroroo.

Pressing paid better than rousting, and it was cleaner and better work. Ed could work at a job like pressing all his life.

Some of the rousties were jealous. They were with the Doleman Brothers far longer than Ed was with them. Years longer.

"Pays to suck up," Sam challenged Ed, his head back.

Ed let it slide.

WOOL-PRESSING WORKED like this. Shearers shore the fleeces from the sheep. Roustabouts threw the fleeces to the classer's table. Other roustabouts and the classer skirted – cleaned - the fleeces. The classer allocated the fleeces to the wire bins according to their wool grade. Fleeces piled ten feet high and ran ten feet deep in the wire bins. The presser pulled the wool from the bins by the body full and pressed it into bales, making sure to bale wool of the same class only.

Ed Kaspar leaned into a massive bin of wool as if he threw himself against an upright mattress and bounced back with everything he folded into his arms. He dragged the load to the hydraulic press, which he previously lined with a bale bag. The press was the size of a very large, oversized washing tub, far larger than Ben's portable washing tub. He loaded the wool and pushed a button that lowered a hydraulic ram. Steel pins shot across between slots in the pressing plate and held the wool in place. The hydraulic ram retracted. Then Ed loaded another armful of wool, released the steel holding pins, lowered the hydraulic ram, and continued until he pressed a bale of wool.

With the holding pins in position, he pulled the top flaps of the bale bag and stapled them with inch-long, two-pronged hooks. He released the holding pins. The wool swelled the bale into an enormous tightly packed unit of wool ready for shipping, again, the size of a very large washing tub.

Ed unlatched the press door, grappled the bale from the press with a Captain Hook's hook, rolled it onto the nearby scales, and weighed it. Some hydraulic presses had built-in scales. Not this one at the Orroroo shed. He stenciled the wool grade, bale weight, station name, and date onto the bale with a stencil brush that resembled a giant shaving brush. He either stacked the bales inside the shed or rolled them to the loading dock where farmhands removed them to a flatbed truck. Ed earned his money and his fitness.

His body changed in other ways.

"What's up?" Warrick asked during smoko.

Ed peered at his inner arms.

For the next year, he would extract wool fibers from the insides of his arms. They embedded themselves into his pores while he handled the wool. They would pop out weeks and months later like little hairs that grew from him. It wasn't so gross. The trick was knowing what was wool fiber and what was body hair.

Machinery was a far, far bigger hazard. When it grabbed someone and did what it shouldn't do, it was not more cold-blooded than a shark. Blood didn't enter the mix, hot or cold. Victims wanted to cry for mercy or find an eyeball to stab. But to cry for mercy from a machine counted for nothing.

Ed used heavy-machinery during his apprenticeship at the engineering plant and to a lesser extent at the winery. He used power-tools throughout his childhood on Zolli's building sites. He used power-tools aplenty at home in the workshop under Zolli's supervision. Even high school taught him to use bandsaws, bench grinders, wood lathes, and arc welders to prepare for a destiny in skilled work.

He heard horror stories of industrial accidents. Most came by way of trade school classmates. When Ed asked for detail, his fellow students usually shrugged in a "you can believe it or not" sort of way.

Without a doubt, nasty mishaps happened for real. In the metal machining process, whether involving a lathe, mill, or planer, swarf curled from metal like rind curled from oranges. In rare cases, it extended a yard long and was as thick as a finger. Trade newspapers recorded an incident where swarf caught a man by his overalls and dragged him into the highly specialized lathe he operated quicker than the eye blinked. It cut him and killed him in ways that Ed had not seen reason to visualize for himself.

He heard of other instances, ones near home, where powered grinding stones exploded and sent shrapnel through

138

unprotected heads or PTO tractor shafts entwined long hair and scalped or killed victims.

Ed, fourteen, jammed his hand in a concrete mixer while waiting for a mix. To alleviate boredom, he poked his hand at the mixing divot - an indentation in the drum skin - upon every rotation of the mixing drum. The divot caught his hand between the mixing drum and the frame and wedged it tight.

Hearing his youngest child call for help, Zolli flew from the site building and switched off the power to the mixer. Fortunately, the drum was fully loaded with concrete. This placed the motor under load. Fortunately, too, Zolli had replaced the fuel motor, which exploded, with a modern electric one. The electric motor jammed under load. A combustion motor would not have jammed.

Ed could have lost his hand or his arm. He could have lost his life. As it was, he received a nasty shock that wasn't serious enough to warrant sympathy from Jean when he arrived home early from work that day. Nevertheless, he wore the scar until a chainsawing incident decades later replaced it with another.

Luke, a wool presser in one of the Doleman Brothers' teams, almost lost his arms in a wool press a year earlier. He was immensely tall, around six-five, and strong, with thick, wavy hair like BJ's. He had a handlebar moustache and wore John Lennon spectacles.

He tried to poke down wool in the mouth of the press when the hydraulic ram caught him by both his arms and partially severed them. A quick-thinking roustie leaped to the kill-switch. Surgery saved Luke's arms, but only just. Luck saved his life.

Ed came to know him at the Orroroo shed. He seemed to see this in Luke's eyes, this acknowledgment of how lucky he was, and of how quickly accidents with machinery changed lives.

"I held him," Rick Bell explained aside.

"Yeah?" Ed asked.

"Till, you know, the meat wagon came."

Ed looked along the shearing boards at Luke, who sensed eyes on him.

Luke, a man in his mid-twenties, underwent multiple surgeries and months of rehabilitation. He was a good guy, but quiet, reflective. Following his accident, so the story went, he viewed things - life - differently. People pulled him into the conversation. When he entered it, the conversation, he conversed enthusiastically. But he was distant, and friends always invited him first.

The Doleman Brothers, great guys, decent men, open-minded, responsible business people, brought Luke back into the sheds on light duties. These men allowed a British accented mother to talk them around into giving her son an opportunity despite him having little to no agricultural experience outside grubbing dead peach tree roots and crutching straggly sheep near his hometown.

Luke helped the classer, Mark Johnson, remove dags from fleeces at the Orroroo shed. He was not disposed to learn how to shear. Nor would he cope physically with shearing sheep while he underwent serious rehab. Probably he lacked the patience to complete a two-year wool-classing course. Most people couldn't face returning to school once they worked for a few years.

It was an irony not lost on Ed that most country boys, barring the odd star like Philip Wagner, merely dabbled in the sheds. They earned pocket money offseason from their real jobs, which were probably on their parents' farms.

Or, those country boys who followed the sheds as a career, barring the stars like Philip Wagner, seemed to live at the edge of town along unsealed roads in small rundown cottages. They drove crappy cars and owned three other vehicles in various states of disrepair, abandoning them out front of fibro-clad houses on lawns long since giving over their topsoil to quarts of used engine oil.

The majority of workers Ed met while working in the

Doleman Brothers' team, on the other hand, drove new cars. They were bright minded and career minded.

And here was the irony. Mostly they lived in metropolitan Adelaide as Luke did. The shearing industry offered them middle-class lives. Stability, not itinerancy. They hadn't read Henry Lawson. They wouldn't know the meaning of "the romance of the swag."

Luke invested his accident compensation money in stocks and shares. He drove a brand-new, newly released 4-wheel-drive Nissan pickup, something that Zolli managed to afford only after decades in the building game, though he owned a Toyota Hi-Lux, and only after his children ceased being a financial expense to him.

***

SPRING WILDFLOWERS COVERED the mid-north of the state. Soon the country would turn brown without rain, and hot beneath a summer sun, perfect for wheat. But that was a month or two away.

Yesterday the last of winter blew in, and the sheep were too wet to shear today. With towns such as Peterborough, Jamestown, and Wilmington nearby, the men went in separate directions. Even Betty, the shed cook, went out for the day. Ed elected to remain at the shed alone, now his fifth shed, his third as a wool presser.

Then, late morning, who visited but Nifty Ronson, the union representative for the area.

"I picked a bad day for it," he said.

"You did," Ed replied.

Shearers had to belong to the union. Roustabouts and wool pressers - Ed - did not.

Nifty, an ex-shearer, was a thin, wiry man with a squashed nose and very gray hair. Three decades earlier, he tent boxed. He traveled outlying towns of the eastern states with his troupe, fighting local-yokels for a fee, usually above his weight-class.

"Just the way it was back then," he said.

Tent boxing occurred long before Ed's day. Maybe it never occurred in South Australia in his milk and honey part of the state. Indeed, during the 1980s, moralizers conveniently misrepresented the pugilistic art and fashionably decried it as a sport for savages. So Ed, in consensus, which was rather the Australian way, pulled his nose at the sport too.

But Ed knew showmen, and Nifty Ronson was a showman.

Ed did not object to the idea of unions. At the previous sheep station, he explored a recently abandoned, rat-infested building that might have served as his quarters had not the union compelled the cockie to erect new accommodation for the shearers.

Nifty related his own industrial horror stories, including one where candidates sprinted around a running track to obtain warehouse work.

He pointed a big finger at Ed, but not at Ed, "What's track got to do with warehouse work?"

Ed couldn't say.

However, he couldn't quite get behind unions. Something about the abandonment of oneself to party lines and the anonymizing of oneself bothered him.

As it was, the conversationalists discussed another topic. The politically inclined men in Ed's team were visiting a nearby shed where it was rumored that New Zealand shearers used wide-combs. Wide combs and cutters were literally wider than conventional combs and cutters by a half-inch or so. Historically, New Zealand shearers brought the cutters to Australia in the early 1900s. The government-of-that-day immediately banned them at the behest of the unions.

Almost a century later, in 1983, the cutters reared their heads again, and the unions called a strike to protest their use. Shotguns interceded between political factions.

Fearful of murder, and with murder in them, some shearers still armed themselves, but none Ed knew.

By 1984, in Ed's day, the law permitted shearers to use wide-combs, even if the old guard of the shearing industry refused to condone their use universally.

The wide-cutter technology allowed shearers to shear more sheep in a day. Shearers earned more money when they shore more sheep. But the union still believed that the wide-comb eroded an Australian shearer's way of life. Nifty couldn't explain how.

During the discussion, Ed made the big man two fritz-and-sauce sandwiches, one for now, and one for the road.

"Spread it thick," Nifty said about the butter.

Fritz-and-sauce sandwiches were extremely popular among South Australians, a favorite staple, up there with vegemite.

Although fritz was not luncheon sausage, it looked like luncheon sausage, the legacy of Silesian Germans who migrated to South Australia in number a hundred and twenty years earlier to escape persecution in their homelands.

Butchers offered little kids a slice of it when they entered stores with their mothers. At least, the butcher in Ed's hometown always offered Ed a slice of fritz when he followed his mother into the store amid blood, sawdust, hooked carcasses, offal, and whizzing meat saws.

The sauce was tomato sauce, Heinz, increasingly internationalized and referred to as "ketchup."

Nifty was very grateful to Ed. As an ex-shearer, he knew that food possessed value. In return, he gave Ed his thumbed copy of "The Ragged Trousered Philanthropists" by Robert Tressell.

The book was about a nineteenth-century house painter who endured terrible hardship in the British building industry.

"The house painter and his workmates were 'philanthropists' because they gave away their labor to rich people for nothing, see."

That was the thinking behind the book title, Nifty explained.

The plight of the characters in "The Ragged Trousered

Philanthropists" really did move Ed considerably when he eventually got around to reading the tome. He found it a genuinely compelling read.

***

AFTER NIFTY HIT the road with his fritz-and-sauce sandwich to go, and with one in the big man's belly, Ed walked to the rolling hills beyond. He lost himself for hours among the green hills and wildflowers.

The sun was warm, but not hot. Along with the gentle breeze, it would dry the sheep for tomorrow, for sure.

Spring insects buzzed in the slanted rays of the long afternoon light.

The air – a dense atmospheric fluid, palpable - exhilarated him.

He forgot wide-combs and industrial politics. Instead, a sort of revelatory intensity moved him while he walked the warm fields.

An indiscernible sense of culture and art intrigued him.

What he remembered of them from his childhood.

What he glimpsed of them as a young adult.

What Jean and Zolli introduced him to.

What he innately knew of them.

Or, if not this, then awe intrigued him.

Awe moved him while he walked low green hills in the state's northern spring

He wanted to explain it, share it, to say it.

The shearing quarters were empty when he returned from his afternoon meander.

He located the writing pad and the Pentel pen that he purchased in Broken Hill.

He positioned the pen above the paper, and he began to write.

***

144

TV MINISERIES WERE significant cultural events in the 70s. When drawcards such as "Roots" came to town, Ed stopped just short of ringing a bell to tell his family that the show was about to begin. The family made the start or missed it for good. At school next day, kids repeated the lines from the scenes and referred to each other by the characters' names. "Kunta Kinte" and "Chicken George" remained in the lexicon for months, years.

Australians went nuts over the show, more so than the audiences of any other country, including US audiences. Maybe ancestral chains, actual chains, played a role. But not in Ed's case. And, let's face it, nor in the lives of most Australians, and especially not in the lives of South Australians, who collectively hadn't any convict ancestry. So, who knew? Underdogs, maybe? Or maybe just the generational nature of the epic? Australians went mad for "The Thorn Birds," too, book and TV series, which was profoundly generational.

As a much younger kid, Saturday morning cartoons demanded total cultural focus from Ed, when he wasn't working on Zolli's building sites or playing junior footy.

After school, "Looney Tunes" provided him with life scripts and "Lost in Space" and "H.R. Pufnstuf" gave him a sense of theater. "Mash" and "Happy Days" influenced him deeply.

Network TV influenced him more than the Bible could ever hope. Hawkeye and Richie sat in his heart to become him as an adult. Meanwhile, the Fonz and Trapper John always made good company.

Repeats of "The Sound of Music" and "Chitty Chitty Bang Bang" and weekly episodes of the "Disney Hour" provided him with enduring glimpses into other-worldliness of grand stature.

Trannies– transistor radios – were a big part of Ed's cultural childhood. The word "tranny" would come to pejoratively refer to transgender persons. But for Ed Kaspar, the word "trannie" meant a social phenomenon like none other.

Sanyo made great transistor radios. BJ owned a Sanyo. Improvident Ed owned a cheaper unknown make branded by the Australian importer, Haminex. Later, he purchased a Realistic, made by RadioShack, from the Tandy store in Salisbury, the city-side suburb, one from Ellaville.

Pocket transistor radios were not only consumer cool among Ed and his friends. They were the "source" of kid-important information. 5AD brought him early morning gags about the Dover family, that is, Ben Dover and his friend Phil McCravitch (bend over and feel me cravitch; yes, classy,) and Run Dover, the family dog (equally as classy.) 5KA provided a raunchier mix of music.

Upon waking each new day, his precious transistor radio – a lifeline to the world - brought him updates from the 1976 Montreal Olympics, news about the death of Elvis a year later and, in 1980, staggeringly, shockingly, earth-shatteringly, the public announcement that John Lennon was dead.

John Lennon appeared in Ed's lounge room along with Zolli and Jean from the earliest of times. That he was dead seemed far bigger news than hearing he was murdered.

"Just like that, gone," Ed explained to Tim Griegson, his friend at the engineering plant, while awaiting the morning work siren.

As a kid, once weekly Ed listened to Casey Kasem's "Top 40 Coast-to-Coast," praying the brickish little 9-volt battery held until the end of the show.

It had not mattered that Casey Kasem's show referred to the US's coasts. "Hotel California" and "Country Road" were Ed's cultural geography.

The lines from "School's Out" were useful to know when Ed and his classmates rose up against a teacher literally in a chorus, simply for the excitement of seeing her pop a fuse.

The transistor radio provided little, tiny, all-meaning, self-selected rallying points. Who knew why the Greeks didn't want no freaks? When the Eagles' classic played over some kid's radio during school lunch, Ed and his classmates danced to the track anyway. They shared inimitable social moments in utterly tactile ways. Real-time social feedback could never keep up because Ed and his friends lived their social experiences in actual-time.

Jean made an effort to introduce Ed to cultural Australia, but not much of one. She gave him a copy of Colin Thiele's "Sun on the Stubble" when he was eleven, actually by way of a hand-me-down from BJ. (Gus went straight to adult fiction, the literary kind, not the sex kind.)) Largely, this was because the story was set in Ed's hometown. Colin Thiele was born and raised nearby, and he went to Ed's school, among others. In some cases, publishers provided instruction on how to pronounce "Thiele," a German surname, pronounced "Tier-lee," not "Therle." In Ed's community, "Thieles" abounded.

Later in his youth, Jean provided him with a new hardback edition of Henry Lawson's collected stories, likely for no other reason than having seen it for sale in the newsagency across the street one day. She gave him plenty, plenty of other books. But these were the Australian books she gave him.

Tom Wagner, Philip's younger brother, Philip being he of local shearing fame, gave him a book about Aboriginal folklore (for kids) at his tenth birthday party, which Ed loved. Steve Donaldson, who died a few years later in a car crash, hadn't been able to attend the birthday party. But he arrived early with his mother to wish Ed a happy birthday and to present him with a beautifully illustrated book of caricatured possums and koalas together with a green ray gun.

Ed loved that, too, the green ray gun.

Otherwise, his childhood was bereft of Australian literary influences.

Maybe the lyrics from the Australian Scout songbook.

But mostly they were British. Or American.

Some kids, bright kids whose parents fostered lofty

national ideals in them, recited Australian poems verbatim, like circus tricks. These kids even sang the soon-to-be national anthem, "Advance Australia Forever."

Ed later wondered if Jean's British leanings influenced his childhood away from national tropes, however inadvertently. It would have been natural enough, as in any immigrant household.

School shared some of the blame. While he heard about the White Cliffs of Dover in class, Ed battled to name what country Sydney was in when Dianna, the grocery store assistant, returned from holiday with a souvenir of the Harbor Bridge for him.

"Over there, near New Zealand," she explained.

"Oh."

Hadn't helped.

The teacher marched the class to a touring art exhibition in the Institute building once. Beautiful scenes of English landscapes and Turner-esque ships mesmerized Ed.

The Australian Broadcasting Commission's school songbook, like the Scout songbook, contained mostly British and US songs.

As a little kid, the "Famous Five" series was his favorite outside of school. Being the kid he was, he read it for the adventures, entirely missing the socio-economic issues that sent serious-minded adults into tizzies. Ah, the whimsy of childhood reading and its impregnability to weird adult hang-ups.

Other British stories such as "Biggles," "Doctor Who," and the wizard and dwarf stories penned by Ruth Manning-Sanders filled his bedroom shelves, though "Biggles," all warsey and espionagey, was never Ed's favorite. BJ loved "Biggles" but.

Literary works from America, a place that was not Britain, such as "The Hardy Boys," the "Nancy Drew" mysteries, and "Encyclopedia Brown" occupied shelf space in Ed's shagpile carpeted childhood bedroom too.

Far earlier in his life, Wisconsin based Little Golden Books gave him his sole literary moment with Zolli, who explained that he once hewed forest timber in the European Alps just like Paul Bunyan hewed forest timber in the frosty climes of North America.

When he became a teenager, Jean purchased him Stephen King stories from the Gawler Book Exchange, his favorites, both the books and the Book Exchange.

Throughout his teens, paperback editions of "Jaws" and "2001: A Space Odyssey" went a long way, though the movies, when he got around to seeing them, went a lot farther.

The Peanuts gang was genuinely a matter-of-heart, later rivaled only by the Footrot Flats dog.

In primary school, Ed subscribed to the school-sponsored "Lucky Book Club," in which he served as the Club Secretary. He collected money and sent away the postal orders on behalf of his book-reading schoolmates from across the classes.

"Encyclopedia Brown" was a "Lucky Book Club" order. "The Jewel of Seven Stars," another. Though he never read the latter.

"Paddington Bear" was his first ever "Lucky Book Club" order, in Grade 2, and his first ever book purchase.

Gus helped him select it. Ed hadn't been tall enough to see over the classroom sideboard to the catalog taped to it.

Jean scolded him when she found out he ordered it without her approval. She argued it was beyond his reading age, and too costly. But she coughed up the cash anyway.

"Only this once, mind."

***

OTHER CULTURE WHISPERED to him on the breeze on clear days. Or in storms and in heavy wind. Or when rain fell, and earth was turned, and water moved, and bees and birds flew. Or at night when the air stung him. And beneath trees.

Culture whispered to him then, too, beneath the trees.

***

CIGARETTES WERE MAJOR cultural forces. TV, radio, print media, billboards, store posters, and buttons promoted the little harbingers of death.

Sporting events spruiked the lung sapping sticks in life-affirming ways.

Cigarette heroes from TV and magazine advertisements were distant uncles with exotic backstories.

In contrast, the immediate family introduced Ed to pipe tobacco and cigars.

Zolli and the boys quartered oranges beside blazing campfires atop Fords Hill every Sunday while they ate squares of "Energy" chocolate and puffed contentedly on corn tobacco pipes. Nothing beat a pipe after an ascent up a hill of mud, loose rock, and moss-covered boulders.

BJ's pipe was a regular size; Ed's was cut down to fit his tiny, stubby six-year-old fingers. Gus's pipe was somewhere in between. Zolli's was a long one. He altered it with curved aluminum tubing to something the length of a Gandalf-pipe.

Cigars, which Ed smoked from four, expressed a morality all their own.

"A woman cried rape in a hotel room," Zolli explained.

"What's rape?"

"It's when a man takes what a woman doesn't give."

Ed's young mind boggled.

"When bystanders arrived, they saw the undisturbed ash of the man's cigar." Zolli showed how long with his thumb and forefinger. "They knew the woman lied."

"How did they know she lied?"

"Because of the cigar ash."

"Oh."

However, Zolli always considered the smoking of actual cigarettes – unfiltered Camels aside – worse than womanizing and gambling. A couple of years later, he counseled Ed, seven, in these very terms – "worse than womanizing and gambling"

150

- after they observed a man tip the contents of his car ashtray onto a public street.

Cigarettes won out, though. By his teens, Ed smoked them socially, a habit that he hid from Zolli, sometimes successfully, sometimes unsuccessfully.

***

LATE FRIDAY EVENING, Ed parked his Ford outside the aesthetically significant Adelaide train station (which featured in the movie "Gallipoli") and collected Zolli, who returned from Europe and the United States via Melbourne International Airport and the Overland Train.

The sheep were wet that day, so Ed waited for his appointment with Zolli alone at the shed. Everyone else left to make a long weekend of things given it was Friday. Uncharacteristically, he smoked a packet of twenty cigarettes to kill time and to make a start on killing himself.

Driving Zolli home with his one suitcase, Ed listened agreeably while he talked about extended family members in Hungary and the Rhine and stuff.

Then, crowded together in the Ford, and with Ed stinking of stale cigarettes, Zolli asked him if he took up smoking.

Ed lied and gave the old "spent the day with a smoker" excuse. Seemed to hold.

Back on Main Street, Zolli expressed his love for his youngest child, a man of twenty, by presenting him with a Citizen digital watch. Ultra-modern, and all the rage, digital watches kept good time. They were futuristic too. These were the days that followed songs such as MiSex's "Computer Games." Also, Ed and Zolli, like so many fathers and sons, shared a thing about watches. This one came duty-free, which was a mysterious tax process that shamelessly avoided government surcharges.

He gave him three gold-plated bicentennial coins encased in a plastic card the shape of the United States. The coin-card (belatedly, where Ed was concerned) celebrated two hundred years of American independence. While visiting his cousins in Philly, Zolli paid his respects to the fallen at Valley Forge. He described to Ed what the troops faced during that winter two hundred years ago. Zolli, himself, experienced wartime winter deprivation.

His father's description hadn't involved tears. It involved description, which in Zolli's case was enough. Ed took the gold-plated coins everywhere. They reached to him from the heroic depths of a significant moment in world history and from the depths of Zolli's rare display of emotion, which invoked a sort of heroics of its own.

Next day Ed fell ill with an awful, terrible cold, as bad as influenza, but not quite as bad.

The very idea of drawing cigarette smoke into his lungs ever again made him nauseous.

Come Sunday, while heading the Ford to his next shearing shed in the southeast of the state, Ed decided never to smoke cigarettes again, even unfiltered Camels.

(He hadn't smoke pipe tobacco or cigars since he was thirteen.)

Within a year, the biggest movie star in the world, Yul Brynner, would posthumously declaim cigarettes, which, in Ed's mind, would sort of vindicate Zolli.

(Yul never apologized for his womanizing, posthumously or otherwise. However, he only ever gambled in the movie remake of "The Brothers Karamazov.")

Some government shuffling later, cigarette heroes exited most cultural platforms altogether.

Occasionally, though, they returned in films and TV shows, secreted like dirty rags.

***

ED'S HOMETOWN IN the north of the state enjoyed a Mediterranean climate, as they say, summer heat and winter rain. A little farther north, and not by a long way, the rain hardly fell at all. There, the Marrabel Rodeo - boots and utes - held pride of place in the annual events calendar, along with the Bachelors and Spinsters Ball, also about boots and utes.

On the other hand, the South East, with the city of Adelaide calling the line between the north and south of the state, was altogether wetter and cooler. That mattered in Australian temperate zones. The southeastern city of Mount Gambier was urban and sophisticated in ways that towns in the north of the state were not.

Leaving the arid north of the state for shearing sheds in the wetter southeast was a big deal.

On his way to the South East, Ed dropped by Adelaide to visit his second brother.

He picked up another couple of books.

"Did you finish the books you borrowed?" Gus asked.

"Not really. Well, no, not yet."

Shearing work gave him a break from routine. It cleared his mind. But it was not an environment conducive to reading dense academic textbooks about Australian history and death and dying.

He struggled to read "The World Is Made of Glass."

While passing through Adelaide, he visited his uncle and auntie too.

Uncle Robert told him that the experiences he gained while shearing would be valuable to him later in life.

"Why?"

He could write about them one day.

His uncle also told him to keep a sense of humor.

***

LUKE'S TERRIBLE ACCIDENT, Ben's learner-stand, and another anonymous presser from one of the Doleman Brothers' teams upping to surf the Australian north coast for the remainder of his life (an ambitious aim for a nineteen-

153

year-old) indirectly presented Ed with a steady job in a tightly held role, wool-pressing. In turn, it gave him the shed experience he craved – the experience of the "Australian bush."

This experience arrived in its purest form in his first South East shed. It involved a type of wool press, the Koerstz wool press.

The Koerstz press was a wooden tower, split in the middle horizontally. The top box swung to the side and lowered to the ground for filling. Each box was, like hydraulic presses, the size of an oversized washing machine. The press was a marvel of cogs, cables, and winches. It harked back to the nineteenth century, back to the days of Henry Lawson.

Ed lined the lower bin with a bale bag. He packed wool in both boxes. Then he jumped inside the boxes and stamped the wool down as much as he could. He loaded the boxes again with great armfuls of wool, as much as he could carry. He stamped down the wool and kept going until both of the boxes were full-to-bursting.

He placed the iron pressing plate on the top of the top box, like a lid. He winched that box up over the bottom box, completing the tower. He removed the pins from the bottom of the top box (a floor for the wool while the box was separated from the tower.) He attached the winching cables to the iron pressing plate up top. He took his position at the long crank, which was about the length of a boat oar, and worked the crank up and down.

A winch pulled down the pressing plate – the lid thing - until it sat slightly below the lip of the bottom box. He released the top box, now empty again, swung it to the side, and lowered it to the floor, ready for the next bale of wool. He pushed the holding pins – forged iron rods - through the top of the bottom box as if they were sabers. They would keep the wool from springing out like an enormous jack-in-the-box once he released the pressing plate.

After he released the pressing plate, he pulled the bale

flaps over, as with a bale in a hydraulic press. He stapled the flaps, extracted the forged pins, and removed the bale from the wooden structure with his Captain Hook's hook.

An engineering masterpiece of wood, winches, iron plates, cables, and forged pins, the Koerstz press was powered by whatever its operator ate for breakfast that morning.

The husband and wife pastry chefs prepared their rich delights at the very shed with the Koerstz press.

Some of the shearers complained that the cooks were meant to "feed, not fatten" them.

Ed ate plenty of rich food – creamy profiteroles and gravy-soaked mains.

"Here he is," the husband and wife chefs happily cheered to Ed when they saw him arrive in the mess.

The excess weight slipped from him, and he muscled up magnificently. No athlete requiring core strength could have better fitness training than working a Koerstz press in a busy shed. No one, nowhere, no how.

Ed loved the Koerstz. He not only enjoyed the physical ardor involved, but also the mental clarity that the hard work gave him. Some hard work brutalized him. It reduced who he was. Working the Koerstz press left him physically sated, yet without a strained muscle or sore joint. The job allowed him to appreciate the uniqueness of it, where "it" was the "everything" it.

He not only experienced the bush of Henry Lawson yore. He experienced the bush. More than this, he experienced life. And it was a gift, just there, from out of nowhere, having waited for him in this shed in stripped hardwood, faded red paint, and ironwork the color of mother earth. He was well aware of just how privileged he was to work the Koerstz press.

The other workers, the shearers and the classer, as well as the rousties, some of whom still harbored niggling jealousies over him becoming a presser ahead of them, respected him on a new level.

Gus told him how a literary outlier, Bob Pirsig, understood

"Quality" through motorcycle maintenance, which in turn provided him with an understanding of the unity of life. A Koerstz press did it for Ed Kaspar.

The Koerstz press proved he could make a life of shearing.

He knew that now.

***

THE STATION OWNERS with the Koerstz press befriended Ed. They were young people in their forties, husband and wife. They held baby boomer if not hippy views. Yet they heralded from an aristocracy of Australian land ownership, a "squattocracy."

A hundred and fifty or so years earlier, men and women grazed sheep on land not yet within the English property system. Usage alone - squatting – gave them rights to enormous tracts of land despite rapidly evolving claims under the English legal system and despite pre-existing ownership on the part of the original Australians.

Eventually, these squatters - well-heeled and well-connected and hardly flea bitten wanderers as the word "squatter" might imply - received ninety-nine-year Crown leases where rent was a peppercorn, that is, a pittance.

The expanses of land that they claimed were unimaginably big by European standards. These squatters became hugely wealthy and powerful. For a time, they ruled the country. Hence a play on the word aristocracy, namely, "squattocracy."

The government upset the applecart when it parceled out millions of acres of the squatters' land to soldiers who returned from the World Wars. War veterans were deserving, they were voters, they had time on their hands, and they returned home with skills in collective violence (always a tricky issue for governments the world over and throughout history following total war. Blackshirts, brown shirts, the bed-sheeted Ku Klux Klan, and D.H. Lawrence's fascist organization, the "Diggers Club," in his novel "Kangaroo"

156

were examples of what could go wrong when soldiers returned home with bees in their bonnets after fighting total wars.)

Meanwhile, back at the ranch, yes, some soldiers had farming skills or learned them quickly. But many squatters claimed their land back when the demobilized men re-entered town life after abandoning their blocks bruised, bloody, and beaten like war never did to them.

Squattocracy did not exist in Ed's hometown, though important landowners once reigned. Nowadays, farmers in Ed's hometown were hard working, modern, responsible business people.

Presently, it hung around them, the owners of the Koerstz station, this fading lineage of squattocracy, like faded silk rugs, lush, thick, and inimitable, but faded nonetheless. It was a very odd property.

"Why keep hundred-year-old junk?" Warwick asked while waiting for Ed to break for lunch. He referred to the Koerstz press. "The cockie's not short of a bob."

He had a point. Unlike the Wilcannia property, miles from anywhere, the Koerstz station was well and truly on the electricity grid.

Nor could Ed guess why the squatters befriended him. A bigheaded poser, he put it down to his incredible bearing.

Maybe it had something to do with this. He never spoke with a plum in his mouth. But he picked up something from Jean, who spoke with a standard British accent and behaved with standard British manners.

Zolli influenced him too. Obviously of a non-English-speaking background, Zolli's accent bamboozled Ed's school friends when he spoke to them through the years. But to Ed's ears, Zolli made perfect sense – and perfect grammatical sense. Zolli pulled his nose at the lousy diction of stereotypical Australian speech, speech that was the exception rather than the rule in Ed's hometown. He couldn't respect the rare local who cussed every second word either.

The station owners introduced Ed to their daughter, who

returned home from Sydney University for the shearing season.

Andrea was a show-off, she was a flirt, and she was hot.

As a rule, the shearers excluded the station owners and their families from the actual shearing shed unless they visited under appointment. The rule let them get on with their work. Sheds ran as incredibly functional units and involved methods developed over a hundred years. Workers needed to get on with things and complete the job for the benefit of everyone.

So, prevented from entering the shed itself, Andrea paraded outside the portholes through which the shearers pushed the sheep after removing the fleeces.

The team members knew what she was up to, although why was anyone's guess. She wore skimpy pants and leaned over in the races, wiggling her backside, trying to distract the men. Perhaps she was a bigheaded poser too.

The father, a bit of a dilettante, smiled in a forgiving way, even in an agreeable way at her flirtations.

When women arrived at the shed or nearby, one of the men – usually one of the older men or one of the old-minded young men - yelled "woman-o." This warned the other men that a woman was nearby and that they had better avoid calling out expletives in anger or in conversation. Rather a quaint practice. Even women who worked the sheds yelled "woman-o" if a stranger to the shed, female, arrived unexpectedly.

At this particular shed, the Koerstz shed, shearers grew tired of calling out "woman-o" whenever Andrea decided to flaunt herself outside in the races. They complained about her when they realized what she was up to, especially the family men. In the end, she was banned from not only the shed but also from the surrounding area.

That did not stop her from visiting the quarters on the weekends.

Ed never played into Andrea's flirtations. He couldn't break from a crippling mindset that understood sex, or anything remotely connected with it, such as flirting, as an

158

emotional relationship, though he wanted to. It would have made things easier for him.

Raven-haired Andrea hung around anyway. She brought, if not some class to the mix, then at least a fresh way of seeing things, and Ed liked her.

His mind drifted back to the day he left Bill O'Brien's packing shed and looked across North Terrace at the Adelaide University campus to a life that he imagined as vastly superior to his own, one rich in learning and diversity.

He recalled the men in Standard Books that day and how he believed they talked down to uneducated people like him. He imagined that the men would welcome Andrea as one of their own. Maybe they would kowtow to her, her a member of the squattocracy and her going to Sydney University and so hot and everything.

And here was Ed, pulling a brush-tailed possum from the rafters beneath the veranda and handing it to her while she drank beer from a long-neck bottle.

"I'm heading back to Sydney tomorrow," she told Ed.

The Koerstz shed cut out a few days later. Ed moved on, and he never saw Andrea or her folks again.

Ed made a lot of friends that year in the sheds, without ever seeing them again.

***

ED WAS DESTINED to press wool at a massive fourteen-stand shed situated on an incredibly unbelievable twenty thousand acre property, a humungous amount of land relative to the munificent agricultural ecology in the southeast of the state. It was replete with its own village of workers, and a manager's homestead, not to mention the actual homestead, a mansion bathed in expansive English gardens. It lay outside the tiny, South East town of Alexander.

"Does Alexander have a grocery store?" Ed asked Warwick.

"It has a pub."

Ed hadn't drunk alcohol since the Wilcannia shed. But alcohol influenced his formative years more than TV, transistor radios, pop songs, books, family, Citizen digital watches, TV uncles and real uncles, and cigarettes combined.

Or if alcohol hadn't influenced him more than these things then it weaved a tapestry from them that he wore as a means to identify himself and to belong with others.

Alcohol influenced him as a child too, though as a matter of family rather than as a gateway to teenage debauchery. Santa left him and his siblings little Tia Marias, Drambuies, and Jack Blacks in mantelpiece stockings. The New Year was a time of Coopers Stout and shandies (beer and lemonade.) Sunday roast was always served with flutes of sparkling red Minchinbury, a red bubbly. Sometimes when pharmaceuticals faltered, and Zolli had his way, foul-tasting alcoholic black stuff arrived as a medicinal. Following the backyard grape harvest, the kids trampled the grapes in rubber boots for Zolli to make his muddy, mule-kick wine. Ed collected wine labels from Valley wineries when he visited them with Zolli on store business. Other kids collected postage stamps and cereal box critters.

Alcohol was about to play a big part at the Alexander shed.

***

DRINKING AT THE Alexander pub four nights a week became the norm for Warwick and his buddies, including a short, stocky, mustached newcomer who went by the name of "Tallboy," named so for obvious irony. Tallboy was thirty. He carried a backpack everywhere with him, though no one knew why.

Even on off-town-nights, Warwick or Tallboy traveled to the town for grog and returned with it to one of the group member's huts.

One night, around midnight, Tallboy led a few men to

Buggsie Somebody's room, a young, diminutive roustabout, who was sleeping.

Ed roomed next door with a quiet, easy-going, bearded family man a few years older than him, named Rocket. Early in their stay together, Rocket advised Ed to "not listen through walls."

Tonight he had no choice. Buggsie Somebody howled like a little kid. Thumps and thuds erupted. Grunts. More shrieks. It continued for around fifteen minutes.

Ed considered helping the kid. But it wasn't like chaos reigned. The kid could have called for help rather than shriek stupidly. If he called for help, the older men would look into things even if it meant getting out of bed to do it. The kid could have told the interlopers that he would raise hell with the contractor come morning. They would let him be. They were drunks, not outlaws.

Ed braced himself should they enter his room next. He would push back, even if it came to blows.

Ed had reason to defend himself in the past.

Also, he witnessed vicious fights from a young age. He watched Australian hoods and English hoods war with each other using knives, chains, clubs, and nunchakus outside the sole government rental house along the street where Uncle Robert, Auntie Anne, and their neighbors lived otherwise respectable lives.

There were plenty of examples. Kids and kids, men and men, women and women, and men and women. He saw them all fight.

Ed would fight if he had to. He would fight tonight if he had to. Resist vigorously enough, and one man can deter a group of attackers, especially if they were half-hearted, and if he wasn't.

But, truth was, he wasn't a fighter by nature or instruction. Nor BJ.

And no one ever remotely considered Gus a fighter, though he had inherited the Kaspar hot head.

Zolli was too law abiding.

As it was, things quieted down in Buggsie Somebody's room. The men went elsewhere to whoop it up until fatigue caught them by their scrawny necks and sent them to sleep.

The attack on the kid was one thing. Nightly disruptions were something again, and they thrived at this shed.

Ed dragged bedding to his green Ford, which he parked away from the noisy quarters. He hunkered down on the back seat uncomfortably on chilly nights behind four locked doors, cracking the windows a tiny little bit for air.

He faced wool-pressing in a fourteen-stand shed each day. His joints ached without a proper night's sleep.

Ed's life in future times would involve searching for homes free of rowdy neighbors to sleep for work.

High-powered stereos, extended licensing of bars and clubs, thudding arterial roads, cheap building materials and bad planning, greater leisure time (which for many would mean purposeless lives without knowing it,) increasingly crowded living, a socially degenerative lack of concern for others, and unemployment and underemployment as social realities, and their reduced need for sleep, would make his quest difficult.

Other craziness ensued at the Alexander shed. Maybe the spring sun caused it. Maybe the nearness of a pub caused it.

Sam, the unionized kid from New Zealand, otherwise a bit awkward and straight-laced, began drinking copiously to fit in. His work motivation slipped. He complained to Charles, a classer, about Rick Bell who asked him to sweep the boards quicker. Charles, (there were two classers at this humungous shed,) ignored Sam's complaint. He filled in for Mark Johnson, who was home ill. So Sam whispered that Charles victimized him too.

Charles was a portly, thinly mustached, button-eyed, black-haired, gentle fellow from Adelaide. His father was a judge. So he – Charles - had a strong view of right and wrong, even if he defaulted to getting along with everyone.

Ed hung with Sam some weekends, and he was a pretty good guy. But he had a chip on his shoulder. Eventually, shed workers had to pull their heads in and get on with their work without calling attention to themselves.

"I'm not backing down," Sam demanded.

He claimed that he was a victim of harassment when, really, he was the perpetrator of subterfuge.

His uncharacteristic foray into the heavy consumption of alcohol made him this way, and this was his real problem. Before Mark fell ill, Sam used his relationship with him, a young guy also, to his advantage, that is, to slack off. The stand-in classer, Charles, didn't jump when the eighteen-year-old from a fourth generation shearing family told him to jump.

Harvey Harvey interviewed every man at the shed. In the end, he made Sam take a break, despite Sam's threats of union action.

It was not so bad. Harvey Harvey put Sam in the sin bin for a couple of weeks, giving him an opportunity to return home and cool his head in a family environment. He rehired him at another shed down the track.

The only people Harvey Harvey had not interviewed that day were Betty, the cook, and Ed. Cooks didn't mix with shed politics even if some of them, Betty included, were great gossips. And Ed had a reputation of an observer who didn't take sides. Maybe his presser's mantle helped with this image. Maybe abstinence from alcohol left him at the edge looking in.

Ed made friends with the quieter guys, although this did not always guarantee a hassle-free life. One guy in his mid-twenties, Ricky, a lean, muscled, sallow, white headed, healthy man with the easy, natural movements of a shearer, comfortable in his own skin, and at peace with it, brought his wife to the shed, herself pretty and quietly spoken. She did not mix with the team. She preferred to stay in her quarters and go for drives or walks alone. But she did befriend a handsome Maori man, Daryl, himself married with children, but alone at this shed.

Daryl was outgoing, a reader of novels. Like all book readers, he knew a lot. He talked to anyone because he had things to say. Sometimes he visited the young wife in her quarters and took her books to read, that sort of thing.

On those occasions, the young husband, Ricky, left them to their conversation. He walked his dog, which, like him, was long-legged, muscled, and lean, a dark-colored Shepherd of some variety, likely a Belgian Shepherd or of that ilk.

Ricky brought the dog to Ed's room and tied him outside. He sighed and smoked a lot while he talked to Ed about football and cricket.

Suffering was in his eyes. And he smoked too much, and too fast.

One time, he pulled the dog into the room. Confused, it barked at Ed. Ed grew up with his dog, Blackie, and there were dogs everywhere in his hometown, so he was not shy of dogs. But this beast was intimidating. Like nearly every dog on the planet, it expressed its master's mind, in this instance, the torture and suffering of a young husband.

His eyes tortured with that weird glint, Ricky, smiling, assured Ed, "He's friendly, he's friendly."

Who "he" was, was anyone's guess. Stress leaked from Ricky and pooled on the floor in Ed's quarters, and the barking dog drew attention to it.

Then there was the incident with the station manager's cousin, Cheryl. This was such a big farm that the farmer hired a station manager and a dozen workers, all having their own single or family quarters on the property, grouped in a community of cottages a short walk from the shearing shed. Ed befriended the station manager, Andy. Often, he walked the well-worn, compacted dust track to visit him and his family in their home.

Andy was around eight years older than Ed. He was one of those men who graduated from high school to a position of responsibility, something Ed, with his wanderlust and anarchic temperament, never attained.

Andy's wife, Patricia, was a year or two older than Ed. Auburn-haired like her husband, she was responsible, thoughtful, and respectful. Already a mother with a baby, she entered the shed during a quiet period one day and tried her hand at shearing a sheep to prove to herself and anyone who looked on that she had not forgotten her shearing skills. She was rusty, but her technique and animal handling skills remained spot on.

Andy's cousin, Cheryl, was a different person. Also a year or two older than Ed, and a lovely woman, she reached for something in life other than what she had, and was going through a marriage breakup with her husband, a Mount Gambier firefighter.

Because the fate of the relationship was undecided, her estranged husband visited the homestead once or twice, and Ed met him. He was not the brute Ed imagined. His work as a firefighter was stressing him, and this compounded the marital complications. Even Cheryl related to him okay on these visits. However, the man looked very lost. He asked questions to prove that he was interested in the conversation. But then his eyes wandered without waiting for an answer.

When they were alone in Andy and Patricia's home, Cheryl pushed Ed against the wall, threw her face into his, and stuck her tongue down his throat.

"Don't you want to?" she asked confused.

Ed derived his theology from "Looney Tunes," and drew on it now. Good and bad angels arrived on his shoulders. He gently put distance between him and Cheryl. He muttered something about a girlfriend back home.

It was wasted opportunity where opportunity was seen as getting it on with a vulnerable woman who, at this random moment in her life, experienced emotional complications. It added up to something else if not seen as that. The good angel won.

Carmen was on his mind, true, and she would be for years to come. But his reference to a girlfriend back home hadn't been a reference to her. His image of her became just that, an image. He no longer saw her, not the real her, not in his mind's eye or anywhere else for that matter.

Perhaps he never saw the real her, which was why he was left with only an image of her now. Honestly, he hadn't really known what her views on life were, even while they dated. He hadn't known what she wanted from life, what she planned to give to life. He hadn't known her favorite song.

He desired her, and that was where his need for her began and ended. With him wanting her. Wanting her was not loving her. Without loving her, how could he know these things, her plans for life, her favorite song?

Their relationship could have grown from his desire for her. He might have ended up loving her by accident or design, it hardly would have mattered which, provided he truly ended up loving her. But he hadn't truly loved her when he broke it off with her. He had merely desired her with all he was.

He lied to Cheryl and himself while mentioning a "girlfriend back home."

***

THE FOURTEEN-STAND shed near the tiny township of Alexander became famous in Ed's memory as the last shed he shared with Warwick.

Warwick took to drinking beer before breakfast. Drinking beer for breakfast.

Latter-day temperance unionists overstated alcoholism. They wanted people to believe they were alcoholics if they drank nightly or even weekly. Sometimes even monthly. Trying to save face, because they knew that what they preached was untrue, and because reformers needed addicts more than addicts needed them, these nanny-weirdos referred to the irregular consumption of alcohol as "binge alcoholism" or some fanciful variant on that phrase. They pronounced their admonitions accordingly.

The truth was, willpower alone set people free of booze whenever they liked if they drank weekly or even nightly.

They were alcoholics when they drank booze every few hours.

Warwick was an alcoholic.

He talked about the hair of the dog in the morning. He spoke of a quickie at lunchtime. He claimed that he deserved a few at the end of a hard day. Then he needed one or two to put him to sleep. He pre-mixed brandy and water and kept it beside his bed for when he woke through the night. The booze caught him at a cellular level.

Forget moralizing. Warwick needed a lot more than attitude to free him. At this stage, the trap was bio-chemical.

Australian careers were severely limited where workers refused to "have a few" with workmates. Less leeway was offered workers with parental responsibilities than was offered hungover workers who homerically "battled their demons" or "fought the black dog" with the aid of grog. Workers who fell ill with colds or the flu or faced family bereavement and required grieving time or workers who arrived late to work after traveling overpriced, subpar, intermittent public commuting-systems were cut no slack either. But "having a few" with the boss set a worker free. Outside of work, social groups were dissolved and re-established according to one's inclination (or not) to "have a few." In Australian social life, no one was worse than a "wowser," someone who elected other than an alcohol-soaked focal point as his or her life's quest. Ultimately, there was no discussion without rolling over on the subject of "having a few," which meant having far more than "a few."

Ed gave away the booze at the Wilcannia shed. In this sense, he went against the grain. Yet, Warwick left him alone on this score. Because Warwick was a chronic alcoholic, and he knew he was in a dangerous place.

Ed saw the long-legged, straight-talking man of subtle humor turn nasty and cruel. Between drinks.

He was not a pugilistic man, far from it. He vented his mean streak on the animals.

He shoved hot cutting combs into the sheep's mouths to "get a taste of this." With the animals lying on their sides for the long stroke, where the fleeces were shorn from their bodies, Warwick fell hard with his knees, bringing down enough force to break ribs and puncture lungs. If he decided to stitch the animal where he cut it, he jabbed it repeatedly with the needle first, sometimes in its eyes. He cut animals in ways that cutters had a tough time doing when used correctly. Or incorrectly. He stomped heavily on the testicles of the rams and more or less pulverized them to show the rams that he was "boss."

Animals experienced extreme pain without context in these circumstances. All they knew – all they could know - was that they were in the hands of man. Resignation reflected from their sad eyes. It was the most damnedest, most pitiable thing to witness on the planet.

Some people get it; some people don't. Those who don't, wait outside, please. Your bus will be here soon. Take care.

Shearing developed over hundreds of years to ensure that sheep were sent from the shearing boards without their fleeces with as little fuss as possible. The method was improved significantly during the 1950s.

Sometimes the best shearers nicked an animal with the clippers. Occasionally rare sheep struggled unusually. But always upon always when things went wrong, and animals were injured, the operator was at fault.

Between drinks were times when life hadn't the same kick for Warwick.

"I'm losing it," he confessed to Ed.

Ed didn't know what to say.

Sure, he needed help. But Ed didn't know how to help him.

Warwick sent sheep into the counting yards cut up, blind, neutered, with flesh and fleece hanging from them, and poorly stitched, if stitched at all.

168

Ed saw it. The men saw it. The expert saw it, the wool classers saw it. The farmhands and the cockie saw it.

The cockie, whose name was Bentley Cache, was a compact, solid man with a rolling, barrel-like walk and a very educated approach to farming. He had black hair and a red beard. He said little, but he saw everything. His men, hard men themselves, strongmen who knew right from wrong, vocally wanted something done about the way Warwick treated the animals.

Firing a shearer mid-shed raised problems. The other men might walk in protest. And it was pointless to think about hiring workers during the peak of the season to replace the fired shearer. Also, even if the contractor found a new worker, which he wouldn't, he risked union intervention if he hired him for the same role. Then the contractor, and of course the cockie, were left without the means to finish the shed expeditiously. That was bad news for everyone. Even for the sheep, which would struggle beneath heavy fleeces.

Bosses could not "counsel" shearers. Shearers weren't office workers. They would get up and leave if someone counseled them in that wishy-washy, loaded, passive-aggressive HR fashion that even HR managers see no point to but get paid for. Then the team would be down one stand. The contractor might even find himself back at square one, with all the shearers muttering words of protest.

No one suggested that Warwick continue unchecked. But some of the shearers would question whether Harvey Harvey handled things right were he to indeed dismiss him. Stuff like that.

Unhelpfully, do-gooders began to advocate indiscriminate testing for the consumption of illicit substances in the sheds. But men didn't want to be presumed guilty until proved innocent. They wanted to work, and work was impossible while serving cruel, supervening, self-defeating, hyper-surveilling, counter-productive Whole-of-Life-Regulation.

A hyper-do-gooder system cheapened people. It

criminalized them. It had them where it wanted. People broke rules just breathing. Meanwhile, as they say, real criminals walked free.

Also, even Blind Freddie saw when a workmate was tanked. You didn't need to test for it.

And what about a shearer who did take a drink the previous night, or a joint, but who worked the next day responsibly despite what some flip with a science kit said?

The world's problems weren't symbolized in an intoxicant. It was imbecilic and lazy to claim it. Surely, it was about harming animals, as in not harming them, and not about drawing false-positives between saliva and crime.

In no time at all, you had Australia, the world's biggest Stanford Experiment. A slippery slope for a nation that began as a prison.

"Why prove he was drunk?" Rocket, Ed's roommate, asked in private.

True. In a job where animal husbandry skills were paramount, wasn't it enough that Warwick demonstrably hurt defenseless animals? Pack your bag and go home.

Warwick left that night. Ed never heard what happened to him.

Harvey Harvey and Dennis Harvey fixed things because that was what competent people did.

**

OTHER EVENTS EXASPERATED Ed at the Alexander shed. While he helped a roustie organize the sheep in the inside pens, he saw a dead lamb stuck halfway out of a ewe, the female sheep. The farmhands must not have noticed while they shepherded her from outside, or else they would have quarantined her. Maybe it happened inside the shed. Whatever, the sight of the ewe and her dead lamb brought Ed low.

Ed isolated the sick ewe. He frantically tried to release the dead lamb. Unsuccessful, he turned angry, and he became mad at shed life.

When the shearers broke for lunch, he called over his roommate, Rocket, a decent, contemplative guy. He showed him the ewe, which he left in the corner of the pen alone. She was in an awful condition.

His roommate, a quiet man, appeared more shocked at how the event affected Ed than the sight of the struggling ewe. He explained that it was not Ed's problem. Or even his job. Rousties – not pressers – ran the inside pens. Nevertheless, he joined him in trying to remove the dead lamb. After a few minutes, Rocket said he would find a farmhand.

"I'll wait here," Ed said, looking stupid.

Ten minutes later, a farmhand, old David, and the cockie, Bentley Cache, showed up with fencing wire, a towel, and a bucket of warm soapy water. They tied the wire around the dead lamb. With the help of the warm, soapy water, they gently relieved the ewe of her burden.

No one sane enjoyed seeing animals suffer. But the sheep remained livestock. No one saw a cockie's sheep as creatures that strained heartstrings. Reliable, intelligent, hardworking Ed suffered strained heartstrings.

It wouldn't be the last time emotion got the better of him in a workplace.

Ed couldn't blame his teammates, the cockie, the sheep, bosses been and to come, or authority figures. It would take him decades to realize this. It would take him another lifetime to accept the universe's injustices, which even the universe was unaware of or couldn't care about.

The farmer, the farmhands, and Ed's workmates didn't look at him the same again. He was never quite "one of us." Now he cracked under pressure. And over a dopey bloody ewe.

***

BETTY THE COOK was older than Ed's mother. A couple of times at the Alexander shed, which was a long one, she drove him to her home by the sea, where he stayed in a guest room out the back of the main house. She introduced him to her daughters. They were three and four years younger than him, and gorgeous, and really casual, and easy-going and trendy in that progressive city way he liked.

They were too young to know the flower power generation as an actual way of life. But they belonged to an 80s culture that was its legacy. It continued as a counter-point to everyday culture. At the same time, Gordon Gecko's Black Monday and Tuesday approached on the horizon like Birnam Wood. Lunch was about to become a thing for wimps. That psychosis would survive as the predominant culture.

Soon the government alone alleged that egalitarianism remained at the country's heart, and only around voting time, there with kissing babies. For the rest of the time, leaders misquoted George Bernard Shaw and counseled that life wasn't meant to be easy. (Forgetting the part of the quote about life being delightful.) So, you know, suck it up.

The rise-and-rise of the vice of one-upmanship began to replace egalitarianism. It would fill the breach left by efforts to play down organizational hierarchy in the name of populism. The biggest mouths would be left to call the shots, un-credentialed in anything except an adult form of schoolyard bullying. Disorganization became organization's hallmark.

Unmitigated economic competition gave rise to a winner, not winners. Society would mutate into economic tyranny.

Workers fell low with hurry-disease and other career ailments. They would turn to the religion-of-buying-things at the not-just-Sunday Church-of-Mall. Then they would go back to the wheel to pay for it, losing family relationships and their souls in the process.

Other workers found themselves unemployed and underemployed. They wouldn't lose their souls. Society would crush them in two-bit TV shows aimed to maim and hurt – to dehumanize for kicks and graft.

Retraining programs would become all the rage, though only guaranteeing teacher, not student, employment as genuine as those programs aimed to be.

Social-justice centers plugged holes. Like sandbags in a tsunami.

Office work expanded exponentially as the robbing-Peter-to-pay-Paul services sector became the new Promised Land but without a national mythology to endorse it. It was a non-unionized factory class of highly qualified, wholly replaceable professionals. Those who kept their jobs politicked better than they performed. They demanded big titles filled with the same stuff that underwrote their claims, zip.

Office jargon, with its specious sidekick, the "key selection criteria" that wanted ten, twenty, no, thirty unbroken years of verifiable career experience, demarcated an otherwise sameness of rather pointless administrative roles, the skills of which were acquirable on-the-job in six-weeks or less. These workers headed toward the lemmings-cliff of New Millennium computer automation.

Manufacturing, the actual foundation of human endeavor, appeared dirty and low class, and was shut down.

Tradespeople became "tradies," a word with the same amount of letters as "teddies." They competed for work in workerless economies. Their betters patted their heads, rubbed their bellies, and withheld pay increases.

Prescriptive regulation conjured a class of newly licensed professionals to solve problems that never existed. Repairing a backyard fence post would soon require five pairs of paid eyes and three purchased government permits. The regulations taxed what incomes they could and fined everyone else.

Unparalleled economic growth fueled by property speculation and the sale of fickle commodities would see the well-being of most people head backward.

Australia became economically useless. It would fool itself into thinking that the sale of hard fought for, tax-funded public assets evidenced its incredible capacity to generate wealth.

Well, yes, like how third generation moguls fornicated their way through life.

Politicians were already slaves to the only advice on offer, that of unrepresentative, dippy, ill-dressed bureaucrats. They announced elaborate rounds of shifting deck chairs. (Imagine it to music. Like the music played at the end of Benny Hill shows.)

Ed knew one thing. The Australian way of life he aimed at turned out to be another short-term stay.

Being Australia and being an Australian wasn't the same.

They weren't close.

They were different books with different themes.

Betty prepared dinner for him and her daughters.

Decay drifted from the nearby sea.

"Love me. Love me, please."

Later that night, with a belly of beer and a heart of broken idealizations, Ed Kaspar walked into the embrace of his host's beautiful daughters, who were as lost as he, and as lost as an already lost man of an Australiana past, Warwick Apotherick.

***

Friday, the wind blew hard. Ed shivered. His head was unclear. Cars honked him for going too slow around mountain elbows. He was sure he took a wrong turn.

He was near the packing shed where he and Quinn worked several months ago, the day the world stormed old Bill O'Brien's gates on the word of a kid who left town giggling.

He drove home the back way through the Adelaide Hills. The Alexander shed cut out early in the day.

The backroads were poorly engineered, with undulations and bumps leading to bad cambers in dangerous places. Invisible gravel lay on bends, making things unexpectedly slippery. Tar was narrow and ran to broken, jagged edges, where it met concealed mud or, at the other extreme, chunks

174

of tire-piercing granite. Corners came up fast.

Other road users seemed dangerous to Ed. Didn't they know how hazardous roads were? Even a slow speed crash broke road victims into pieces.

Few farms around here had gardens, unlike Ed's house where Zolli grew everything from daisies to watermelons. Here topsoil was so fine that the breeze carried a handful of it to the nearest town and blinded people in the street.

Dogs out here in the backcountry lay tethered to corrugated iron water tanks. They lived until they worked a full day no more. Then the farmer walked the sad thing behind the shed and blew out its brains with a .303 cartridge.

Even when he arrived back in the countryside of his home, and he saw the rooftops of his town sprinkled in low hills like in a Women's Weekly picture, Ed felt unfamiliar with things. He could not figure out why. He was not away from home so long.

He parked the Ford in the garage and shut down the motor. With cramped legs from the five-hour drive, he stepped from the vehicle and waited for his blood to flow again.

The shelf beside the driver's door that once belonged to BJ remained empty all these years.

"It's his. When he wants it," Zolli would say.

He knew full-well that the time when BJ would reclaim his shelf had long passed.

Stretching, Ed looked at his own meter-deep wall-shelf. He reassessed the neatly stored engineering tools of his trade. It took the years of his apprenticeship to acquire them. They included expensive micrometers and Vernier calipers. Other tools – spanners and sockets - were German or American made. Literally, and not only as a matter of promise at the point of sale, they would last a lifetime.

Other tools were cheap rubbish, not many.

Some he acquired from the two places he worked while an apprentice, the engineering plant, and the winery. This latter category of tools included consumables such as worn files and drill bits, or dollies sawn from off-cuts of brass rod.

Buying his tools satisfied his instinct to buy things. Later in life, he would purchase many books, not to read them all, though reading was essential to him, but because shopping was his totem.

When he purchased spanners and calipers, he purchased logos, just the same as when he purchased clothes with logos. He curated an image of himself that he wanted people to see.

In search of himself, he lost himself.

As far as the real he was concerned, he – it – might not exist.

He was as real as the place he never came from and never was or would be.

He purchased his football club pullover when he wanted to project himself as a town patriarch, a young one. He purchased high-cut running shorts and head and wrist sweatbands when the jogging craze hit. He picked up a squash racquet when the world went nuts for the game and its heroes. He smoked Black & Whites as a fourteen-year-old, thinking himself Jimmy-Dean-cool. He bugged his mother to buy him black ripple-sole-suede-shoes, a South Australian specialty. When he was eighteen, he purchased Windsor Smith cowboy boots. They weren't manufactured to horse-riding standard. But they looked neat. He purchased a horse to go with the boots. And between the ripple-sole-shoes and the cowboy boots were motorcycle boots, along with motorcycles.

Recently, he remodeled himself into an image of Australia, one of warmth and humility, an iconic, nationally acceptable, and globally admired ideal. It was the best armor he came up with.

His self-image lacked xenophobia, thin-facedness, laziness, moodiness, a need to play people against each other, endless excuses, sycophancy toward authority and belligerence toward the weak, sycophancy toward the weak and belligerence toward authority, righteousness and telling people how to live, a moral elevation of the disreputable, impulsiveness, pathological worry and hyper-sensitivity, material greed, and neuroses that encompassed all these things plus more.

Before the "tick, tick, tick" of the Ford's cooling motor died away, Zolli walked into the garage to greet his son.

"Oh, it's you," he said.

Ed watched him, curious.

Zolli was not the sort of man who raced to greet his son. He wore tailored purple Bermuda shorts from the 70s and an unbuttoned collared short-sleeve white shirt. Beneath his unbuttoned shirt, he wore a white singlet.

Zolli rarely drank himself into a stupor, even if he often drank to the point at which he sang along with old records in the evening while wearing padded headphones.

Currently, he came perilously close to the sort of functioning-not-functioning alcoholism exhibited by such shearing shed luminaries as Warwick Apotherick.

Ed never judged Zolli. He wasn't above judging his father. It was that he lacked the insight and explanatory power to judge him. An odd form of impotent hatred and withdrawal sometimes took the place of judgment.

Here stood Zolli in his singlet, unbuttoned shirt, and purple Bermuda shorts, drunk. Born following Hungary's collapse from world politics, he survived global economic depression, the childhood diphtheria that afflicted him and killed his brother, his mother's religious autocracy, and his father's breakdown caused by policing Budapest's treacherous interwar river docks. He survived the war that killed a hundred million people. He survived Nazi occupation and Allied internment of dispossessed Europeans. He watched Communists break what was left of his land. A little older than Ed was now, he survived his arrival to a continent of deserts and deserted suburbia. Then the real fun began: life. Against this background, he succeeded. He married, made a home, raised three children, and remained self-employed all his working days, something - self-employment - so vital to his sense of self. Along with his immigrant cohort, he terraformed a continent.

Now, his youngest child stepped into his own future, and Zolli and his wife, Jean, were left without an immediate way to reinvent themselves. Instead, they regressed into the only life alone together they knew, one of courting and promise, often jumping aboard the pop-canopied Hi-Lux to venture to faraway places as they had in the 1950s. But after a lifetime of incompatibility and tit-for-tat arguments, the future would not hold the hope it held for them when they first embarked on the exhilarating unknowns and sometimes impossible responsibility of parenthood. Zolli saw the end of the road, without knowing what it would bring.

He was left with a land he owned, but that wouldn't own him, except by way of duty, but not by way of belonging.

What did it mean? Where was everything he worked for? What happens when futures end but life holds on?

After returning from his father's grave in Szeged, Zolli drank two of the three bottles of aged French brandy reserved for the weddings of his three children. The third he opened this morning, and he explained as much to Ed now. He talked of the Alps and of rivers that tumbled through many nations.

"You can have my tools," Ed told him, without thinking about the brandy or the Alps and the rivers.

"What if you need them again?" Zolli replied.

"I won't need them again," Ed said.

***

ED SLEPT POORLY and felt awful when he woke through the night. He dragged himself in pieces downstairs to the bathroom in the morning. He stayed home through Saturday. His body imploded with sudden inactivity, with lethargy, with exhaustion.

Ed was pleased that Zolli hadn't barbecued dinner that evening.

"I can make you something if you like," Jean told her son.

He explained he would get something "out." But he had no intention of eating.

He left the green Ford in the garage and walked the short distance to the Woolshed Hotel. Red and brown dust lay on Main Street and gathered in crevices. A dust storm blew through the town while he was absent. Enormous billowing clouds of red dust brought an uncanny night to day. The town, its occupants ever proud of its streets, cleaned up as best it could.

At the height of last summer, golf ball hailstones fell and turned the hot ground white. Ed was home on that occasion.

The year before that, Ash Wednesday fires threatened the streets.

Once, locusts swept through the small town. From the back window, Ed watched as swarms of insects approached from the hills a few miles to the west. Just like in the books, they arrived in dark clouds. And when they came, they covered every square inch of grass. When they left, they left behind dead stalks.

Years ago, fearless, crazed, starving mice plagued the town in wriggling carpets of desperation and gray fur.

One time, unprecedented rainfall flooded the town. The river lapped the railings of the main highway bridge. Everyone got out of bed at midnight and drove to see if the bridge would hold.

As Ed reached for the door of the Woolshed Hotel, he felt chilled. He knew he would stay this way through the night, a night that felt dark and silent around him. Words lacked cheer enough to reach him. His ears were closed to words of happiness, closed to words of warmth.

Old man MacArthur tended the front bar. His knuckles pressed the bar counter like his son Stew MacArthur when he tendered bar. He was a tall man, with a considerable paunch. His naturally long face was rounded in fat. His eyes hung with a droop.

179

His wife, and mother of several children, was seated on a barstool to the western end of the bar, trim, well-made-up, dressed well, pretty, a middle-aged woman bringing sophistication to the curtain call of a rapidly closing era of country life.

The old man asked Ed what he wanted, and Ed ordered a schooner of beer, though he had no appetite for it.

Dickie Hewitt, a small man with thin, oiled back hair, styled conservatively from the 1950s, nodded to Ed like an equal, as if Ed was equal to him in adulthood. But it wasn't enough. Ed wanted more from Dickie Hewitt. They worked together at the carriage plant.

What was Dickie's image? Humphrey Bogart?

He drew on a cigarette and pushed out his lips to blow away the smoke.

"That's good, that's good," he said in reply to Ed's word or two about his life during the two years since they last met. Dickie Hewitt explained how old Bobbie Hanes, "Left us. Lung cancer. Lost his hair. That was the toughest part, seeing him like that. He always had a great head of hair."

Alan Dyson died from a heart attack. Garlic chomping Dreyssig too. Ted Biggins died from stomach cancer.

These men were Ed's father's age. He worked with them at the carriage plant. They died two years of its closing.

The world opened for Ed when the plant closed. It was not so for the men who worked there long ago enough to qualify for special dispensation from joining the troops in World War Two, in recognition of their importance to the manufacturing sector.

Now manufacturing, along with farming, followed that great bell curve to the sky, along with the men and women who worked in it.

Ed sat on his beer, without the appetite for another. Old man MacArthur watched a talent show on TV, laughing now and then, turning to Ed and Dickie for their responses. Ed gave his everyman smile where required. When asked. Dickie stared at the TV along with the barman.

But Ed had a distinct feeling that Dickie stared somewhere else entirely. Only he, Dickie, saw it, even if everyone alive stared in the same direction. Everyone saw much the same thing, though believing they saw it alone. That we see it alone. Like Dickie, Ed believed that he saw something radically different from everyone else when he stared into the same place. In thinking it, he imprisoned himself.

Mrs. MacArthur left her barstool and walked to Ed. He was seated and she, tall and thin, leaned into him.

"They've gone to Bali on a football trip," she said. "Are you looking for them?"

He looked for his friends in the same fashion that he ordered his beer and then sat on it without a thirst.

He felt god-awful lonely, and he felt shivering-cold, and he wished old man MacArthur switched on the radiator that hung from the ceiling behind the bar. He just felt so damn unconnected. He felt so damn not a part of this place. And Bali! For a football trip! Two years ago, the club chartered a couple of buses, purchased onboard beer kegs, and drove the players up the road to the Riverland. The adventure of the trip was to see who cried next for a piss stop. Bali! For a football trip!

Ed Kaspar knew things were changing. And what had not changed as a result of him seeing things differently had changed because things always change.

Now he was here. Forever. A place that couldn't last past the previous still.

***

ED MET DES in the final shed scheduled before Christmas outside the town of Meningie near the Coorong. The Coorong, a couple hours' drive south of Adelaide, was a ninety-mile long lagoon protected from the ocean by a thin, permanent spit of sand. Colin Thiele's "Storm Boy" belonged here.

Des was a couple of years younger than Ed. His father was a preacher. He lived in one of Adelaide's newest suburbs with his parents and his three younger sisters.

Ed could not remember the name of the suburb, and may not have even registered it when Des told it to him.

Years earlier, Zolli drove Ed, a kid, to grocery wholesalers in Adelaide weekly through new subdivisions and criticized the houses as "all the same." This meant something to him, a builder, even if at the time he ran the grocery and liquor store. He disliked the sameness of the low-quality subdivision houses, which were a total eyesore to him. He claimed that the residents were "packed in like sardines."

It suited Ed's present sense of superiority to look down his nose at the sameness of the new suburbs of today such as that inhabited by Des and his parents and sisters. He clung hard to what he had worked so hard to believe in, to build his life around, to build his future around, namely, a bush ethos. He clung even harder to it when he realized it didn't exist as he imagined it. But cities always intrigued him, and now Des intrigued him. Des impressed him.

City life impressed Ed. Busy, civilized, clean, permanent, and diverse. In contrast, one man nodded his assent in a country bar, and all the men nodded their assent. One man may argue the toss. But that was the point. He argued against something as fatalistic as a coin toss. Ed imagined that city-folk expressed whatever views they liked, whenever they liked.

Des was tall, lean, and muscled in an agile way. He had a goatee beard and a mess of black curls. He spoke about studying to become a preacher and following in his father's footsteps. He might not too. He was at that stage of his career life. He had the look of a young professor or cleaned-up, latter-day beatnik.

He played association tennis. He claimed that he kept fit by catching public transport everywhere, and walking or running the rest of the way. He explained that he didn't possess a driver's license. He didn't want one.

To Ed's ears, this very sentiment, this idea of a young guy not wanting a driver's license, amounted to an enormity of waywardness. Whoever heard such things!

Admittedly, Ed's brother, Gus, didn't own a car, and probably he wouldn't ever own one. But at least he had a license.

As far as Ed and his close friends were concerned, they claimed a driver's license and ownership of a car, or a motorcycle, as their first adult reward.

When Ed met Warwick, Warwick talked about his plan to one day live in a city and to bicycle or catch buses everywhere, and not to own a car at all. Cars, he argued, offered independence. But they also depended on fuel, registration, upkeep, tires, hoon modifications, and insurance where obtainable, big expenses collectively.

Ed and his friends sought lower-cost third-party property insurance to protect them from claims brought by the owner of the proverbial Rolls Royce they crashed into. Some young drivers couldn't even afford that level of coverage. Ed had not always afforded that level of coverage. The Ford, mercifully, had full insurance.

And cars themselves were expensive, even old pieces of junk. Especially old pieces of junk. Old pieces of junk required ongoing maintenance. A broken fan belt, a blown radiator, long-motors, short-motors, "new" gearboxes from the wreckers, re-machined brake drums, shredded tires, likely cheap re-treads to begin with, and any amount of other things imaginable, points, spark plugs, mufflers. The expense was measured in time, too. Repairing the dog-boxes late into the night and on the weekends was a continual chore.

Warwick had good reason to idealize a day when he might live without the expense of a motorcar. But he would never live in the city. Or, if he did, he would never walk or run to and from bus stops as Des did. He wouldn't put up with long, long, long, long waiting times for public transport, particularly on weekends and afterhours when public transport in Adelaide dried up.

Des managed it. He was born and bred a suburbanite.

Ed had not expected to meet someone like Des in the sheds. Des hadn't walked from a Henry Lawson story into Ed's life. Warwick hadn't either. But Warwick might have if Henry Lawson was alive today and writing stories about the bush.

Des was only a start. Steve Bridges, a gun shearer with gently parted bangs, practiced Pilates in the evenings at the Meningie shed to maintain his back muscles. He refused to overeat at mealtimes, always leaving a morsel or two on his plate.

"Overeating affects my nutritional balance," he told Ed.

Nutritional balance! Wasn't steak nutritional? And beer the balance?

He ate salad too, as in lettuce, something Ed's cohort referred to as "rabbit food."

Ed wanted to denounce Steve Bridges a douche.

But he wasn't a douche. He was a cool guy.

With great bangs.

Ed's other surprise came when he encountered Quinn at the Meningie shed. Ed bunked with him at Bill O'Brien's packing shed six months back. He heard that Quinn worked for the Doleman Brothers. It all seemed too much to figure out where. Then they just walked into each other on the property beside the Coorong.

"Do you wanna bunk?" Ed suggested.

Quinn explained that he bunked with an English immigrant, Mike. They hit it off a few sheds back, whiling away their time talking about the historical development of London pub rock and New York garage bands. Not much for Banjo Paterson to see here.

Even Tallboy sobered up, the crazy man who led the troop of marauders into the hut of the kid on the state border a few weeks ago. He reflected over the contents of his backpack

184

more and more and went by his real name, Aloysius.

He stuttered through his explanation to Ed as to why he wanted to invest his savings in the burgeoning forestry industry and short, medium, and long-term life insurance policies, which were a type of financial instrument before the days of government mandated superannuation.

The huge man with damaged limbs, Luke, wisely invested his compensation money and already reaped the rewards. Now he talked of a house down payment.

Sam, the fourth generation shearer, was politically savvy.

Ben read books like athletes kept fluids up.

Ed's ride was over.

Not just shed work, but the whole thing.

With it, his future ended too.

***

LATE MONDAY, ED went to his room and fell into one of his dreary, twilight funks. He felt miserable and very cold. He was outside before he left home for the shed thinking the late morning sun wouldn't burn him. It did.

Some people avoided eating while they felt sick. Not Ed. Like a little kid, he crept to Betty's larder and made sandwiches.

Instinct warned him off fatty, meaty, buttery, sauced sandwiches. He settled for tomato and cheese sandwiches. But afterward, he overate Betty's cookies.

Back in his room, stuffed with food, his sunstruck head pulsated with his heavy heartbeat. He felt more miserable than ever and so hopeless about everything. He sensed that this was who he was.

Living his outback dream for real, he faced the truth that he remained him.

He thought that going somewhere else would make him someone else. It didn't.

He woke at midnight to read one of Jean's Alistair

MacLean novels. He could not connect with the whole thriller storyline, which seemed to offer zero insight into the stuff going on around him, life. He accepted the dark truth that Henry Lawson's stories no longer guided him as they once had. Yet, he wasn't ready for Gus's collection of books, which included William Faulkner's "As I Lay Dying" and "Go Down Moses." He stroked the covers of the Faulkner books, wondering as to their hidden messages.

He reached for his lecture pad, the one he purchased all those months back at the Broken Hill newsagency. He had not written in the pad – not really – not since he re-discovered the wonderful effect that writing had on him in the mid-north of the state following his meeting with Nifty Ronson, the union organizer.

After meeting Nifty and walking the spring fields, culturally and artistically inspired as he was, he scratched a paragraph in response to a newspaper article that whined about the economic cost of old people.

How on God's green planet were old people a cost? They were the ones who created the wealth.

The way Ed saw it, young people owed old people everything. Earlier generations laid the roads Ed drove on, built the house he lived in, taught him at school, cured his ailments, wrote the songs and stories that narrated his world. They provisioned him to this point in his life.

But he resisted the call at the Dawn of Causes – which would prove to be a mighty church without a spire in the decades to come. That was to say, he hadn't written anything else on the topic or on any other topic since.

However, a couple of weeks ago, he used the writing pad to pen an application to study for a para-engineering diploma. After completing the course, he might get work helping a university-degreed engineer, or even work as an employee in his own right in a lower order role, for example, as an in-house drafter.

The winery employed a drafter, and that was something to

recall while Ed contemplated the next stage of his life.

"Boydie told me to drop this to you," Ed nervously said to the drafter in his office a week after he started at the winery.

It was a spigot for one of the grape crushers. Boydie, Ed's boss, wanted Scottish Nick to tool it. First, he needed the drafter to spec it.

The drafter drove a Jaguar motor car, an E-Type, one of those low slung, cigar-shaped coupes famous in the movies. He wore his gray-black hair over his ears and sported muttonchops and a moe. He wore checked suits with fabulously broad lapels. His office walls were stained yellow with cigarette smoke, and he died quite young, in his fifties.

"Leave it here," he told Ed without looking up.

Alternatively, Ed could use the diploma to enter a degree course in engineering at one of the ramped up tech colleges, which were joining Australia's established universities as providers of higher education.

If accepted, he would study for the para-engineering diploma at a college of Technical and Further Education, a TAFE, one similar to where he studied his apprenticeship lessons, somewhere in an outer suburban industrial estate, ringed with a ten-foot-high cyclone mesh fence and six-foot tall weeds. Middle-aged men in dust coats and patriarchy-beards – perhaps the same men who taught him as an apprentice - would teach him.

The experience would be lonely because men were always lonely where there were no women unless there was booze. When there was booze but no women, men were lonely and sad, or lonely and sad and cruel.

Ed thought back to the day when he parked on the roof across from the University of Adelaide. Boys, young men actually, had not worn steel-capped, elastic-sided work boots with scuffed toes. Their hands and fingernails were clean of engine grease, Ed was sure of it. And there were girls, and just by being there, girls brought a dimension to the learning institution that boys wouldn't have brought on their own.

In Ed's imagination, everyone at the university campus was raised well. They were intelligent and inclusive and had grand plans, just like the kid who wrote a play on his typewriter on the lounge room floor when Ed joined his friend, Brent Edwards, and his Marist college buddies one Saturday night years earlier.

Smart people didn't argue, or squabble, or white ant and bait one another.

Not the intelligent people in Ed's imagination, an imagination already fueled by what he saw in the university that day and in scenes from "2001: A Space Odyssey."

He switched off the light in his shearing quarters for the second time that night and took what sleep he got.

***

TUESDAY MORNING, JEAN got word to the contractor, Harvey Harvey, who got word to the owner of the Meningie farm, who got word to Ed.

The farm owner permitted Ed to telephone his mother from the farmhouse during his lunch break.

Afterward, Ed replaced the hallway phone and thanked the taciturn cockie.

"I'll pay for the call," he offered.

The cockie pulled his head back and led Ed to the door.

The para-engineering course accepted him.

The news hadn't wowed him as he hoped.

Rather, he planned a new odyssey, one aimed at 2001, where intelligent, educated people like Poole and Bowman, didn't argue or white-ant each other in petty and trivial ways. The idea of Adelaide University filled his mind.

Ed Kaspar never completed high school.

***

SUMMER HEAT ARRIVED and the evenings were bright.

188

"Emotionally pleasant," Ed remembered saying to his good friend Brent Edwards a year ago on a similar evening.

Brent called him "the poet."

The beauty Ed saw at the Meningie shed before the sun set late amazed him. Christmas was near, which meant festive gatherings with his family and friends.

Iron sheets that flapped in the wind and rusted farm implements made for evil scenery in the shivering, perennially unheated Australian winter. But in early summer, they were windows through which he watched breezes sway golden crops. Here at the Meningie shed, he experienced Colin Thiele's "Sun on the Stubble" firsthand.

Ed heard sounds that he would have heard a thousand years back and would hear in a thousand years to come were he ever to arrive in those future times where only life grew.

***

ED'S LIFE CHANGED forever when Quinn entered his room with a big, fat, unread weekend newspaper around eight o'clock Tuesday night.

Newspapers were everything in the 80s, especially Saturday newspapers. The "everything" in the newspapers was a whole lot less than the "everything" on the Internet-to-Come. But at least the "everything" in Saturday newspapers was not a message in a bottle that floated on cyberspace oceans awaiting God and Google for the mention.

Quinn wore his freshly laundered black baseball cap, as he did even while roustabouting during the heat of the day. He showered and washed and dried his long, straight, chestnut-brown hair. He wore a checked flannel shirt and Levis, freshly laundered, which would be his work clothes for the next two days.

He sat on the bunk against the wall across the narrow room from Ed. He drank beer and played with the rolled up three-day-old newspaper. He kept his bare feet from the mattress.

Ed sat on the edge of his bunk, feet on the floor, head rested in his hands, elbows on his knees.

They talked about the possibility of working another shed before Christmas, a short one.

The world, this local Australian world, pretty much closed for a couple of weeks over Christmas. With summer at its height, and with test cricket on TV, and TV tennis around the corner, and with parties and open-air discos, and day visits to the beach, and rock concerts and street pageants and family celebrations and gift giving and well-wishing everywhere, it was a great festive time.

Ed and Quinn were lucky. They cherished things.

After a half-hour or so, Quinn said, "I'll leave you to it." The sun was down. "Oh," and he left the newspaper on the spare bed. "I can take it with me if you don't want it. It's Saturday's. I remember how you liked the inserts," and he sorta growled this and twisted his face, because men don't want to appear girly when being nice to each other.

"Yeah, leave it," Ed growled softly.

He waited until Quinn walked the wooden veranda back to his room. Then he closed the door to keep out mosquitos. The door was part windowpane. It was nice to see the fields redden with the absolutely last rays of sunlight.

He let his mind buzz with the sound of the insect world and the silence of the hidden sun. His residual fatigue carried him somewhere nice too. Then with the arrival of the dark, and no moon yet, he switched on his lamp and opened the newspaper, which appeared barely read. He knew Quinn was thinking of him when he kept it.

Funny, or scary, or just "was," how chance played a primary role in life.

All Ed needed to do was remain open to it.

Quinn's castoff paper fascinated him.

He would read it all in time.

Meanwhile, something in the nature of the newspaper, and its separated sections, each a hefty lift-out magazine in its own

190

right, or something in the nature of the early summer night, or in Ed's heart, or in the spiritual world he inhabited right now but couldn't know, or could not know directly but knew indirectly, drove him to a bland notice taking up less than a fifteenth of the broadsheet page.

The state government invited applications from adults who wanted to return to school to study for their matriculation certificate.

Technically, to "matriculate" was to sit exams across five subjects, the passing of which allowed "matriculants" to apply to university to study for a degree. Practically, it was Year 12. Other states had higher school certificates. Same thing.

To matriculate in South Australia in 1984 was a big, big deal. A big, big deal.

A couple of years earlier, high school officially terminated with the "Fourth-Year" (Year 11) Leaving Certificate.

Kids attempted to matriculate only if their parents paid for their attendance at a private school or if they were fortunate enough to attend a state school that offered a matriculation course – or if they lived within commuting distance of such a state school.

Ed's brother, Gus, hopped buses to a neighboring town in the Valley to study for his matriculation.

Zolli or another parent drove him to and from the bus stop in an intermediary town. Commuting always presented immense difficulties of a logistical nature, which invariably festered into difficulties of a family nature.

Mostly, kids had to be bright and eager. Matric was not a waiting room to become adults. Or a means for governments-of-the-day to manipulate youth unemployment statistics.

It was a faster racetrack than Nifty Ronson's warehouse racetrack by a factor of ten. Candidates needed to want it, and they needed a reason for it.

Ultimately, teachers suggested it to them and their parents. Which was to say that plenty shoulders weren't tapped.

Matric was as good as it got for most young people. It led

to bank jobs and post office jobs at a time when the banks and the post office meant something in society. Some kids with good matric scores got cadetships in journalism, though this was rare, because not even Ed's lifelong friend from class, Michael Leichhardt, obtained a journalism cadetship on his Year 12 grades alone, and Michael possessed all the flair in the world. In some states, but no longer in South Australia, kids entered the legal profession in their old man's firm on Year 12 grades.

Generally, well-heeled farmers' kids around Ed's prosperous hometown only ever aspired to matriculate.

Ed's high school introduced matric as part of its curriculum, but only in the year that he left to work in the engineering plant.

Anyway, no one suggested that Ed study for his matriculation.

No one tapped his shoulder, which was for sure.

Boys far brighter than Ed left high school when they were fifteen or sixteen and entered trades. The competition for a "good" apprenticeship was significant. This swelled the ranks of blue-collar life with gifted individuals and had done for decades. A certain proportion of men in their middle years who wore grease-stained engineering overalls were inventive geniuses. Others were crippled geniuses. All tradespeople adhered to seriously high work standards.

Money and heritage got kids into university. Or luck of the planets-aligning variety might get less entitled kids there. But aptitude scored kids good trades.

Apprentices nominated for Apprentice of the Year were revered. They were boffins in overalls and future leaders.

Talented girls became bank tellers, a distinguished career move in those days.

One girl from Ed's class became a lab technician.

Others became teachers' aids.

It wasn't a time when bright kids from rural backgrounds went to university in number. As such, trades and clerical

192

roles were stacked solid with really bright kids. Other bright kids who had a year or two of private schooling and parents with civic ties sometimes joined the police force. Some chose the military.

Trades and clerical roles, military grunt, and beat cops would all suffer talent shortages toward the new millennium when kids from all backgrounds headed straight to university to take degrees in everything from medicine to makeup artistry.

Maybe Ed would have tried harder had he sensed this unprecedented arrival of educational and career opportunity in the air.

Maybe he would have trained for a profession like teaching.

Zolli encouraged his children to aspire to a university education. He always told them that he saved money for it.

Indeed, Ed topped every subject in Year 10 and won book prizes. He interviewed a World War One returned soldier. Carolyn Coley, the school's top typing student, transcribed the interview from recorded cassettes. Things looked promising on the academic front. But he lost interest by Year 11. He convinced himself that Year 10 was an accident, and he was no hero during Years 8 and 9. He took Jean's lead. She would be proud of her children if they swept the streets provided they were happy doing it and they did their best.

Yes, Ed's poor attitude figured in his substandard school performance. But despite talking up education's strong points, Zolli always bugged him into helping on building sites or in the workshop on the weekends and in school holidays. Barely had Ed opened books on his desk Saturday mornings when Zolli requested his help with something.

After school, he performed chores, from "running messages" to chopping wood.

And Zolli shouted a lot in those days, and he banged doors. His behavior jarred Ed's nerves, which weren't in a great state anyway, what with eating packets of cheap cream filled cookies weekly and handfuls of jelly babies daily.

Emotional turmoil hung around long after BJ fled the home. No one knew where he was. Ed, the younger brother, worried himself sick over Zolli's comments.

"The police will knock on the door one night with the news he is dead, I tell you." Zolli said.

He always looked away when he said this.

Jean openly blamed herself for the estrangement of her eldest child. But secretly she blamed Zolli. No wallflower, she continued her quiet but visible war with him. Invariably, they argued. The tension was thick enough to cut with a knife.

On top of this, images of girls competed with his school lessons for his finite mental energy, supplemented by occasional real-world dalliances of a frustrating nature with actual biologically constituted girls in his class.

And he had to leave school if it meant escaping the weekly P.E. locker room pubic-hair and dick-length count.

In all, matriculation just hadn't happened for Ed Kaspar.

Rightly, his high school teachers would have persuaded him against wasting his time and theirs.

In contrast, the carriage plant cleared Ed's head. He struck gold when it employed him. Its whistle measured town hours. Its workers were community leaders. The plant focused him, reconnected him with his town, and paid him wages, small as those wages were.

Of those tiny wages, less than unemployment benefits, he paid thirty percent of his before-tax earnings in board-and-rent to his mother. He became a responsible member of his family, a fact that fulfilled him and kept him broke.

But he always knew that he had more to give to educational pursuits. He just hadn't known how until now.

Now, he forgot dull paraprofessional classes. Definitely, he would never complete his diesel mechanics correspondence course.

He re-read the government notice inviting adult matriculation applicants.

194

It defined suitable applicants in terms of social justice categories. And as everyone knew, but did not say, to define was to exclude, no matter the righteousness.

Ed wondered if the notice excluded him by virtue of including not-him. But it had not explicitly excluded young second-generation workingmen with strangely spelled names. So he would try his luck.

Ed never appreciated that the government offered a free course, with free teachers, a student pension, a healthcare card and a transport concession card, paid administrators, classrooms, a library, and librarians! All an enormous, enormous expense, all free. Priceless knowledge capital on the part of highly trained, well-versed, and committed teachers – free!

He couldn't see that this opportunity represented the changing face of Australia and that he was a part of it.

"Do you want to work with a hammer or a pen?"

Ed still couldn't answer Zolli were he to ask the question.

But he knew that the matriculation course would change him forever if he got in.

He applied to study at Carrington Woods College, which was in the tree-lined avenues of Adelaide's genteel eastern suburbs. He wanted out of industrial wastelands.

Before he switched out his light, he completed the final draft of his application, ready for the morning post.

***

A WEEK AND a half later, the Meningie shed cut out. Ed was home on Main Street when a letter of acceptance arrived from the Sheraton Hotel resort in Alice Springs. He forgot he applied for the job, which was for a sort of handyman role. It came with brilliant conditions, good pay, an embroidered uniform, and a chance to travel to other Sheraton resorts for work and play. The job had an exciting feel to it. Ed sent the recruitment officer a photo of himself, a requirement, along with a densely worded application letter where he told his life story.

"Your looks will get you the job," the photographer in the city booth said,

"Really? You think?"

Ed never photographed well. He always backed away from the camera and squinted, possibly to stop the lens from sucking in his soul for keeps. Maybe his antipathy evolved from his and his siblings' disdain for Zolli's photographic pursuits in child portraiture of the family snap variety. But this photo – a squinting mugshot – was passable, and Ed took the photographer's words as an omen.

Then, on receiving the letter that morning, he immediately declined the offer in writing and mailed his rejection letter that day, genuinely thanking the resort manager for giving him a chance. He made up his mind to go back to school to study for his matriculation, and he told the resort manager this in his letter.

He wrote another letter to the TAFE college that accepted him in the para-engineering course, and he formally withdrew his application.

Next day, Jean took a long distance phone call (from Adelaide.) Ed heard the STD pips from his room. The administration officer at the TAFE college wanted to make sure that Ed knew what he was doing when he withdrew his application to study for the para-engineering diploma.

Ed shook his head in the negative as Jean offered him the phone. He shook his head in the positive as she mouthed whether he was sure he wanted to pull out of the course.

Jean explained Ed's decision to the caller, thanked him in her best Queen's English, and rang off.

Ed had one more shed to work before Christmas, a four-day impromptu shed that the contractor squeezed in after the Meningie shed.

Friday, before he left for it, the Carrington Woods matriculation college telephoned.

196

"Six-six-two-zero-nine-five. May I ask who's calling?"

Jean always answered the phone if Zolli was at work or outside in the workshop.

She answered very correctly because she and Zolli ran a business. The automatic exchange was a mere eight years out of the switchboard operator's hands.

Again, Ed heard the STD pips that introduced every long distance call.

Jean held him back with a hand gesture.

Harold Sands, the principal of the Carrington Woods matriculation college, personally telephoned in deference to the well-meaning application that Ed penned. But, at this point, the college must refuse his request because he showed little hope of completing the course.

The principal took into account Ed's trade schooling and his high marks in his diesel mechanics correspondence course. His application letter read very well, and that was the reason behind the call this morning. But his high schooling was not up to scratch. Places in the college were limited, and better-qualified candidates had applied.

If Ed thought about matters rationally for just a second, something he avoided like hell, he would see Harold's reasoning, and mix it with some of his own: he was all-points dumb going on his high school efforts. He'd better just head back to a life of grease, engine or sheep grease, his pick.

But Jean wanted the opportunity for him. Her family hadn't bags of money or entitlement. So she had to find other ways to get him an education. She brought out her best British accent, still a thing of force in 1980s Australia. She was the eldest child and was a mother for twenty-five years. She trained and worked as a nurse in major UK hospitals. When called upon she was tactfully and relentlessly merciless. By the end of the telephone conversation, she convinced Harold Sands to meet with Ed after Christmas. The school term started in early February.

"Now, are you sure it's what you want?" she asked Ed

after she rang off.

Only a loophole and luck saved him.

And a willful mother.

What Jean had not given Ed through an inherited title, a thing so defining in Australian life, where social mobility constituted an act against nature, especially in the South Australian city of Adelaide, she gave him through her force of will and intellect, his actual birthright.

It made for a very, very slim opening.

***

MANUAL WORK WAS dirty and destructive. Ed rose before dawn most days. During winter, he found a warm place if he could, the long rays of the first of the morning sun, the slightly warmer air pocket four steps to the left of the plant generator. In summer, midday heat killed.

His hands calloused-up six months into his apprenticeship. Engine grease tattooed itself on his fingers and palms.

His work clothes were spent clothes, or purpose bought blue and khaki twill cotton that turned Jean's washing machine black and never totally washed clean of workshop odors, and never washed clean of stains. Work boots were heavy, ill-fitting, tiring, clodhoppers with steel caps that showed through the leather after the third or fourth wear.

He lifted heavy objects that punished his hips, spine, and knees. He worked up to his thighs in trench water swinging picks. He twisted two-foot long spanners on oversized bolts. The bolts gave. He drove his knuckles into metal casings and removed the skin to the bones.

Daily, his lungs filtered industrial particulates. He fell from a twenty-foot tall storage tank and bounced from other tanks to the asphalt below. Power tools ripped him up, vibrated him to bits, and deafened him. He slipped on broken flooring and wrecked his ankles. On one occasion, doctors cleared the waiting room as Scottish Nick manhandled him to the surgery

198

in blood-soaked overalls.

"Olympic swimmer, Chester, coming through," Scottish Nick yelled, his voice tremulous, his face as white as a sheet.

Many days, anger, Ed's sole source of vitality, supplanted his work ethic. It was all that pushed his body past its limits on cold, cold days while he lifted heavy, heavy objects with sore, sore hands.

This was Ed's work life. No respite. Not a gap year.

Into his middle years, or earlier, his body would be an intricate system of pain and injury. Alcohol would be a medicinal cabinet mainstay. At forty-five, regular employers wouldn't employ him.

"Give the younger blokes a go," interviewers would tell him.

When he retired from work altogether, unsure what to do, with his body crying for a rest after a lifetime of monotonous, spirit-killing, bruising activity, and with his hips, knees, and shoulders rigid and awfully pained, he would topple headlong into an unhealthy stasis. He would worry how to afford to feed himself and pay heating bills.

Unable to pay medical insurance when he needed it most, after paying hundreds of thousands of dollars for it through his work life when he needed it least, if at all, he would die a year later of one or more of any variety of maladies.

This was manual work: pain and deformation.

With an absence of reward.

***

ED WASHED HIS hands with Solvol soap in hot water before heading to his meeting with Harold Sands. He remained wary of the ingrained engine grease he hadn't removed.

"Use turps," old garlic chomping Dreyssig told him at the carriage plant. "Cleans your hands. Drink it too if you want." (Ha, ha.)

The stuff burned, stank, and leeched skin lipids.

Anyway, he didn't have any turps.

However, six months of working with sheep lanolin removed some of the engine grease tattooed into his hands. He was thankful for that.

But he could not conceal the damage to his hand from when the concrete mixer grabbed it as a boy, a sort of scarred hollow above his knuckles.

He would pluck wool fibers from the insides of his arms for months to come too.

He quickly checked his inner-wrists now.

While checking for rogue wool, he worried about his right inner-wrist. When he was fifteen-years-old, he carried a large rock at one of Zolli's building sites. The rock slipped. There was little to no bleeding. But the wound left scars that made Ed appear as if he took to his pubescent wrists with ill intent. He lowered his shirt cuffs now.

Diversity policy was one thing.

Like shelf ornaments.

But gatekeepers didn't examine people like Ed for winning attributes. They watched for damning traits.

Ed wasn't giving Harold Sands a reason to exclude him.

***

FOUR YEARS OUT of high school, and hardly a year out of trade school, and only a few months from his correspondence course in diesel mechanics, Ed was not entirely uncomfortable sitting across from Harold Sands in the principal's office at Carrington Woods College.

Harold explained that the education department expanded the school twenty years earlier to accommodate late-stage baby boomer girls. With the last of the girls moving on, Harold Sands and his team moved in.

"We specialize in matriculation courses for adults," he said.

Ed was in the right place.

At the right time. In a year or two, the state would decide that educating future doctors, judges, lawyers, teachers, artists, computer scientists, and engineers wasn't what it wanted after all. At least, not where the fodder was drawn from non-private school backgrounds. A construction company would purchase the school at mates-rates and level it to considerable short-term profit and swinging parties that included ministerial helicopter joyrides.

Harold Sands, suited and aged in his fifties, was a bit stiff at first. Ed knew hard men and women all his life, and never feared them, or felt uncomfortable around them. He knew where he stood with them. He only ever feared mean men and women. Unstable men and women. Harold was hard, not mean or unstable. Harold was an enlightened headmaster by another name.

Ed began school with a "headmaster." Daily, he marched to what were even back then forty-year-old war tunes. He sang "God Save the Queen" along with the entire school at morning assembly while a designated kid hoisted the flag. The cane – the "cuts" -wasn't spared. Sometimes teachers flipped and general beatings eventuated too. But by Year 5, a "principal" took over. Corporal punishment was out. School assemblies were out. "Where Have All the Flowers Gone" replaced "God save the Queen" before "Advance Australia Fair" had even a chance. Garden studies replaced religious studies. Classes went from fifty kids in rows to sixteen kids in groups of four sitting on molded chairs around laminated tables with brightly painted legs. Though teachers still flipped violently from time to time.

Harold emanated from this juncture precisely, now ten years on from its advent.

Out of his work clothes, and dressed casually neat, concealing hand calluses, scars, and tattooed engine grease, Ed spoke to him enthusiastically and mannerly.

"I'll work hard," he pleaded. Sort of.

Zolli and Jean weren't pleaders. They argued their

positions convincingly, Jean according to "what's proper and fair" and Zolli on the more black and white basis of "right and wrong." They never pleaded. And nor did Ed now. Instead, he set about convincing Harold that he wanted to study at the college. Pleading, where apparent, comingled with enthusiasm.

When Harold gave in on the study point but told Ed to attend classes at the Ellaville campus in the northern suburbs, which was close to Ed's hometown, Ed lied and claimed that he was already living here in the city with his second brother in the neighboring eastern suburb of Magill.

Ed didn't want to study at the Ellaville TAFE College. He attended trade school there. The surrounding suburb was comprised of heavy industry and tiny brick houses constructed in the 1950s. Knee-high cyclone-mesh fences and weedy lawns encompassed homes. Desolate train platforms. Motorways and highways that relegated pedestrians to second-tier existences. The sun was hotter, the winter wind colder. Shopping malls that only ever lived come weekends, or lived with the wrong kind of life come weekdays. Traffic lights stopped drivers on the barest stretch of lonely road and kept them there for what seemed to be soul-crushingly unendurable times. Factories utilized "flexible" workforces comprised of the unemployed and the casualized employed who were scared of being unemployed. The flatness. The sameness. The real, the truthful, the indelible "Australianness" of it all. Only the minds of youths and rare minds at that aspired to something more, and often in fruitless and misguided ways. Generally, youth expired at the grand old age of seventeen or eighteen anyway, when marriage and newly born kids, not in that order, and low rent housing and government benefits took over, and life outside a narrow range failed.

Proselytize about the working classes as he might, Ed preferred a middle-class existence.

Like all his country-people preferred, were truth told.

Or if not this then a life interestingly lived.

202

Despite Ed's lack of formal education, and despite his working-class experiences, and despite the calluses and engine grease on the hands that he hid from Harold, and despite his small-town origins, and second-generation beginnings, he was none of these things. He was what Harold was. All Harold had to do was see it.

Ed was certain that many of the men he met in the sheds would not be welcome here, in spite of the newspaper ad's promises of social inclusion, not unless, as Ed was doing now, they showed they could fit in.

His whole future turned on it.

Life was about the gates that kept you and the gates that freed you.

Maybe Harold thought back to his conversation with Jean. Likely he did.

***

ED AIMED THE Ford home, thrilled. He had a place in the Carrington Woods College matriculation course, the absolute last and final candidate accepted for the year.

Plenty of other men and women missed out, like him, kids really.

One actual person with a name and birthdate missed out because of him, which he avoided thinking about for now.

He immediately set out to remedy his lie about living in Magill. He had not lied completely. He saw an ad in the newspaper for a Magill apartment late yesterday, and he liked the idea of living in it. That much was true.

It was still a time of near full employment where Ed lived. So country roads were quiet during the week, with everyone at work. If he saw a rare car or farm vehicle, likely he knew the driver. He gave the open-handed wave from atop the steering wheel, a little double flick of the wrist, index finger extended relaxedly, a sort of rural salute, as was custom.

He knew when Uncle Pete, the local police officer, set a

speed trap, and where, and when the Freeling police set their speed trap. In country-stations, staffed by one or two officers, a lot had to do with available time.

Fixed speed cameras were too new and too few and at the mercy of semi-automatic rifles owned by voters.

The metric system was in Australia for a decade. The Ford was new enough to have a metric speedo. However, Ed's first cars were in miles because they were old jalopies. And the road signs of his childhood were in miles. So now he always rounded eighty kilometers per hour to the old measure, fifty miles per hour. He still rounded one hundred and sixty kilometers per hour to one hundred miles per hour or a "ton" in the lingo of days past.

Yes, Ed and his friends, with as many passengers in the car as possible, "cracked the ton" a few times while heading their barrels of bolts along the straightest stretches of road they knew. Preferably on a slight downhill run, and with a tail breeze.

"Go, go, go, go," but for the grace of God, might have been the last words they spoke.

Ed drove these same stretches of road on his way home from his meeting with Harold.

The Ford was a big-motored, highway vehicle. The "ton" was in its stride. Nevertheless, Ed rode home at one-twenty-clicks (one hundred and twenty kilometers per hour) which still exceeded the speed limit by ten kilometers per hour, but was not the "ton," was not one hundred miles per hour or anything like it.

It was the next day, the day following his meeting with Harold when he "cracked the ton," and this was how it came about. After a long wait, Gus commenced a career as a paramedic, actually in the spirit of Jean's old career as a nurse. He was spending a few days at home. Things weren't working out with his housemate, Katherine McKechney, in the tiny workingman's pug cottage they shared on the downtown fringe, and no one blamed either of them for that. It was long

204

decided that if Ed studied at Carrington Woods College, he and his second brother would share an apartment together. Ed wasn't aware of Jean's thoughts on the issue, but Zolli thought it proper.

"You need his guidance," he told Ed.

And it probably wouldn't hurt Gus if he had Ed around.

In Zolli's view, living together would be good for them both, despite their yet unacknowledged differences in their ways of seeing life – and in living it.

And despite Ed returning to school, not childhood.

That morning, Jean telephoned a glamorous real estate agent and spoke with her about the Magill apartment that Ed saw advertised on the eve of his meeting with Harold Sands.

A mother's voice could achieve amazing things where country siblings were concerned. Suzette, the agent, agreed to meet Ed and Gus at the apartment at eleven o'clock. It was a little after nine o'clock now. It would take only an hour to get there because morning peak-hour traffic would clear before the Ford hit the metropolitan fringe. And they could take the city bypass to Magill from the northern road.

Within twenty minutes, Ed and his brother were in the Ford heading to their meeting. Someway from home, Ed realized he forgot his ATM card. He pulled over and u-turned the Ford with a roar and headed home for it, the auto-gearbox kicking the vehicle forth. At one hundred and sixty kilometers an hour, with a few Ks for adjustment, or one hundred miles per hour. Cracking the ton.

Four years ago, Zolli told Ed the road "narrows so much you can't see it" at one hundred miles an hour. And that "you feel every little bump."

It came with Zolli's only driving lesson to his son. He dropped Ed at the river-ford out of town along an unsealed road one Sunday beneath the hill they climbed religiously for years as weekly outings during Ed's childhood. Then he hiked the reedy river per those old habits. Ed's first motoring victory was in narrowly missing him as he drove a car for the first time. Quartzite gravel crunched beneath the wheels. Steering sort of floated. This must be what driving was.

Maybe Zolli confused driving at one hundred miles per hour with interstellar spaceflight when he talked about the road disappearing at that speed. He was right about one thing. Ed felt every little bump.

Cracking the ton with Gus was dangerous, truly. But the big-motored Ford cruised okay. And Ed had that morning focus. Then they turned around on Main Street and headed back to the city. At one hundred miles per hour. Gus was not a nervous passenger.

For Ed this morning, cracking the ton was about fixing loose ends while finally making a start in life. Again.

***

ED KNEW A guy named Harley Stanton at trade school. He was tall and had a great physique, though he hadn't been athletic. Ed respected this, him not being athletic. Athleticism was a big thing back home. But the world was bigger than that, and Ed got it.

Harley had a manner about him that made Ed and his classmates think that one day he might be a trade school teacher.

When the teacher threw and caught his own whiteboard marker, Harley threw and caught his own mechanical pencil. Uncanny. Everyone saw it.

To whisper that Harley might one day be a trade school teacher was to say great and kind things about him. It removed him from the everyday factory life in which Ed and his classmates placed themselves without demurrer. Harley existed somewhere higher, somewhere Ed couldn't ever expect to go. Go, Harley. Do it. Make us proud.

"Guys. Oh, you guys," he laughed.

That was two years ago.

While driving to the Magill apartment, Ed pulled the Ford

up at traffic lights along the Main North Road in a suburb with, in the political-correctster parlance to come, a lower socio-economic demographic.

While waiting for the lights to change, Ed saw Harley Stanton push a pram toward an all-you-can-eat-diner. A red, snot-faced, chubby baby screamed from the stroller. Beside Harley walked the infant's mother, most likely the infant's mother. She hardly kept pace. She struggled for breath.

This was when it began, really, in the mid-80s.

The Obesity Era, together with the medical professionals, dieticians, fitness coaches, bureaucrats, and scribes, Pharisees, and soothsayers that caravanned along with it.

True, Ed recollected one obese person from his childhood, Mrs. Ringwood. Then again, perhaps she was just overweight. Some people, including Ed and his mother, Jean, carried a few extra pounds. But most kids – and adults – were bean-thin. Obesity was barely a word in the dictionary and far from a societal health issue.

Widespread societal changes such as widespread obesity required widespread catalysts. They required widespread subcultural acceptance, even where that acceptance was marred with despair. They required widespread mainstream reinforcement, too, even where that reinforcement was marred with sympathy.

The 80s advent of the entire McDonald's restaurant chain, a favorite scapegoat then and now, was not big enough to create adverse change single-handedly on that scale.

Social dislocation played a part. Boom and bust economics was and is Dislocation King. Boom meant people mattered; bust meant they didn't. Unemployment was becoming a way of life in the 80s, rather than something people did while without work. When they did work, increasingly robots did the heavy lifting for them. They commuted to their jobs in the air-conditioned comfort of one of two or three motorcars owned by the household.

Gender roles changed too. This was for the better. But, in

the zero-sum-game of employment, where one person's job was another's dole, it still brought dislocation.

Women thought, "Wow, engagement with the workforce. Finally, I get to see what life is all about." Men thought, "Wow, disengagement from the workforce. Guess I get to see what life is all about."

Food technology improved, a biggie. Foods of commerce became incredibly, incredibly cheap. Takeout became the new eat-in. Previously it was an experience enjoyed rarely if ever. The retail sector entered the bulk sales phase of shopping evolution.

Zolli, he of an older generation, wandered newly built supermarket-acreages agog, like a tourist vacationing somewhere off-planet, not buying anything, just staring. Agog.

Supermarkets sold packets of choc-coated cookies in bulk, two for one, three for one, four for one, free packets with car fuel purchases, a double choc-coated ice cream for ten cents more.

Packets of produce doubled, tripled, in size, without an increase in cost. A bucket of cheap soda swished it down.

"Want soda. Want more, want more."

"Stick your mouth over the nozzle, as nature intended."

The small change made big money for corporate heavyweights and their shareholders. "Thou shalt loss-lead," became Corporate Food's refrain.

No one needed to bake bread-'n-butter puddings again unless for the sake of ye ole' reminiscence.

A decade earlier, Ed's entire family sampled an eight-ounce block of chocolate, say, as a monthly treat, judiciously shared among five people.

"You break the chocolate, your brothers choose first. It's fair," Zolli would decree.

(The same decree applied to cutting cake, the idea being that the cutter tried extra hard to cut equal pieces while knowing that everyone else would choose their pieces first.)

Not only teeth health but sheer cost barred gorging.

Not anymore. Gorging was in. Required of all citizens. A.K.A., "consumers." All-you-can-eat. At eleven A.M.

Strange to consider how other Australian households, such as that run by Harvey Harvey's wife, became "fat-free" at this exact juncture in food history.

And how the Steve Bridges of the world sought "nutritional balance" after shearing three hundred sheep in a day.

Society was ever a fulcrum of counter-poised weights.

Harley Stanton, unlike the child's mother, was not yet obese. Instead, he was a big man run to fat. Someone else's body imprisoned him. The tall man leaned low to push the tiny stroller with his flabby duck feet.

Ed sensed that Harley knew that an alien growth surrounded him.

Fate grabbed everyone in as many ways as there were people.

Tripped them up, too.

"Good-natured Harley. Harley will do the right thing."

That was what people said of him. And look at him now, walking behind an infant mid-morning to an all-you-can-eat-diner.

Ed would not do the right thing. Not if it meant living a life alien to him.

***

IN NO TIME, Ed and Gus arrived at the Magill apartment.

The Adelaide foothills, that iconic realm of genteel dominion, open cut quarries, olive trees, hiking paths, and marginally higher-than-average rainfall relative to the city's low-lying plains, were within a stone's throw of the apartment if Ed possessed the throwing arm of Hercules. If not, it was within a bike ride, which still made it pretty close.

Ten clicks out of the city center – a long way in Adelaide distances - the two-story apartment block rose above the neighboring Californian bungalow. To the other side was a tire fitting workshop. To the other side of that was an off-street shopping village, which had a video store and an independent-chain supermarket, aptly named "The Food Place." Out front of the apartment were a brush fence and a bus stop.

Suzette drove a Jaguar saloon. Parking lines counted for nothing. Her hair was stylish beyond anything Ed might see in Australia. Her fingernails were manicured and polished. She over-wore her lipstick. She enjoyed meeting and talking with Ed and Gus, and helping them.

Here in Suzette was Ed's Adelaide, his aspiration.

Perhaps not an aspiration for a Jag.

More for the chutzpah.

The apartment was new, clean, and tidy.

"No weekend gardening," Ed mused.

"Aren't we lucky?" Gus said.

Ed thought nothing of the busy road outside or the paper-thin walls and the potential threat of noisy neighbors.

Or that upper levels of units would prevent him from hearing the rain on the roof.

He admired the bathroom door. A year later, he would put his fist through it – almost through it – when frustration overwhelmed him for some eminently forgettable reason.

As they left the unit, the neighbor stepped from her apartment wearing a bikini. She pushed into the group, taking Ed's hand.

This woman, Lorraine, and her housemate, Bernadette, would become characters on Ed's stage during the coming year, along with the neighbor to the other side, Nicholas, a simple-hearted man who developed a real attachment to Gus. He would always light a cigarette at a bus stop because with his luck, he claimed, a bus would immediately arrive.

Lorraine was gorgeous and tall and blonde and entirely without pretense and from the country also, although not from near Ed's hometown, but from the South East, where Ed worked the old Koerstz press those months back.

Where was that place? Those months back?

Here was now, that world gone.

The late morning was not as hot as late mornings in Adelaide could be in mid-summer.

Ed and Gus rode the green Ford behind Suzette's Jaguar to her home-office beside downtown parklands.

Such a refined, genteel life was Adelaide city.

Such a clean, fresh busyness without the clutter.

Such a sense of movement.

People can be places in Adelaide without always wishing to be places.

Redgum's song about "boring" Adelaide was not long out. Entitled "One More Boring Night in Adelaide," the song left little to the imagination.

As a result, from the late 70s, and very definitely into the mid-80s, Adelaidians talked about their city as "boring."

"What's it like living in Adelaide?" interstaters asked.

"Okay, but so b-o-o-o-o-ring," locals replied.

The reply was entirely unwarranted. If an impenetrable metropolitan expanse choked the city, as was the case with Australia's so-said world cities, where the only beat of life was that of its traffic-clogged heart, sure residents might not be totally bored. But that was because they were totally exasperated. They lived on the edge of a big-pimple, namely the Australian CBD and its uber-inflated, speculative property market. All the cluttered tracks led to it, and nothing but inadequate side roads cut across it.

In contrast, people were free to move around Adelaide.

People were free to live.

Living is anything but boring.

Adelaide remained the nation's bolthole of The Good Life.

After Ed parked the Ford, he ran to the Hutt Street branch of the National Australia Bank, which was the bank the carriage plant did business with. It was Ed's first bank after his school bank, the Bank of South Australia, and two banks after his very, very first bank, his parents' bank, the Bank of

Adelaide, where he deposited his building site wages as a preschooler.

Presently, he withdrew cash for the security bond and four weeks rent in advance from the ATM and ran back to Suzette's home office.

There, he met the agent's husband. He was suited, slightly chubby, and pleasant, pleasant urbane. Genteel.

A few weeks ago, Ed would have dismissed him as someone who inhabited another world and useless to the world he then inhabited. Now he was someone from whom Ed intuitively learned, even if by way of the passing insights offered during his brief meeting with him.

***

A FEW DAYS LATER Ed and his brother, Gus, arrived back in Adelaide in the Ford and parked behind Zolli's canopied Hi-Lux and trailer outside Timbo's Bargain Emporium.

Timbo's Bargain Emporium sold used furniture. It did not offer bargains at all. Instead, it sold used furniture at three quarters the price of new furniture, actually bargaining with itself that its customers couldn't quite afford the new product. Everyone had a ceiling, and old Timbo's job was to guess what that ceiling was.

Ed and Gus couldn't afford new furniture. Cheap, brand-new, whole-of-house, flat-pack furniture was fifteen years away. And Ed would not buy it on credit. He was a child of Zolli and Jean, and Zolli and Jean were children of the Great Depression and World War Two. The synaptic loop was not an intricate one: "Must Pay Back One Day If Obtain Credit." And how could he do this while a poor student? Ergo, do not use credit.

Another peculiarity of the times was that credit card providers required at least some evidence of an ability to repay credit card debt. Ed was about to support himself on a measly student pension. His Bankcard maxed at three hundred dollars, hardly enough to finance a house of furniture. A bank would not have increased his card limit given his inability to repay the money. In any event, he saved money from shed work. He could pay for Timbo's used furniture in cash.

Timbo, hunch-shouldered, followed Zolli and the kids around his emporium of junk.

"How'bout this scratched, broken pile of crap?" Timbo ought to have asked. Instead, he merely said, "Arrived this morning."

Sure, along with an inch of dust and a spider zoo.

They kept touring the store.

Two hours later, Zolli, Ed, and Gus unloaded a trailer of used furniture at the Magill apartment - bookcases featuring significantly - and then they locked up.

Gus was free of his lease in Stepney in a week, and Ed had other fish to fry.

***

ED DROVE THE Ford a few hours back to the southeast of the state in a last-ditch effort to amass funds for his year of full-time study ahead. He dreaded crashing out of the course before the year's end for want of money. But he wasn't headed back to wool-pressing.

His shearing life was done. Ed finally squeezed the life of the outback from his image of Australia. On the day he and Gus inspected the Magill apartment, he visited Dennis Harvey, thanked him for everything, and resigned from shed work.

"Pretty hard to quit from subcontracting work in a purely legal sense," canny Dennis quipped.

But the meaning was there. He and his wife wished Ed well in his studies.

Now he focused on harvesting wheat on the wealthiest wheat farm in the state.

While working at Bentley Cache's massive shearing shed a few months earlier, he befriended the station manager, Andy, as well as his wife, Patricia, and of course, Cheryl, Andy's cousin, the estranged wife of the Mount Gambier firefighter. Andy arranged wheat-harvesting work on the property for Ed and invited him to stay in his house, the station manager's cottage, a five-room bungalow.

Farmers harvested wheat in November and December in the hotter north where Ed lived. Farther south, near the border with Victoria, with a colder and wetter climate, they harvested a month or two later, in late January.

Really, Ed focused on the money. He would earn maybe two months wages for two weeks' work while harvesting wheat around the clock.

He had his eye on a Commodore 64 computer, and they didn't grow on trees, although without a real idea of what to do with one. At least, he had no answer when Zolli asked him why he wanted a computer.

"What do you do with one?" Zolli asked, his hands raised and turned outward.

Of course, buying a Commodore 64 computer had something to do with moving beyond Henry Lawson to Stanley Kubrick and Arthur C. Clarke.

***

A LIGHT SHOWER of rain or even heavy night dew sidelined wheat harvesting. Moisture levels in the grain had to measure precisely right. Otherwise, the wheat board wouldn't take the wheat, and it would be almost impossible to store. Damp grain rotted in storage or smoldered and burst into flame when the hot sun eventually shone.

Ed joined the men and mended fences, actual fences, the fire retardant paint burning him like rays of sun. But when the crop dried, when it became right to harvest, then, whammo, the work was on. Machinery didn't stop. Men didn't stop.

Ed drove the pickup tractor. He never drove a tractor before, let alone one like the eight-wheeler on Bentley

214

Cache's property. He climbed the fixed ladder to an air-conditioned cab. It contained a bucket seat and a stereo-player as well as a radio, as in two-way communication. Everything was power operated, right down to the adjustable armrests.

The tractor was as fat as a planet. It towed a massive trailer. As fat as a planet.

Ed sidled the tractor-trailer beside the rolling harvesters and siphoned the grain while on the move. He drove the wheat to the big grain trucks and grain bins, off-loaded it there via the auger mounted on the pick-up trailer, and returned to the harvesters for more, and kept everything operational.

The big combine harvesters chewed nonstop through the crop. Bentley owned one of them, two contractors, the other two.

One of the contractors drove his harvester around Australia with a little Subaru four-runner linked to it, which he unlinked on jobs and used as a town car.

"One day I'm gonna harvest the wheat plains of North America," he professed, with that wistful look of self-deception.

Ed moved the portable silos around the property, and positioned them, ready for the grain in the next paddock.

Sometimes he moved the massive grain trucks, big, barely controllable field-beasts they were too.

Later, Bentley Cache decided to help a neighbor, an old, bald, vigorous man named Dan Randall, who was as deaf as a doorpost.

Old, bald, vigorous Dan was more hands-on than the aristocratic Bentley. Bentley supervised his farm from the side window of his paddock thumping, current model, fully optioned Mercedes sedan. Dan worked the fields.

Ed couldn't help himself. He crept up behind Dan one day a mile from anywhere and shouted into his ear as loud as he could. No response. At all. Yes, as deaf as a doorpost, and then some.

When old Dan realized Ed was there, he turned his big,

bald, leathery face toward him and exclaimed in a voice louder than Ed used in his attempt to call the old man's bluff, and pointed him to the corner of the field.

"Government put it there. Some science thing. Haven't paid me as they promised yet."

Yes, as it might turn out, genetically modified crop, secured by a strand of sun-ruined, red binder-twine and a weathered piece of paper even at that time unreadable.

At the end of the harvest, Bentley Cache grudgingly handed Ed his enormous check. Ed took the money without a qualm. He had plans. Gus arranged with his friend with a car in Adelaide to pick up a new Commodore 64, a catalog sale item from a Kmart across town. "2001, A Space Odyssey," here came Ed Kaspar.

See, while working for Bentley during the extreme hubbub of pitch point crop harvesting, and without experience going into the role, Ed managed to ruin the axle on a portable silo when he forgot to raise the wheels before loading it with twenty tons of wheat. He crushed the casing of the auger on his trailer when he came in too fast to the grain bin one day. And he managed to snap the tractor towbar when he crossed a culvert too quickly.

"Never saw that before, snapping a tractor towbar," old David said, the farmhand who helped Ed with the ewe and stillborn lamb in the shed those months back.

The other farmhands agreed.

Not that they saw a crushed auger or a wrecked axle assembly on a portable silo, either.

Thence marked the end of Ed's adventures in the Australian agricultural sector for the time.

On to the next windmill.

Induction day at the Carrington Woods College of Matriculation was but a week away.

***

HERE ARRIVED THE dawn of one of the most exciting periods in Ed's adulthood.

Perhaps it was the most exciting period in his entire life, including the bit that he willfully and later regretfully chose to forget, as if he hit delete in a spring-clean forever, namely his childhood.

He prepared for it by watching daytime soaps and morning TV.

Advocates who wanted to mandate a dull, dry, sawdust version of the English language of colorless, characterless, indeterminate, unintelligent caveman (cave dweller) grunts guaranteed not to offend were merely the loudest voices in the room. They were the stupidest people on the planet. They weren't averse to dragging everyone into their misguided righteousness of hyper-regulated, bureaucratized language known as Plain English (which was miles from natural English.)

The stereotypical Australian bushman, the so-said quiet achiever, national icon, advertisement for mining companies, was a dill without enough on his mind to speak a single engaging sentence.

"Um…you bet."

In fact, real workers, including real bush workers, men and women both, Ben aside, talked plenty, and with as colorful vocabularies and twists-of-phrases as they could muster.

Ben made up for his dearth of words by consuming ten bestsellers a week – close to.

Like Jean told Ed, "You have to open your mouth if you want people to listen."

Jean was right, and he would do that, open his mouth, once he owned a vocabulary to deploy.

Soaps weren't great vocabulary builders, though, because most of the drama was in the eyes. And in the hairstyles. But Ed picked up a word or two.

Morning TV talk shows might not seem to offer Ed much from a vocabulary point of view either. But watching them from where he came from, namely a place of sheep and beer, they offered a lot. And intro music was always attention-grabbing, the big thunder, the mission, the sliding directorial cut to the anchor. Let the zaniness commence.

Ed madly scribed new words into his small notebook, the first of many journals for that year of transition and learning.

He flicked through his newly purchased hardback edition of the Concise Oxford Dictionary, which, bigger than two bricks, was not so terribly concise at all.

Throughout his childhood, books, TV, the radio, school, and life generally fed him words aplenty. Zolli, foreign-born, was a stickler for diction, and, dare it to be said, a hater of Australian slang. Like many in his generation (of native English speakers.)

Up until the 1970s, Australians spoke as eloquently as possible. Why would they not? Look at the elegant suits they wore, even on Saturday afternoons when they weren't working, and most definitely on church days, Sundays. Old photos of Jean and Zolli camping and canoeing in the 1950s still saw them dressed rather rakishly casual.

Ed merely chose to play the role of a taciturn bushman, an imaginary one, who refused to move his jaw unless eating, and especially not while talking.

Now, on the morning of his matriculation year, his new world of his making portrayed him as eloquently loquacious, with a sort of cadence, lyrical and inquisitive, explorative, rather than mysteriously taciturn. It eschewed the national three-word vocabulary of two words, "yep, nup, yep."

He left his cream brick apartment in Magill, waving to gorgeous, semi-naked Lorraine through her front window, rode his bicycle (living Warwick Apotherick's dream) to the matriculation college, and attended the induction day.

This took more nerve than might be expected, to ride his bicycle. Sure, a few adults cycled. But it was not like decades later when the world of cycling would gear itself toward adults in lycra and spermatozoa-shaped helmets to the absolute, brutal exclusion of all and every child in Westerndom. In the 80s, kids rode bikes. That was because they couldn't drive cars. Seeing a kid of license age ride a bike made you think something was wrong. You avoided him. You assumed he was making up for lost time spent in youth detention, especially if he sported a full-growth beard that put to shame a woodwork teacher's beard.

Actually, Ed rode a bicycle to work at the winery in the Valley like a champ those few times. That was a year earlier. Fortunately, lycra hadn't been his thing.

***

IT WAS A beautiful day, as it turned out. Students drifted around the college grounds in that way they did when still new and strange to each other. They sat on lawns chatting like people released from a dreary destiny of lowbrow employment or messy unemployment. Like people with purpose. Like people with futures.

Inside, students smoked in hallways like cigarette heroes from TV. Floor ashtrays caught discarded stubs on their slow burn to nothing.

The TAFE college that Ed attended in Ellaville during his engineering apprenticeship was the same. But the people here were different. They didn't mumble so much. They didn't boast about screwing chicks and fighting over the weekend. And "dropping acid" and when pressed couldn't explain what "dropping acid" meant.

Not that everybody in his apprenticeship classes mumbled. Or talked about screwing, fighting, and dropping acid. Just the ones Ed Kaspar hung with.

Men at Carrington Woods College wore loose-fitting scrubbed denim jeans that tapered slightly at the ankles (just to put distance between them and the outrageously flared jeans of the 70s.) They wore short sleeve polo shirts. Which meant that Ed got it right. Together with his barely worn Tiger Asics, his most expensive clothing purchase during the Christmas period, he fit in. And maybe he even stood out – in a fitting-in sort of way.

The induction took three hours. Ed formally registered for classes, English (literature and writing skills,) Australian History, Modern European History, Geography, and his requisite one-in-five pick from the maths-science stream, Biology. He chose his subjects with the horse sense to get from A to B, nothing fancy. He paid his administration fee, which was minimal. He ordered a student card (useful for cheaper public transport.) He would collect it from the admin office later in the day. He met teachers, and he was very, very shy around them, almost debilitatingly so, mainly the liberal ones, whom he wanted to emulate, but experienced pangs of guilt whenever he tried.

He attended Harold's general welcome.

Harold gave everyone what they wanted, a symbol of connection, stability, and future.

Afterward, Alan McGinn, a thin man with a thorax-length beard, highlighted the sort of obstacles that students might face during the year of study ahead. All that back to earth stuff. He talked dropout percentages. Dropout percentages figured during Ed's talk with Harold those few weeks earlier too.

According to Alan McGinn, dabblers saw the matriculation college as a vacation from life's responsibilities. They underestimated the workload and dropped-out months or even weeks in. Genuinely motivated applicants who hadn't made the intake quota, a numbers thing, missed out for naught.

"Are yah dabblers?" he asked with a whine. "Are yah?"

No way. Useless dabblers, Ed thought.

Actually, he didn't think this. He just listened. For the first time since deciding to head back to school to study for his matriculation, he felt normal. Yeah, it was happening. To him. He wanted to learn. He wanted to avoid the traps that dabblers walked into. He wanted to succeed.

220

Higher education wasn't for kids like him. It just wasn't his reality. Now, very quickly, higher education was a reality for kids like him. A reality for him.

Too quickly it became a reality for him.

Fit in with scrubbed denim jeans and Tiger Asics as he might, Ed suddenly questioned his sanity for returning to school.

At the business end of things, he wracked his nerves over whether he was a dabbler, over whether he could pass his exams.

Ed spent Year 11 making up whatever excuse imaginable for not handing in his assignments. He never wrote an essay. Ever in his life! He wrote "compositions" since fourth grade. Matriculation essays couldn't be that much different from fourth-grade compositions, yeah?

Ed always allowed grand schemes to propel him. Now while listening to Alan McGinn, he allowed grand gremlins to spook him.

And curriculum textbooks? Alan McGinn talked about the importance of reading them before the semester commenced. Before the semester commenced? Hell, Ed only knew what subjects he would study when he enrolled in them an hour ago. He was pulling wheat from combine harvesters and working short sheds near the Coorong. How could he possibly read all those "curriculum textbooks" now?

When the flow went with him, reading was a magical experience. But when the flow did not go with him? When he had to churn through several chapters at velocity? Then words blurred after the first sentence. Like Zolli's road at a hundred miles an hour.

Suddenly, he convinced himself that he didn't fit in, but, instead, just stood out, and in a bad way.

To compound his self-doubt, he feared that his friends back home might think him crazy for returning to school, as in genuinely crazy. Real crazy, finally. Crazier than adults who rode bicycles.

Then, of all things, Alan McGinn questioned the fairness of the college for accepting "all-comers." Ed was an "all-comer," even if Harold questioned his academics back when he spoke to Jean over the phone and when he and Ed met in his office.

Alan McGinn touted a scheme that scaled-back "all-comers" in favor of "meritorious" applicants. He mentioned a student who studied Year 12 at an elite private college with tuition fees in excess of average annual incomes but missed getting into law school at university by a few points.

"Law school requires the highest matriculation score anywhere," he informed everybody.

Giving kids like her a second chance, even if it meant scaling back "all-comers," that is, excluding people like Ed, would improve the school's ranking as well as right the terrible injustice done to a private college student who missed getting into law by a few points.

Oh, no. What had Ed Kaspar done?

He stopped a private-school chick from getting into law school.

Ed preferred old-time Harold. Harold wanted to exclude him because he was too dumb to pass his exams, which was fair enough. Ed didn't want to hear induction speeches with double meaning. Ed had sufficient trouble with single meaning speeches.

Again he saw himself as an outsider to a middle-class life. Because, right or wrong, that was what he heard in Alan McGinn's speech.

In this, he mischaracterized his upbringing. Zolli was a self-employed builder. He met clients, scoped costs, prepared contracts, drafted complex building plans, obtained municipal building consent, paid advance taxes, purchased indemnity insurance, argy-barged with banks for overdrafts, worked tools onsite, arranged trades to work onsite, and liaised with engineers, architects, and building inspectors. He, himself, passed the building inspector's exam with distinction. The

222

occasion was serious enough for the local police officer, the one before Uncle Pete, to invigilate the exam in Zolli's study over a bottle of beer and salted cashews, courtesy, naturally enough, of the house. Before that, Zolli imported fine wines and liquor for his retail business. He fluently spoke five languages and some Greek. He boomed out classical music on his stereo and had his own photo lab. He practiced yoga when most Australians thought yoga was something they shouldn't eat without a doctor's prescription. He assiduously studied the Bhagavad Gita because in his youth – as a matter of chance – it stirred him spiritually. He discussed Hindu "fakirs" (pronounced "fuk-eers") with a giggling ten-year-old Ed.

Jean nurtured a library of books and read widely. When she arrived in Australia, she was a highly trained nurse. Though she didn't know it at the time, or at any time while alive, her ancestry was documentable back several hundred years. And what she did know at the time was that her auntie was the first female mayor of Cardiff when Cardiff stood for something and that her father, the other granddad Ed never met, played rugby for Wales.

But Ed felt guilty when Alan McGinn reminded him of how lucky he was to not be excluded by a narrower college intake model.

Then who did he see among the groups touring the college grounds following the induction speeches, but Cat Anderson?

Cat was a year under Ed at school. She was the daughter of a mogul from a neighboring town. If she missed the school bus, a driver chauffeured her to Ed's school – an area school - in a limousine. There she was, cruising into the schoolyard, swallowed by big limousine leather. Cat attended her senior year at an expensive private school in the city.

Was she the sort of person Alan McGinn wished to include in his quotient of meritorious students? Likely not. Daughter of a mogul as she was, she hadn't been born and raised in the prosperous middle suburbs of Adelaide where Alan McGinn and his children and the children of his peers resided. Likely she remained a country girl in his eyes, an outsider.

Back in high school, Ed mixed with Cat Anderson but only ever under truce conditions. She was hardheaded and tough-minded. He was autocratic and emotional. Quarrelsome people like Cat and Ed had a way of identifying like-souls with whom they might quarrel.

But here at Carrington Woods College was a meeting space of a different sort. Ed tried to catch her eye. She looked away, glowed red, and he thought he saw her mumble. He never saw her again, not ever.

In some ways, Ed loved how Carrington Woods College leveled the field. Here he and Cat Anderson were, he the son of an immigrant, she the daughter of a mogul, and yet both at the crossroads of identical educational opportunity. He even felt a sort of "take that" toward Cat, as if she was no better than him, despite her background.

But he felt for her too. He knew that she experienced the same highs and lows as he experienced in returning to school as an adult.

Seeing her here, he realized that he was not so special after all. Sure, he faced unique issues. But he wasn't special because of them. He was human because of them.

At last, Ed accepted that the only way in which Ed Kaspar was special was in the stories he told himself.

"Oh, I'm working class."

"Oh, I'm a child of immigrants."

"I'm from the country."

"I'm this, that, or the other."

"I'm Australian. No, I'm not. Yes, I am."

He issue-fied his life and he imagined himself special - superior - because of it.

The truth was, he was who he was, and that was why he was, and that was all he was.

He collected his student card and rode his bicycle home to Magill.

The next day, Zolli telephoned to announce that he sold

Ed's Ford. Remembering stiffly suspended jalopies and bumpy dirt roads of another era, Zolli told the buyer that the green Ford "rode like a Mercedes." When the guy (city-folk) returned from the test drive, he said he wanted more time to decide. But then, Zolli noticed a small scratch on the front fender, and genuinely believed that the test jockey put it there. Zolli wasn't having a bar of it. He wanted reparations. Zolli never gave ground. Ever. The guy just ended up buying the car for the asking price. Zolli receipted the cash.

There was no turning back for Ed Kaspar.

***

ED ATTENDED STANDARD Books to buy his curriculum textbooks, the bookshop he visited several months earlier when he left Bill O'Brien's packing shed and drove his Ford to the rooftop car park and looked across North Terrace to the Adelaide University campus.

Now he entered the store with his matriculation booklist in hand and money in his pocket. The same university educated men as several months earlier were talking about the same topic, namely, that high school dropouts didn't fit in.

Actually, they were not there. But were they there, Ed would move among them easier than he moved among them those several months ago.

The bookshop had a special section for matriculation students. "Sons and Lovers" was in the curriculum. When Ed read the first line of the novel, he wanted more. Here was a book about a young man who needed out. Words pinged Ed's synapses with startling clarity.

Later, he learned how some readers recoiled from squeamish themes in D.H. Lawrence books.

Much, much later, he learned how some readers declaimed another all-time favorite, "On the Road," as drug-addled and misogynistic.

Indeed, a time would arrive in the future when correctsters

would damn both tomes (and others) as works "Offending the Insipid."

Ed saw things differently. Like life, novels were full of contradictions, contradictions that existed within a novel and within and between readers.

Literature was *the* truly interactive art, the oldest, oldest variety. Ed brought himself – his experiences and beliefs - to the outlines of life that he found on the book pages. Characters lived in the light *he* shone on the pages.

Ed read "Pride and Prejudice" with his own eyes, as readers do in any part of the world and at any point in history.

Silly, captivating Lydia Bennet was never a weird, fixed, antiquated figure who talked odd. She was Cynthia, Ed's neighbor, the one who asked him why he jogged, and then twisted her head like he was off the wall when he told her.

Cynthia played Lydia's role in Ed's imagination. Even the words "silly" and "captivating" belonged to Ed. And Cynthia.

Literature lived as he read it. Meanwhile, movies saturated him with the totality of the times. The next generation would see the same movie as corny. Movies need to be remade every twenty years to connect with their audiences.

Literature fomented Ed's individuality.

Movies, in saturating him and leaving him with no place to go, ripped him back to the communal hymn sheet.

Ed rewrote novels in his imagination.

Even when he reread them, he rewrote them.

Lawrence's and Kerouac's heroes weren't working class heroes. They weren't even working-class villains, as in the minds of some readers. They weren't victims, as was the house painter in "The Ragged Trousered Philanthropists." They knew better. They wanted more than what their backgrounds offered them, and they found it. This was what connected Ed Kaspar with Paul Morel and Sal Paradise.

In future times, Ed would read similar messages in the supremely incredible and equally controversial novels, "Valley of the Dolls" and "Peyton Place."

He witnessed something of himself in the characters. Not someone of economic class or of a national trope. Not someone of freewheeling misadventure or cataclysmic bondage. But someone of the universe, of soul, of living, of being.

He read themes that the works triggered *in him*.

He and the books were in partnership.

He and the book he read shared the same moment.

In that moment.

The truthfulness in "Sons and Lovers" attracted Ed.

Not so "Left Hand of Darkness," which was also on his reading list. A perfect novel in many ways, the writing style of "Left Hand" nevertheless felt so damned devoid of juice to Ed. A run-on sentence might sink the boat.

Later in the year, he read "The Dispossessed" as elective reading in his English course. He valued it tremendously. But he didn't get why working class men revolted in support of a skinny physicist dude from the moon, not unless workingmen were latter-day noble savages in the imagination of a chic educated writer, A.K.A. a young Urshie Le Guin.

Ed purchased Australian history textbooks. Well, these indeed were not the books he remembered from high school. "The Tyranny of Distance" read as interestingly as a novel. It contained titbits about early Australia that Ed really wanted to know. "Triumph of the Nomads," likewise. Incredible stuff. Michael Cannon's picture books too.

"The Australian Legend," which Ed purchased that day, pivoted his perspective later in the year in class. It stated that Australia was egalitarian because of the nation's bush history. Well, that wasn't altogether true, neither the egalitarian bit nor the cute reason offered for it, namely bush ethics, at least going on Ed's experiences of contemporary bush culture. Australia, like anywhere, was about as egalitarian as a chook house (of people.)

Some of his classmates treated him as if he sullied God's image when he got around to expressing his thoughts on the subject later in the year.

"Who do you think you are, eh, professor? Just follow the rules," one guy ejaculated.

Ed waited for him to ejaculate a "go back where you came from." But the guy didn't know Ed's history. So it never came.

While completing his shopping excursion for textbooks in Standard Books that day, he saw enormous hardback, twin-apiece, first edition volumes of the collected works of Henry Lawson and Banjo Paterson. He wanted them, and he purchased them, even if he never read them. They were too damn big, and he preferred his smaller hardback edition of Henry Lawson's collected stories that Jean purchased for him.

Also, Banjo Paterson's works, excepting "Waltzing Matilda" and "Clancy of the Overflow," never really took his heart as had the works of Henry Lawson. Kids who wore their school ties done all the way up and later left for city schooling seemed to enjoy reading Banjo. Some of them even recited his poems off the cuff. Ed preferred the grit and simple verse of Australia's most famous drunk.

Outside the bookstore, life was vibrant with color and movement.

Another thing about Adelaide city was its downtown mall, a shopping street mercifully exposed to the elements, but closed to cars, known as "The Mall."

Ed never saw a happier, busier bunch of shoppers. That was because The Mall was not just a shopping street. If it were, it would be dead like every other retail strip in the world. Dead in a Midas way, where every community experience turned into consumer items. It would be like buying justice or love, leaving a bitter aftertaste. Sometimes, people needed a town square to hang out in, one that had a feel of life about it, like with a European plaza. Or a country town main street. A place where they were members of the community, without relegation to a consumer status, nasty business.

228

Often you bumped into someone at The Mall you least expected to see. Ed bumped into Ben, Sam, and Luke.

Luke, the mountain-size man, just saw a surgeon about getting the rest of the pins removed from his arms. He was eager to return to wool-pressing. He drew on his cigarette, a hand-rolled Log Cabin. Ben stood back smiling, his heavy, square chin thrown forward, his hands deep in pockets of a lightweight jacket. The angular shape of a bestseller took the place of a gun in his pocket. Sam, the unionized New Zealander, voiced his respect for Ed for returning to school.

"I'm going back too," he said, "when I save the money."

That was a good one, saving the money. It was what people said when they knew they would never do it. Ed kept his tongue. The men shook hands and parted as if they would catch up at the next shed.

They never did. Nor anywhere else.

***

AFTERWARD, ED RETURNED home for a few days. He still hadn't worked out how to tell his friends that he was going back to study his final year of secondary schooling.

What a dork thing to do, to go back to high school. He was afraid they might laugh at him.

He also feared that home life – i.e. partying - would reel him back and prevent him from reaching to the stars, as it were. In a manner of speaking.

In this, he was very lily-livered. His friends might have supported him at this crucial moment in his life. But, caught in his own hang-ups, he never gave them a chance.

Ed disappeared from their lives. Some of them hung "wanted" posters in the local pubs.

"Cheka, Cheka, Cheka," they yelled while driving past his house at two AM.

The occasional "Chester" thrown in betrayed the caller.

Ed knew this, even while he hid in his parents' home

waiting for his new life and year to begin. Alone.

***

HIS MOTHER HELD him the morning he left for his matriculation course. He might have aimed to save the world, but she would hold him because, in letting him go, she would miss him. Thank God for fathers.

Ed waited in the front yard for Mick Williams to roll up in his big-six Holden from three blocks away. Mick worked in Adelaide as a non-certified accountant and drove to the Gawler train station each day to catch the city train. Like a Swiss clock. In times past, Ed set his bedside clock while hearing Mick whip around the corner on his way to the ole' Smoke an' Noise.

Today, Mick beeped his horn at the corner of Main Street. The code over the years was that if Ed didn't show when Mick beeped his horn, Mick drove away and left him. Fair enough.

This morning, Mick almost left without Ed. But he saw him behind the oleanders and waited. Jean was always big on hugs. Ed, now a man, moaned and jimmied away from her.

All he had with him was a crew bag. He and Zolli moved his other essential possessions to the Magill apartment a few days ago.

Mick, white-haired like his dad, smiled when Ed hopped into the vehicle.

"Got everything?"

"Yup."

Then he concentrated on driving the car. Not much conversation passed between them. It never did.

Jean held Ed with her eyes as the car drove away. Ed was confident she wouldn't relinquish her image of him until sometime around mid-morning.

Whether memories of Humphrey B Bear TV and honey sandwiches, the watching and the eating of which were rituals that occurred during Ed's toddler years around late morning,

230

broke her down again, Ed never knew. The sudden sound of nothing in the family home now the last child left it, more permanently than not, had to affect both Ed's parents.

Mick always broke the speed limit along the road to Gawler, but not like a maniac. He knew every little bump and twist, and he knew when the police speed traps were out. He took the town bypass, which was quicker than navigating the Gawler main street each day. He arrived around the back of the train station.

"Got everything?"

"Yup."

Then it was a commuter scurry to the train and a packed but not too packed ride to Adelaide's station downtown, with a few express stops along the way.

Zolli was working today. However, he arose especially early, earlier than usual. While Ed waited for Mick, but before Jean arrived outside to prevent her son from entering the world on the basis that she would miss him, Zolli went out to wish him well.

They spoke few words before Zolli, oddly vulnerable, said, "I can't help the way I am."

In all his days, Ed never heard his father reveal such sentiment.

Pre-day peace sat around him. Zolli, opinionated and argumentative, confessed what Ed always knew anyway. Among Zolli's children, Ed spent the most time with him. He was the least critical of him, and the most understanding of him. He whiled away hours with him in the photo "lab" and later around the billiard table while listening to instructional tales about Eddie Charlton, the snooker champ. He whiled away hours with him in the workshop fixing trailers, making dinghies, and trialing dovetail joints, willingly sometimes, but often reluctantly. What would you expect of a boy when cartoons and friends beckoned? He spent weeks and months and years with him on building sites when the only sound was that of the silence of hot summer days and the kid a couple of blocks over aiming his cricket ball at a disused wooden door with wickets painted or imagined on it.

Zolli's photographs comprised a form of art that captured his children's laughter and conspiratorial scowling, and that caught his own passage through life, before the children arrived, and afterward.

Ed knew that Zolli was a man of perspective and reason during his quieter moments, such as on mornings that preceded days, but sometimes Ed struggled to get him there.

He always suspected that Zolli possessed a peaceful heart. The day and life changed it, this peace, this inner calm, this knowing.

The morning he left for his matriculation course, Ed saw it in Zolli, however fleeting.

Fleeting, as it was with everyone.

***

ED TOOK BIOLOGY, his quota from the maths and sciences stream. He was cunning enough to leave maths alone and to avoid subjects like economics that were strange to the ear of an almost-graduate of his hometown high school. He left foreign languages well enough alone. Egy, kettő, három – Hungarian for "one, two, three" – wouldn't get him far.

Although the curriculum thrust Biology upon him, the subject ended up fascinating Ed. It gave him some of his best highs and lows for that year, and had the neat advantage of vaguely tying in with David Attenborough's incredibly popular natural sciences TV show, "The Living Planet."

"You watch it too?" he asked.

"I never miss a show," she said.

It was where he met Ariana.

Short, dark-skinned, Ariana colored her hair orange, green, and crimson. Her eyes were a deep shade of blue. She wore colorful leggings. She smoked cigarettes, and she couldn't care less, and she seemed very new wave to Ed.

232

He met plenty of women who dressed this way, in a new wave or neo-punk style, as might be expected in the mid-80s. These women appeared to offer an understanding of life that went beyond what girls in his hometown had, what with the girls from his hometown wearing knitted pullovers and without cosmetics and other adornments. But in the end, he discovered what most people knew already, that these neo-punk girls weren't priestesses of a movement but followers of fashion. They costumed themselves accordingly. They turned over wardrobes when the next trend arrived, nothing more profound in it than that.

However, Ariana was anything but the clothes she wore. Sure, she chose her outfit to express how she saw herself. And her appearance was excruciatingly vital to her. But Ed saw her better in her eyes, and in the way that she animated herself, and in her living colors rather than the colors of her garments, and in the way she stood, and in her facial expressions, and in the way she spoke. He saw her better in her. She was always provoking, questioning, offering. Caring, caring for victims of injustice. Fighting for them. She was anything but somber and moody. This alone made her a total opposite to Ed, who was somber and moody. She pointed out something positive in the world to reach for, something other than what ambition wanted to clutch and keep, and something more real than what hope drooled over.

She was older than Ed, but not by much.

Returning to school created relationship dramas for her. She surmounted them while remaining brilliant in college, and met someone suited to her new life down the track.

Ariana served her own apprenticeship, just as Ed served his. She was born to immigrant parents, who, like Ed's parents, arrived in Australia from both sides of the Channel, her father from England, her mother from the Ukraine.

Ed and Ariana challenged each other in class.

She even read "The Ragged Trousered Philanthropists."

"You've read it too?" he asked.

"I didn't skip a word," she said.

Other students in the group chimed in here and there. But Ed connected with Ariana most. He felt not so alone after meeting her.

***

ED SCRIBED A Tolstoian narrative for his Biology homework. Next day, he read it out in class. The teacher applauded him in a way that made his classmates crack with laughter. Or, as they would say in future times, made them "laugh-out-loud." Or as they might say in those future times, or at any time, were they so inclined, made them "laugh aloud."

A succinct answer was called for, not a Tolstoian narrative. By year's end, Ed topped Biology in the college. He was a mark from topping the state. He never proved his biology teacher wrong or tried to. Day One, his biology teacher proved him wrong, and Ed got with the program.

He got a D for his first English assignment. The English teacher, Will Paternoster, explained to the class that a D exhibited a passable ability to meet course demands. Any lower grade (right down to E) and you backed a loser. Bearing in mind, though, that a D might not equate to a pass in the state exams.

Possibly Ed had the best English teacher in the world if "best" was assessed against his impact on him.

This was saying something because, throughout school, Ed's English teachers, and his history teachers and one maths-computer teacher, as well as his primary and high school librarians, were all the best in the world.

Will's elaborate grading system hadn't figured greatly in Ed's estimation of him.

More so, Will acted in all sorts of modern plays. With his long, black locks, Richard Burton voice, clean-shaven, expressive face, he was made for theater. He was writing his own play, one about a green locomotive. One of his similes was "as fat as a planet," earlier borrowed herein and applied while describing Bentley Cache's tractor and trailer, hopefully in a fashion that befitted its genius.

He introduced the class to Bruce Dawe, a poet who wrote about suburban Australia in a way that made incredible tragicomic sense to Ed.

Will enjoyed teaching D.H. Lawrence and debating his works in class with a student, a brilliant lady, Mandy.

"He's verbose, repetitive, and sexist," she said of Lawrence.

Mandy explained to the class and to Will that she wanted to retire as a literary-lady-of-leisure before she was forty. She was currently thirty-two.

Literary-ladies-of-leisure were a thing in the 80s.

Sometimes, Will arrived at evening class tipsy. Ed attended morning class, so he received this particular intel secondhand, and had no way to assess its veracity. But he wanted to believe it. Teachers needed to be real before Ed learned from them. Not every teacher perhaps. Ed learned from Will because he was real.

He would remember much of what he taught him in the years to come. He couldn't claim this where his other teachers were concerned, not in the same way, not in that deeper way.

It made sense. Stories were about life. Language spoke them. Therefore, literature was what we were.

Roger, the affable, quick-witted guy sitting next to Ed in English, a mechanic by trade, and an aspiring art teacher, got the same result for his first English assignment as Ed, a D. He shrugged it off as what he expected.

Not much later in the year, Roger offered Ed some weedy, scratchy pot during a geography outing to the Morialta Conservation Park, which Ed declined. Roger offered the grass as if they were partners in kiddie crime, a couple of schoolkids breaking the rules. Ed hadn't seen sense in it. They voluntarily attended the college. They weren't schoolkids any longer. No one forced them to study.

Moralizing never played a part in Ed's response to Roger's offer that day. Law, less so. Ed wasn't sure, but South Australia, the nation's progressive state, might not have even criminalized the use of pot. The truth was, as with Will's touted lifestyle, Ed knew he had to withhold judgment about Roger handing around dope. He had to open his heart to the diversity of people and experiences around him if he was to stand any chance whatsoever to learn. But that didn't mean he wasn't firm about these matters on his own account. If he abstained from alcohol to study, that is, to take his study seriously, then why smoke pot? That sort of thing. And, don't forget, Ed just crawled out of years of partying. So, he didn't feel as if he missed anything in rejecting Roger's offer that day.

Ed liked Roger a lot because he was a really great guy but chose against accepting him as an equal-in-enterprise. Roger shrugged off the D, hadn't he? In contrast, Ed wanted to give it everything, wherever it got him, against the wall, or through it. This was Jean's take on life, trying your best. Like most of his parents' adages, Ed took them as words of real-life guidance.

And, as Australians near and far never tired of repeating until the cows came home, while Australia had a bad reputation for cutting down tall poppies, it had an excellent reputation for encouraging people to keep trying even when they failed. Especially when they failed.

Ed would try till the end.

Then try some more.

Throughout the year, everyone at the college congregated in the most fantastic fellowship he ever knew. Everyone pulled away from where they didn't want to be and headed somewhere better. They were doing it together. They were alive in their hearts. Ed hadn't found that often, being a part of this.

There were casualties. Ed felt for one guy, Bryson, a

236

former bricklayer. Ed felt his hurt as if it were his own. During recess one day, Ed just happened to remain in the classroom alone while one of the history teachers pretty much told Bryson to withdraw from her subject. She counseled him as to what was best for his welfare. She was very professional. But, no mistake, she was throwing him out of her class. She hadn't the administrative power to chuck him out. But she didn't reveal this quiet little fact. She let her meaning talk for her.

Bryson was a big guy, hunch-shouldered, woolly-headed, and bearded. His hands were more prominent and more scarred than Ed's shovels-of-hands. His head hung. His eyes teared up.

Ed believed that the teacher drove Bryson from her class because he was a working man in his former life. On these misguided grounds, he imagined the swish of the ax near his own neck. Any moment he would be found out, not just found out as a working-class kid going through a specialized state educational facility, but as a working man who broke ranks. An escapee. Any second, someone would find him out, likely a middle-aged guy with an uncool patriarchy-beard whose weekly highlight was watching Harry Butler hunt frogs on TV. And out he would march Ed, back to where he came from.

Truthfully, Ed found no personal meeting ground with Bryson, and he sensed a while back that Bryson wasn't the brightest guy around. But, after he saw what he saw during recess that day, he feared that the college would issue him his own marching orders. So he tried even harder at his studies. He sucked in a big breath of front and went for it.

However, he couldn't wholly come-out about his own working background.

One day, the Australian History teacher asked the class if anyone knew a shearer.

"Shearing's a big part of what we learn about in this course," he articulated mesmerizingly.

Wondering if anyone knew his secret already, or if the

history teacher tried to pull him into the lesson knowing his background for himself, Ed raised his hand from the back of the room and mumbled something about his experiences.

"Care to elaborate?"

Ed glowed red. Shyness caught him. The stuff of train wrecks. He could have heard a pin drop. All he heard was his heart thump.

The teacher, a considerate man, moved to the next topic. Quick.

Here was Ed's new world, as much an inner world as his former one, despite the efforts he made to free himself from his own bondage.

Dreams released him. Dreams trapped him.

***

BACK AT HIS Magill apartment, his first time in his own digs away from home, and with grocery prices falling in ways they hadn't fallen before in human history, Ed fried four beefsteaks in a sitting, no veggies, and stuffed himself. He turned life-long vegetarian by year's end.

Night after night, he watched single episodes of "Family Ties" on network TV while he eliminated his other staple food of choice, choc-coated, mint-slice cookies, the upmarket type.

What newfound freedom. Packet after packet.

Daily, he donned headphones and ruptured his head with one or the other of Midnight Oil, Alan Parsons Project, Alison Moyet, Supertramp, Dire Straits, especially "Telegraph Road," and The Cure, or Mozart, Beethoven, and Tommy, it not being the US's year in song, except for later in the year with the release of "Scarecrow," which Ed would listen to repeatedly and excessively.

He wore out Gladys's "Georgia" just for the sweet suffering it brought him.

He carried a pocket edition of poetry. Going a step further, he tormented himself with composing his own tortured lines.

238

He stared at his Commodore 64 without software to run on it. He loved the little blinking cursor.

His neighbor Lorraine was happy, warm, and friendly toward him whenever they met. She always had a word or two to share, and she always hardly wore a thing.

As for Carmen, "what-ifs" weren't enough to postpone life, his or hers. Which wasn't to say he forgot her. He hadn't. He only hoped for her to have a great life.

Throughout his year of study, classmates considered him a workhorse.

"Get some sun," one classmate, a muso, told him.

Ed wasn't the healthiest he had been in his life. Jogging a lap of the nearby sports field was a health hazard. He was at a loss without town life pulling him into team sports. But he was his most alive, which meant he suffered as much pain as he experienced joy. But he was not a workhorse.

He didn't even work effectively. Rather, he struggled.

He was a struggle-horse.

He wrestled. He was a wrestle-horse.

These were his best and only options, to struggle and wrestle with his subject matter.

Biology was the exception because the teacher provided easily digestible, bite-sized notes. Ed found other bite-sized answers in curriculum textbooks and Gus's medical books.

But history books and novels presented problems. The pressure of volume reading brought him to his knees.

He held the books in his hands for hours. Words beyond first sentences melted.

Hadn't he experienced reading blocks in the sheds? Well, okay. But now he was a scholar of some couple of months. And he wasn't hungover. Surely, he should devour libraries.

While writing essays, he felt like he wrenched something from mud. And it showed on the page.

On a brighter note, he integrated new facts he learned in class into his mind like films replaying.

He had no trouble with concepts where he got hold of

them, and he remembered and applied new knowledge readily.

He lucked-out with the teachers at Carrington Woods College. They were on another level. Ed couldn't describe them in any other way. He trusted them and adored them.

Throughout the year, he came close to annihilating himself with his only natural talent, an ability to withstand more risk-taking and stress than many people got close to.

He de-stressed by writing private sketches about his teachers and classmates – mini-plays.

He saw his year of study through a prism of a farfetched fantasy to be a writer. It was more guided than it seemed.

Zolli and Jean visited him and Gus monthly. Between times, which was all the time, they bounced around that big old home on Main Street alone.

Ed never appreciated the hardship they endured. No, it was all about him, as far as he saw.

Zolli parked the Hi-Lux outside the door to the cream-brick apartment. Ed and Gus helped him unload twenty-liter tubs of country rainwater. Because everyone knew Adelaide water was bad. The chlorination alone provoked tears. Jean brought homemade jams, cakes, and pullovers. They disguised store-bought food as "surplus" and bequeathed it to Ed and his brother Gus to help. Undoubtedly, they kept Ed on track.

He couldn't believe classmates when, following the mid-year exams, they told him his grades would let him do whatever he wanted in life. He thought they were being nice. They weren't. They were being truthful. They faced scholastic limits. Ed didn't. And they saw this, even though he couldn't. He faced motivational limits, just as his teachers wrote in his report cards ten years back.

During the second half of the year, he applied to law school without expecting to get in. The entrance score was too high. Also, law school appeared like so much hereditary privilege. But it smelled like something that led to a real job. With prospects.

And Andrea applied to law school. Without her or him

knowing it, she was his beacon. He watched her carefully because nearly everything else confused him.

In contrast, the idea of studying for a bachelor of science or arts seemed like a return to high school, this time to teach.

The idea of being an actual scientist or historian seemed pretty cool. Like wanting to be a Hollywood actor. You know, nuts.

He read a sexy article about traders, the wild ones of the financial markets. Briefly he thought to study economics.

Close to final exams, Ed crafted all-purpose, miniaturized essay plans from a chaos of materials. He carried them everywhere with him in a little dollar notebook that he purchased in a deli beside the Carrington Woods bus stop. He memorized them when he could.

Then, leaving his micro-notebook at the exam hall door, he unpacked and adapted the tiny, condensed plans from memory alone to any exam question posed, like little big bangs.

He prayed that his final exams were in the morning because afternoons were never his best hour.

Immediately before his exams, he got himself all mellow. As mellow as he could.

Valium by the gram to sleep the night before and lights out at eight thirty helped.

The exams savaged him. But they were the best things for him.

In contrast, final assessments based on one or two years of interim assignments would have made him wonder when the action was about to start. He would have lost interest. He wouldn't have excelled in a system adapted to mediocre effort.

As it was, his grades improved steadily, and at the end of the year, they soared.

Ed topped his matriculation college and was merit-listed in the state rankings.

It knocked the wind from him.

He didn't know who he was anymore.

He had been a hotheaded, partying, trouble-finding nobody

from an unknown rural town.

Now he was merit-listed, and he had no plan.

Trying and failing was very Australian. But success was unusual, and perhaps even un-Australian. Unless you were a horse. Or other sports identity, not excluding sports stadiums.

No one guessed success on Ed's part when he had only a desire like no other to matriculate. Back when his dreams and hopes burned crystalline, and essay writing was a complete unknown to him. Not Harold the Carrington Woods principal guessed it. Not Jean. Not Ed in a month of Sundays.

Law school accepted him, the highest-placed faculty on offer, just as Alan McGinn said.

"A waste of talent," his biology teacher declared when Ed told him he got in.

"I don't have chemistry for med school," he guiltily explained to his teacher. "I'd have to study the bridging course over summer."

Anyway, medical school was down-market in terms of entrance requirements compared to law school.

But it was "pah" to med school too. Ed's biology teacher thought Ed should study science and major in biology.

Ed felt even guiltier.

He always found something to feel guiltier about.

Will Paternoster told him he knew an ex-student lawyer who bought a Jag. He didn't want one. He thought he had to have it to fit in. Lawyers lived tragically, not seeing it until the end, like Macbeth.

Ed felt hollow just listening to Will's story.

Jake Williams explained how country people without contacts struggled to obtain work as lawyers. He gave an example of a kid Ed never heard of.

Hearing of another kid from town who studied law surprised him. The warning surprised him too.

Yet Ed felt vindicated. He did do the right thing by going back to study after all. It wasn't a dork thing.

Who said it was?

Jean counseled him to stick with law school. She hadn't pressured him. No one thought he would amount to anything anyway. Prospects this side of alcoholism, other indeterminate but equally reprehensible social failure, or early death were a win. No, she counseled him to stick with it because she knew he was impulsive. She knew that some opportunities don't come again.

Zolli reacted incredibly badly when Ed told him that the state's only law school accepted him. He threw the timber he was carrying to the ground and denounced lawyers as parasites. He had a bad experience when he transferred his liquor license a decade earlier. When he calmed down, he confessed that small town lawyers benefited their communities. They sat on football club committees and helped with hospital fundraisers. In a few months, he would find little jobs for Ed to perform, such as writing to the council about a fencing issue. Still, he advised Ed to study something useful, like engineering. But to study something useful required maths, and Ed didn't have it.

Anyhoo, everything had its reward. That was what wise people said.

One thing was for sure, being Australian became something different from a year ago.

During his year of study, shearers became textbook anecdotes. Aborigines he grew up with, schooled with, played sports with, worked with, and knew by name and foible, became social justice statistics. His hometown and other country towns became studies in regional economic decline.

Henry Lawson was a brief Australian History elective topic, ranking behind, believe it or not, Banjo Paterson.

Yet, while working the sheds, Ed connected with a life that he wouldn't have connected with through ancestry alone, whether his ancestors walked down a ship's gangplank thirty years ago or across land bridges thirty thousand years ago.

He heard songs sung beneath the starry nights that followed the days on which people first arrived here.

The unadorned continent immersed him in the nation's truest cultural past, and in its truest present and future.

His, all, the stuff he was proud of, the stuff he must be sorry for.

Warwick, Rick, and Ben and the others remained realities in his heart.

They and he were as real as their country.

The place they were and therefore came from.

The country of their clay.

Bonus Material: The Romance Of The Swag

by Henry Lawson

THE AUSTRALIAN SWAG fashion is the easiest way in the world of carrying a load. I ought to know something about carrying loads: I've carried babies, which are the heaviest and most awkward and heartbreaking loads in this world for a boy or man to carry, I fancy. God remember mothers who slave about the housework (and do sometimes a man's work in addition in the bush) with a heavy, squalling kid on one arm! I've humped logs on the selection, "burning-off," with loads of fencing-posts and rails and palings out of steep, rugged gullies (and was happier then, perhaps); I've carried a shovel, crowbar, heavy "rammer," a dozen insulators on an average (strung round my shoulders with raw flax)--to say nothing of soldiering kit, tucker-bag, billy and climbing spurs--all day on a telegraph line in rough country in New Zealand, and in places where a man had to manage his load with one hand and help himself climb with the other; and I've helped hump and drag telegraph-poles up cliffs and sidings where the horses couldn't go. I've carried a portmanteau on the hot dusty roads in green old jackeroo days. Ask any actor who's been stranded and had to count railway sleepers from one town to another! he'll tell you what sort of an awkward load a portmanteau is, especially if there's a broken-hearted man underneath it. I've tried knapsack fashion--one of the least healthy and most likely to give a man sores; I've carried my belongings in a three-bushel sack slung over my shoulder--blankets, tucker, spare boots and poetry all lumped together. I tried carrying a load on my head, and got a crick in my neck and spine for days. I've carried a load on my mind that should have been shared by editors and publishers. I've helped hump luggage and furniture up to, and down from, a top flat in London. And I've carried swag for months out back in Australia--and it was

245

life, in spite of its "squalidness" and meanness and wretchedness and hardship, and in spite of the fact that the world would have regarded us as "tramps"--and a free life amongst men from all the world.

The Australian swag was born of Australia and no other land--of the Great Lone Land of magnificent distances and bright heat; the land of self-reliance, and never-give-in, and help-your-mate. The grave of many of the world's tragedies and comedies--royal and otherwise. The land where a man out of employment might shoulder his swag in Adelaide and take the track, and years later walk into a hut on the Gulf, or never be heard of any more, or a body be found in the bush and buried by the mounted police, or never found and never buried--what does it matter?

The land I love above all others--not because it was kind to me, but because I was born on Australian soil, and because of the foreign father who died at his work in the ranks of Australian pioneers, and because of many things. Australia! My country! Her very name is music to me. God bless Australia! for the sake of the great hearts of the heart of her! God keep her clear of the old-world shams and social lies and mockery, and callous commercialism, and sordid shame! And heaven send that, if ever in my time her sons are called upon to fight for her young life and honour, I die with the first rank of them and be buried in Australian ground.

But this will probably be called false, forced or "maudlin sentiment" here in England, where the mawkish sentiment of the music-halls, and the popular applause it receives, is enough to make a healthy man sick, and is only equalled by music-hall vulgarity. So I'll get on.

In the old digging days the knapsack, or straps-across-the chest fashion, was tried, but the load pressed on a man's chest and impeded his breathing, and a man needs to have his bellows free on long tracks in hot, stirless weather. Then the "horse-collar," or rolled military overcoat style--swag over one shoulder and under the other arm--was tried, but it was

246

found to be too hot for the Australian climate, and was discarded along with Wellington boots and leggings. Until recently, Australian city artists and editors--who knew as much about the bush as Downing Street knows about the British colonies in general--seemed to think the horse-collar swag was still in existence; and some artists gave the swagman a stick, as if he were a tramp of civilization with an eye on the backyard and a fear of the dog. English artists, by the way, seem firmly convinced that the Australian bushman is born in Wellington boots with a polish on 'em you could shave yourself by.

The swag is usually composed of a tent "fly" or strip of calico (a cover for the swag and a shelter in bad weather--in New Zealand it is oilcloth or waterproof twill), a couple of blankets, blue by custom and preference, as that colour shows the dirt less than any other (hence the name "bluey" for swag), and the core is composed of spare clothing and small personal effects. To make or "roll up" your swag: lay the fly or strip of calico on the ground, blueys on top of it; across one end, with eighteen inches or so to spare, lay your spare trousers and shirt, folded, light boots tied together by the laces toe to heel, books, bundle of old letters, portraits, or whatever little knick-knacks you have or care to carry, bag of needles, thread, pen and ink, spare patches for your pants, and bootlaces. Lay or arrange the pile so that it will roll evenly with the swag (some pack the lot in an old pillowslip or canvas bag), take a fold over of blanket and calico the whole length on each side, so as to reduce the width of the swag to, say, three feet, throw the spare end, with an inward fold, over the little pile of belongings, and then roll the whole to the other end, using your knees and judgment to make the swag tight, compact and artistic; when within eighteen inches of the loose end take an inward fold in that, and bring it up against the body of the swag. There is a strong suggestion of a roley-poley in a rag about the business, only the ends of the swag are folded in, in rings, and not tied. Fasten the swag with three or four straps, according to judgment and the supply of straps. To the top strap, for the swag is carried (and eased down in shanty bars and against walls or veranda-posts when not on the track) in a more or less vertical position--to the top strap, and lowest, or lowest but one, fasten the ends of the shoulder strap (usually a towel is preferred as being softer to the shoulder), your coat being carried outside the swag at the back, under the straps. To the top strap fasten the string of the nose-bag, a calico bag about the size of a pillowslip, containing the tea, sugar and flour bags, bread, meat, baking-powder and salt, and brought, when the swag is carried from the left shoulder, over the right on to the chest, and so balancing the swag behind. But a swagman can throw a heavy swag in a nearly vertical position against his spine, slung from one shoulder only and without any balance, and carry it as easily as you might wear your overcoat. Some bushmen arrange their belongings so neatly and conveniently, with swag straps in a sort of harness, that they can roll up the swag in about a minute, and unbuckle it and throw it out as easily as a roll of wall-paper, and there's the bed ready on the ground with the wardrobe for a pillow. The swag is always used for a seat on the track; it is a soft seat, so trousers last a long time. And, the dust being mostly soft and silky on the long tracks out back, boots last marvellously. Fifteen miles a day is the average with the swag, but you must travel according to the water: if the next bore or tank is five miles on, and the next twenty beyond, you camp at the five-mile water to-night and do the twenty next day. But if it's thirty miles you have to do it. Travelling with the swag in Australia is variously and picturesquely described as "humping bluey," "walking Matilda," "humping Matilda," "humping your drum," "being on the wallaby," "jabbing trotters," and "tea and sugar burglaring," but most travelling shearers now call themselves trav'lers, and say simply "on the track," or "carrying swag."

And there you have the Australian swag. Men from all the world have carried it-lords and low-class Chinamen, saints and world martyrs, and felons, thieves, and murderers, educated gentlemen and boors who couldn't sign their mark, gentlemen who fought for Poland and convicts who fought the world, women, and more than one woman disguised as a man. The Australian swag has held in its core letters and papers in all languages, the honour of great houses, and more than one national secret, papers that would send well-known and highly-respected men to jail, and proofs of the innocence of men going mad in prisons, life tragedies and comedies, fortunes and papers that secured titles and fortunes, and the last pence of lost fortunes, life secrets, portraits of mothers and dead loves, pictures of fair women, heart-breaking old letters written long ago by vanished hands, and the pencilled manuscript of more than one book which will be famous yet.

The weight of the swag varies from the light rouseabout's swag, containing one blanket and a clean shirt, to the "royal Alfred," with tent and all complete, and weighing part of a ton. Some old sundowners have a mania for gathering, from selectors' and shearers' huts, and dust-heaps, heart-breaking loads of rubbish which can never be of any possible use to them or anyone else. Here is an inventory of the contents of the swag of an old tramp who was found dead on the track, lying on his face on the sand, with his swag on top of him, and his arms stretched straight out as if he were embracing the mother earth, or had made, with his last movement, the sign of the cross to the blazing heavens.

Rotten old tent in rags. Filthy blue blanket, patched with squares of red and calico. Half of "white blanket" nearly black now, patched with pieces of various material and sewn to half of red blanket. Three-bushel sack slit open. Pieces of sacking. Part of a woman's skirt. Two rotten old pairs of moleskin trousers. One leg of a pair of trousers. Back of a shirt. Half a waistcoat. Two tweed coats, green, old and rotting, and patched with calico. Blanket, etc. Large bundle of assorted rags for patches, all rotten. Leaky billy-can, containing fishingline, papers, suet, needles and cotton, etc. Jam-tin, medicine bottles, corks on strings, to hang to his hat to keep the flies off (a sign of madness in the bush, for the corks would madden a sane man sooner than the flies could). Three boots of different sizes, all belonging to the right foot, and a left slipper. Coffeepot, without handle or spout, and quart-pot full of rubbish--broken knives and forks, with the handles burnt off, spoons, etc., picked up on rubbish-heaps; and many rusty nails, to be used as buttons, I suppose.

Broken saw blade, hammer, broken crockery, old pannikins, small rusty frying-pan without a handle, children's old shoes, many bits of old bootleather and greenhide, part of yellowback novel, mutilated English dictionary, grammar and arithmetic book, a ready reckoner, a cookery book, a bulgy angloforeign dictionary, part of a Shakespeare, book in French and book in German, and a book on etiquette and courtship. A heavy pair of blucher boots, with uppers parched and cracked, and soles so patched (patch over patch) with leather, boot protectors, hoop-iron and hobnails that they were about two inches thick, and the boots weighed over five pounds. (If you don't believe me go into the Melbourne Museum, where, in a glass case in a place of honour, you will see a similar, perhaps the same, pair of bluchers labelled "An example of colonial industry.") And in the core of the swag was a sugar-bag tied tightly with a whip-lash, and containing another old skirt, rolled very tight and fastened with many turns of a length of clothes-line, which last, I suppose, he carried to hang himself with if he felt that way. The skirt was rolled round a small packet of old portraits and almost indecipherable letters--one from a woman who had evidently been a sensible woman and a widow, and who stated in the letter that she did not intend to get married again as she had enough to do already, slavin' her finger-nails off to keep a family, without having a second husband to keep. And her answer was "final for good and all," and it wasn't no use comin' "bungfoodlin'" round her again. If he did she'd set Satan on to him. "Satan" was a dog, I suppose.

The letter was addressed to "Dear Bill," as were others.

There were no envelopes. The letters were addressed from no place in particular, so there weren't any means of identifying the dead man. The police buried him under a gum, and a young trooper cut on the tree the words:

SACRED TO THE MEMORY OF BILL WHO DIED.

About Joe Jeney

Joe Jeney was born in 1964 in the South Australian town of Kapunda, 75 kilometers from Adelaide. The town (and state) flourished after locals discovered copper in 1842. Bob Hawke's grandparents, among many people, settled there at the height of the mining boom. Bob's uncle, Albert, was born there and later moved to Western Australia, where he became Premier. Sir Sidney Kidman, the world's greatest pastoralist, centered his agricultural and horse trading operations in town. The writers Geoffrey Dutton and Colin Thiele lived there. Author Alice Rosman was born there, and author Rosanne Hawke lives there. The town continues as a prosperous hinterland, farming, and tourist community.

Joe's father, Laszlo, was Hungarian and his mother, Joan, was Welsh. They moved to Kapunda just before Joe was born. His older siblings were born in Adelaide.

Joe attended Kapunda primary and high schools with children nursed beside him in the town hospital. He left school in Year 11 to work as an apprentice in the local foundry, "Hawke & Co" (unrelated to the former Prime Minister or author Rosanne Hawke,) which manufactured and exported weighbridges and iron lacework for one hundred and fifty years. The foundry abruptly closed during the 80s recession. Joe continued his apprenticeship at the Penfolds-Kaiser Stuhl winery in the nearby Barossa Valley.

With the completion of his apprenticeship, he worked in shearing sheds as a roustabout and wool-presser for six months. This role took him into the Australian interior in three states, South Australia, New South Wales, and Victoria.

The following year, 1985, he completed his matriculation certificate at TAFE, the Kensington Park campus, in the middle suburb of Kensington Park in eastern Adelaide.

The next year he commenced degrees in law and arts at the University of Adelaide. He graduated into the "recession we had to have," the 90s recession, and moved to Melbourne to look for work. He returned to Adelaide sixteen months later to complete his training as a legal practitioner and to gain admission to the Supreme Court of South Australia.

With the 90s recession continuing, Joe moved to the New South Wales south-central agricultural city of Griffith to pick oranges. He soon obtained work in a processing plant, Bartter Enterprises, where he worked in laboring and minor managerial duties, and left two years later.

After many false starts, he found work as a lawyer in the Hawkesbury Valley on the Sydney outskirts. There he worked until he returned to Adelaide a few years later to continue his work as a lawyer and to be with his aged parents. A few years later again, he moved to Melbourne, where he settled with his spouse and puppies and worked in legal educational fields.

Joe Jeney has written stories and journals since he was a child. Australian literary journals, defunct now, published his early stories (written as an adult.) His early novels remain unpublished. As the new millennium arrived, and the Internet changed the publishing industry forever, he found opportunity to publish eBooks and POD paperbacks.

His works are available in bookstores as varied as the South Australian Museum bookstore and "Wangfujing" bookstores, China's national chain of bookstores. They're widely available Online in eBook and hardcopy formats. Other novels include:

- Europa: A Thousand Years of Oil
- Human Gods: Live Forever
- Human Gods: Ancient
- Naskie World
- Max Dreyssig: Human Skeleton
- Beautiful Goo
- Name Thief.

Several other novels await final edits after abortive earlier releases. In addition, Joe has a wish list of future projects.

www.ingramcontent.com/pod-product-compliance
Lightning Source LLC
Chambersburg PA
CBHW030535030726
47495CB00004B/1002